REDNECK REVENANT

BOOKS BY DAVID R. SLAYTON

THE GODS OF NIGHT AND DAY SERIES

Dark Moon, Shallow Sea

THE LIBERTY HOUSE SERIES

Rogue Community College

THE ADAM BINDER NOVELS

White Trash Warlock

Trailer Park Trickster

Deadbeat Druid

Redneck Revenant

REDNECK REVENANT

DAVID R. SLAYTON

Published in 2025 by Blackstone Publishing
Series and book design by Sean M. Thomas
Cover design by Sarah Riedlinger

Printed in the United States of America

First paperback edition: 2025
ISBN 979-8-212-91377-5
Fiction / Fantasy / Contemporary

Version 2

Blackstone Publishing
31 Mistletoe Rd.
Ashland, OR 97520

www.BlackstonePublishing.com

For Neva

Thank you for braving the rain in Venice.

1

Adam Binder closed the front door, let out a long breath, and told himself whatever he felt pressing against the edge of his Sight was just a passing shadow.

"Think that's the last of them?" Vic asked.

"I hope so. All the good stuff is gone."

He lifted the candy bowl with its dregs for Vic to inspect. The neighbors' purple floodlights still illuminated their fake graveyard. The giant Oogie Boogie from *The Nightmare Before Christmas* across the street remained inflated, so Adam left the light on.

"Come on," Vic said, hooking a finger into a belt loop on Adam's jeans to tug him toward the couch.

The living room had changed over the last few years. No longer a formal space, Bobby had given in and let it serve its purpose once the den had been claimed as a quiet study area.

Adam preferred things this way. The place felt more like a home and less like a showroom at a furniture store.

"Ready?" Vic asked, remote aimed at the screen.

He'd picked the movie *Happy Death Day* and swore it wasn't too gory or full of jump scares.

Vic never teased Adam about his aversion to horror. He got it. He'd been there for some of the bad stuff and seen quite a bit more in his role as a Grim Reaper.

The house felt quiet, settled. Bobby had a shift at the hospital. Spider was off somewhere. Jodi had moved out, and Vran was well, not dead, not exactly, but Adam didn't expect to ever see him again.

Adam sat and something twisted in his chest, near the warlock wound but not quite on it. He put a hand to his heart to feel the pulse.

Vic caught the gesture and straightened.

"What is it?"

Adam sorted through the sensations. He could taste something beneath the last piece of waxy chocolate—a hint of lemon and a wet wool coat on a rainy day.

He didn't know this magic, didn't know its flavor or source.

"Something's coming."

"Like red alert something?"

Vic turned back and forth, looking for signs of a threat. That was Vic. You could take the Reaper out of the police force, but the training remained.

Adam sifted through the sallow-colored achy feeling. It felt like an old loss, not quite sad, like remembering his great-aunt's humming.

"I don't know."

"Has anything hit the wards?"

"No."

Adam didn't have enough strength to keep much out, but the wards he'd set at the edges of Bobby's property acted like an early warning system. Anything really powerful would blow through them, but he'd at least know it was coming.

The bell rang.

"Do we answer it?" Vic asked.

Adam shrugged.

"It could just be another kid."

Candy bowl in hand, he swung the door open to find two figures standing on the other side.

Adam laughed.

"Who are you two supposed to be?"

"It should be obvious," Argent said. "If I understand the tradition."

The elven Queen of Swords wore a blue-and-white blouse, looking something like an adventurer from a fantasy novel. Her ears were masked by a pair of larger plastic points jutting from her head.

Her brother was dressed in green with a pointed hat and similar ears. He had a foam sword strapped to his back that Adam did not doubt would transform into a real one if the need arose.

Adam wore his blade on his back, a gentle but constant weight. It remained invisible on the mortal plane, sleeping, waiting to be drawn.

"Did you want some candy?" Vic asked.

Argent narrowed her eyes, not offended, but uncertain how to take his teasing. It wasn't like she could eat it.

"It is part of the tradition," Adam added.

"Fine." Silver held out a slender palm.

Adam dropped a piece into it and tried not to smile.

Silver's security detail was stealthy, but Adam could spy them on the roofs of the houses across the street. He did not think they were what he'd sensed and wished his Sight would just spit it out for once.

"Now what?" Argent asked, looking at her piece of candy as if a bird had perched on her hand.

"You go to more houses and say 'Trick or Treat!'"

"But you know it's for little kids, right?" Vic asked.

"Hey, we give candy to teens," Adam corrected. "Bobby would be annoyed if we got the house egged."

"Why are you doing this?" Vic asked.

"We are visiting many mortal practitioners tonight as a show of goodwill," Silver said.

Adam understood.

"It's part of your community outreach?"

"Just so."

Argent's expression indicated that she didn't think they'd have much success.

Still, it was a valiant effort. The King of Swords was trying to build more bridges between his world and the mortal realm, but so far his efforts had shown mixed results.

Adam wasn't certain that trick-or-treating was the best approach, but witches did love Halloween. He took in the quiet street.

A few tiny witches and cartoon characters were still out, accompanied by parents wielding flashlights or the bouncing rectangle of a cell phone screen.

Adam had always wanted this, the chance to give out candy to trick-or-treaters. When it had finally come, the pandemic began, robbing him of the chance. This was the first year things had truly gotten back to normal.

A gust of wind, on the edge of chilling, rushed up the street. It sent the leaves skittering along the road.

He blinked and the elves were gone, vanished while he'd considered the changes of the last few years.

"See you at the office. You're welcome for the candy," he muttered.

"That wasn't it, was it?" Vic asked as he closed the door behind them.

"No, I don't think so."

Adam's Sight would be sharper with a new tarot deck, a channel, but he hadn't found one that felt right, not since he'd given his to Jodi. That had been the right call. He still believed that. He couldn't say what part it had in his cousin's life, but she'd flourished. She was well on her way to a degree and her teaching certification. She'd moved out a while ago, into a house with several roommates and even joined a local coven, getting more focused in her craft along with her studies.

Adam sorted through his feelings, trying to get a fix on whatever was coming, and started when someone knocked.

He gripped the candy bowl in both hands to keep from dropping it.

Vic looked to him, and he gave a nod of confirmation.

Adam nodded and set the bowl on the little table beside the door as Vic swung it open.

"Hi, Adam."

He had to blink. He'd never really met her. He knew her mostly from photos, the ones hanging throughout the house, framed and carefully dusted by Bobby on his days off, or her emails, the regular updates she'd sent back when he'd lived in Oklahoma.

Her strawberry blonde hair was long and straight. She wore a wool coat, a bit heavy for Halloween in Denver, but it had just snowed.

She looked well, really well, with full cheeks and an awkward half smile, which made no sense.

His clearest memory of her was of when he'd killed her.

"Annie?"

Annie didn't look or smell dead. Most importantly, she wasn't drooling and growling about tasty brains.

"What are you doing here?"

"Well, it *is* my house," she said playfully before glancing around them at the changes to the living room. "I mean, technically."

"But, uh . . ." Adam almost blurted out something like *you don't live anywhere, because you're dead.* Instead he managed to say, "You've been gone for three years."

They'd seen it. They'd left her on the Other Side, buried beneath a cairn of rocks on Lookout Mountain where the local dragon's presence should have let her rest in peace.

This couldn't be her. It had to be someone, or something, else, and yet his Sight didn't react to her, didn't warn him of danger. He couldn't sense a glamour or magical disguise.

"I know, and I'm sorry." She sighed and smiled nervously. "When I woke up in the hospital. I needed some time to recover, time to think."

"Woke up where?" Vic asked. "What hospital?"

"Back in Chicago. I was visiting my parents. There was an accident."

But that wasn't what had happened.

Possessed by Mercy, a primeval spirit—heavy emphasis on evil—Annie had exploded, her body unable to contain the magic the spirit had absorbed. Adam had shot her with arrows, a binding spell to trap it inside her wrecked form.

"Things were so hard, you know, with everything that happened with the babies." Her face fell and Adam remembered what Bobby had told him about the miscarriages, about how they'd devastated her, devastated both of them. "I was running back to my parents, to spend some time with them, but I didn't mean to just disappear like that. Robert must hate me. The longer I stayed away, the worse it got, but it was time to come back, to come home."

She peered over Adam's shoulder with a hopeful expression. "Is he here?"

"He's working at the hospital."

"Can I come in and wait for him?"

Adam didn't know what to do. He didn't sense any evil or malice.

Then he spotted the car, a limo, long and black, loitering at the curb. He saw Vic notice it too. Those dark brown eyes didn't miss much.

Adam knew his boyfriend very well. Vic didn't tense. He didn't shift his focus from Annie to the car, but he would memorize details like the model, make, and license plate.

Annie looked over her shoulder and waved at the driver.

"My parents paid for it," she explained as the driver moved on.

"That was nice of them," Adam said.

"Especially since they didn't want me to come back."

"Why didn't they want you here?"

Something in her expression twitched.

"They were never happy about Robert, but he's my husband, and this is my home."

She clearly wasn't saying everything, but she wasn't wrong. If it was Annie, this was her house.

Adam stepped aside and let her in. If she wasn't what she said, if she was some *thing*, then she'd quickly learn that he could pull a trick or two of his own.

"You must be Vic," she said.

He nodded, still silent, still assessing the situation.

"How do you know about Vic?"

Annie gave an embarrassed smile.

"My parents kept tabs on Robert for me, to make sure he was okay."

"What kind of tabs?" Vic asked.

"Private investigators, that sort of thing."

Adam tensed. He'd never noticed anyone spying on them. Then again, if the observer was entirely mundane, he might not have been aware of them. He wouldn't even have spotted them crossing the wards.

"That's a bit invasive," Vic said.

"I know. It's just how they are. Old money and a bit paranoid."

"Well, you picked a heck of a night to make a mysterious return." Adam nodded to the plastic skeleton hung on the door.

"I know, right?"

She laughed.

He'd never met her in the good times, but he'd lived with her pictures, her ghost, for three years.

"You can take off your coat," Adam told her.

She hugged herself.

"Yeah. I'm sorry. It just doesn't feel real, being back here."

She shrugged out of the garment. Adam waited for bats to fly out of it or something like that, but nothing happened when he hung it on a hook by the door.

She took in the living room and the kitchen.

It hadn't changed too much, but it felt less pristine, more lived in, since Adam and the others had come to stay.

He might be the only one left now, but the house that had once felt so unwelcoming now had a sense of home. It was a bit ironic, since he and Vic were ready for the next step. They had been for a while, but the rental prices in the city were insane. Neither of them made that much money.

"Let's have a seat." Adam led them to the kitchen table. "I could make some coffee."

"It's too late for coffee," Vic said. "How about tea?"

"That would be nice." Annie chewed her lip as she pulled out a chair at the kitchen table.

Vic went to fill the electric kettle.

"You said you were in an accident?"

"Yeah."

She pulled up the sleeve of her sweater. There were scars, thick, pink ropes knitted into her pale skin. She tugged at her collar and showed him another corded, forking line.

He could not suppress a wince. He'd seen her explode. Seen her die. He'd piled the stones atop her body.

There was no coming back from that.

"I was in a coma for a long time. Then I woke up and it was a lot of physical therapy. They said it's a miracle that I'm even walking."

Adam didn't say anything.

She couldn't be Annie. She couldn't, and yet, she appeared to be.

Vic brought the tea, an herbal mix of lavender and lemon.

He set a tray down with a little jar of honey and a small pitcher of cream. Becoming a chef had only made him more conscious of the details, the little things that Adam never would have thought of. It was a natural fit, an extension of the way Vic took care of people.

"You never reached out," Adam said.

"I didn't know how. I left so suddenly. It wasn't Robert, not really. I just didn't know what to do. It was all so much. I felt like I was drowning."

Annie had been depressed. That had been how Mercy had taken her, using her sadness as a doorway, but he'd never doubted that the unconscious woman he'd seen when he'd first arrived in Denver had been his sister-in-law. The problem was that he hadn't known her before Mercy. He didn't have enough experience to compare then to now.

The front door rattled.

Adam stiffened. He hadn't heard Bobby drive up.

"Guys, I brought pizza. Cheese and vegan pepperoni. I hope that's—"

Bobby trailed off and everyone froze.

Adam thought his brother would drop the cardboard box, but he set it carefully, slowly, on the little table, balancing it atop the candy bowl.

"Hello," Annie said.

Her eyes shone with tears.

"Adam, what is this?" Bobby asked.

"I don't know. Honestly."

His brother's eyes, brown where Adam's were blue, locked on his.

Adam could almost hear the unasked question.

Are we safe?

Adam shrugged.

"We should let you two talk." Vic moved around the kitchen island to tug at Adam's sleeve, pulling him the short distance into the living room.

Adam didn't resist, but he really wanted to.

"Anything?" Vic whispered.

"I'm not sensing any danger or magic. Just a shift, a change."

Vic sat them on the couch. The movie remained paused at the opening credits.

"Do you think it's her?"

"It looks like her," Adam said. "I mean, we'd know if she had a twin, right?"

"Some sort of magical duplicate?" Vic suggested. "A shape-shifter?"

"I don't think so. Changing your shape is really hard, and I'd know if it was a glamour."

The front window held enough of a reflection that Adam could watch them. Annie was crying. Bobby had gone stiff, detached, like when he went to work.

"If that's her, there's going to be trouble," Vic said.

"Yeah."

He could follow the train of Vic's thoughts.

The Reaper didn't stir, the thing in Vic that Adam called Boney simply because it creeped him out less to do so. If Annie really was back from the dead, then Vic had a conversation coming, a visit to Death. She didn't take kindly to anyone breaking the rules of nature, and resurrection seemed like a pretty big infraction.

"Happy Halloween," Vic said.

"Yeah." Adam took his hand. "Happy Halloween."

Bobby came out of the kitchen a while later.

"Can I talk to you in private?"

Adam followed him to the top of the stairs.

It was a smart move. If Annie were trouble, Vic could handle himself, and anything that messed with him would have to answer to Death.

Still, they didn't go far, just out of earshot.

Bobby pulled a hand through his hair. It was darker than Adam's, browner instead of dirty blond, and he'd gained a lot of gray these last few years. Losing Annie, and working around the clock during the pandemic, had added wear.

"So?" Bobby asked.

"Like I said, I don't know. You?"

"I think it's her." Bobby slid down the wall, sinking toward the pale carpet. "What if it is, I mean, really *is* her?"

Adam shook his head, not because he didn't want it to be true, but because he didn't know how it could be. There weren't a lot of constants in magic, a lot of absolutes, but dead was dead.

"She told you she was in a coma?"

Bobby nodded. "After a car accident in Chicago. She says

she left to go back to her parents for a while. But that's not what happened. I'm not crazy, right?"

"No, you're not. We see her too. You never told anyone what happened, right?"

Bobby scoffed.

"Who would have believed me?"

"She said her parents had PIs watching you, keeping tabs. They never asked about her, never came looking for her?"

"No. I felt bad that I didn't reach out to them, talk to them. I assumed they just thought she'd cut contact."

"Would she do that? Did they get along?"

Bobby made a so-so gesture.

"Mostly. They were cold, even at the wedding. She always said they were WASPs, really reserved."

"If she was back home, it would explain why they never bothered you or came looking for her, but it's weird that they'd have people watching you and that they never told you she was there."

"Yeah," Bobby agreed.

It also meant they might know about Adam and the spirit realm, though he wasn't certain how. It didn't hurt that they'd barely left the house the last few years. He'd spent lockdown between here and Jesse's shop, fixing and selling used cars during the shortage.

Bobby stared at the floor like he wanted to sink into it.

Adam tensed. His brother had pulled himself back together, inch by inch, when they'd returned from Oklahoma. He'd been recovering from losing her.

It hadn't been easy to watch.

It must have been a hundred times harder to do it.

Now he might fly apart again.

"What do we do?" Bobby asked. "Do I kick her out into the cold?"

"I don't think she's dangerous," Adam said. "At least not magically."

"Me neither."

Adam exhaled. He still wasn't 100 percent all right with his brother. He didn't think he'd ever fully be. Therapy helped and, boy, would he have some material for his next session.

"You have to do what you think is best, but I'm going to look into it, okay?"

"Okay." Bobby let out a breath. "Thank you."

"We'll figure it out."

Adam wished he knew how.

Unfortunately, he did know where to start.

"I'm going to spirit walk to her grave and see what I can find."

Adam didn't like the idea of getting that close to a dragon's lair, but hopefully he could avoid attracting its attention.

Bobby clasped Adam's arm.

"The elves . . . Death. What will they do?"

"I don't know. They might think she's dangerous."

"I don't want them to hurt her."

"I'll do what I can, but they will find out, and it might be better for all of us, her included, if I'm the one to tell them."

Bobby tensed and let Adam go.

"I'll do what I can," Adam offered, knowing it wasn't much.

He had a place in the court. He had Silver's ear, sort of, but neither of those things amounted to any actual power among the immortals, something of which they constantly reminded him.

Downstairs, Adam paused long enough to turn off the TV before he headed for the finished basement that Vic called the Batcave.

"You going under?" Vic asked, catching up when Adam turned on the light.

"Yeah. I need to see what I can find out. Keep an eye on them?"

"Of course." Vic laid a quick kiss on Adam's forehead. "I'll be here when you get back. Be careful."

"Thanks. You too."

Adam retreated into his bedroom. It would never be his, but he had made it someplace he felt safe. It didn't hurt that Vic spent the night on a regular basis. They had no privacy at his mom's place, and he'd had to give up his apartment when he'd quit the police force.

Adam stretched out on the unmade bed and tried to relax. Once upon a time, spirit walking had been the thing he'd looked forward to the most, his way out of the real world, but now that he had something and someone to come back to, his walks felt more like errands.

They were also more dangerous as the immortals vied for dominance.

Adam shifted so he leaned to the side, his feet apart as if planted on a hilltop. The image fit, considering his destination was Lookout Mountain. He positioned his hands as if to grip his sword.

The blade remained hidden, unsummoned, but he could feel it, hovering on the edge of real, nearly solid in his grip.

It was a weapon of office, the symbol of his role as the Page of Swords in Silver's court.

He still didn't know how he felt about it most days. The role was mostly ceremonial, which was good, because as cool as the sword looked, and while he couldn't deny that it fulfilled some dream he'd had about looking like a hero from a fantasy novel, it hadn't come with a boost in magical firepower. Adam wouldn't be up for defending Silver from the threats that came for him out of the dark.

Still, the blade contained magic. Adam could call upon it

if he needed it but never had. The elves might be the immortals he trusted most, but he remembered his lessons, the tales of caution his great-aunt Sue and Silver himself had repeated over and over. Power could be an addiction. It would be too easy to sell himself as a vassal or a thrall. That was a path he never wanted to walk.

He settled into something close to sleep, then quickly woke on the Other Side.

As always, the spirit realm was cast in emerald light, a green glow that came from the ever-present crescent moon.

Adam moved through the house much like he would in the mortal world, but everything was a little softer, a little glossier as he climbed the basement stairs.

Annie sat beside Bobby at the kitchen table. He'd put a hand atop hers and looked worried.

Adam peered at her. Neither magic nor malice floated on the surface.

Focusing, he pushed his Sight to look deeper. The scars crossing her body were jagged. They could be from a car accident, or they could be from an explosion of energy. He didn't see how she could have survived either.

Then he found it—a hint of magic lying far beneath the surface.

Adam reached for it, brushing his senses over the trace. It felt old, faint and fading, like a scent in a kitchen that hadn't been used in many years.

Then he had it.

Not a hint, *hints*. Plural.

Someone had cast a lot of spells on Annie. A lot of someones, probably a coven. Adam guessed it from the way the different magics wove together, touching each other cooperatively, almost amicably.

It had been a while since the casting.

Adam extended his senses, reaching carefully.

He found no defenses, no traps, and no magic of Annie's own. That aligned with what Bobby had told him when she'd died, that she'd given her magic, her life, to bring Bobby back from the brink when Mercy had drained him.

Adam could not resist a glance in Vic's direction. The Reaper slept, but he knew what to look for now, the vein of black thread sketched faintly over Vic's skin. A little taller than Adam, and more muscular, Vicente Martinez was a handsome sight.

He let himself enjoy the view, and the sense of cottony warmth Vic put in his chest, for a moment longer.

He knew he was stalling.

Now for the dangerous part.

Adam willed himself elsewhere, to the northwest and deeper into the spirit realm, further away from the mortal world.

He hadn't gone to school and wasn't certain even the elves' new college for wayward practitioners would have the answers he wanted, but he read a lot. He'd decided the spirit realm was metaphysical, at least in the sense that it was as much of an idea as a place.

Perhaps it was where the dreams of the mortal world and the higher planes met and mixed. He could say for certain that it wasn't objectively measurable, which was why it bent and changed so often, sometimes a little at a time—sometimes in a rush like an earthquake.

The spirit realm remembered, which was why it clung to the past. Forgotten things lingered here, as did monsters that had never been real in the mortal realm. They walked beside creatures long extinct. Perhaps they were memories too, or perhaps they were the idea of what people thought they'd been like.

The deeper you went, the farther from the known landmarks,

the weirder things got, and the more likely that a creature out of myth would come to snack on you.

In the mortal world, Lookout Mountain sported an antenna farm lined with lights like cherries blinking to warn passing planes. Here, the tree-lined rock stood dark and imposing, marked by a rising, curving road. Buffalo Bill Cody was buried at the top, but he wasn't the only one laid to rest here.

Sometimes, on patrol, Adam would see the dragon. It liked to fly in lazy circles, gliding over the mountain as if in warning to lesser things.

He walked the road now, scanning the hollows between the trees, trying to remember exactly where their battle with Mercy had ended while keeping one eye on the sky.

On the horizon, the watchtowers glowed. The north, pale and white, seemed the brightest.

The light of the eastern tower almost matched the emerald sky. Adam had been there, to the school Silver had started, but it would always hold a little pain for him, and not only because its anchor was set at Liberty House, the institution where Bobby had committed him when his Sight had become almost unbearable. That was where Vran had gone, and where he'd never come back from.

The dwarves, in their fortress-like brewery, held the southern tower. Adam knew them the least, but he liked their biker gang vibe. They felt a bit like Oklahoma, like home.

He tried to ignore the tower closest to his position but could not.

The leprechauns had moved their western anchor recently, perhaps to put more distance between themselves and the elves, though in the mortal world it wasn't that much farther. Now they occupied a towering mausoleum in a historic cemetery.

Perhaps their King of Coins, Seamus, had wanted an

outward expression of his grief. He'd lost his love, and the fate of her murderer had left bad blood between the elves and leprechauns. Adam was the cause of it. He hadn't quite understood the ramifications of the deal Silver had offered him, but the elven king had assumed the debt Adam owed Seamus. Now Adam avoided the western watchtower, not wanting to flaunt his rank or the mercy Silver had shown him.

He focused on the task at hand, keeping his senses open but quiet. He did not want to broadcast his presence to whatever lurked among the pines and boulders.

Vic had taken him hiking in the summer. The experience had been boring, though the view had been pretty, but it hadn't been enough to train him for this much uphill walking, and his legs soon protested the climb.

There. This was it—at least he thought it was.

It felt right, though the ground had risen. The trees loomed taller than he remembered, their shadows longer in the moonlight.

This was where they'd buried her. It had to be, but if Annie was here, he had no way to know. The place had changed too much for Adam to discern whether she still lay beneath the ground.

He closed his eyes and let out his breath.

That left him no choice. He'd known it would come to visiting the tower and reporting this to the elves, but he had no idea how it would go.

He hadn't lied to Bobby. He had to report any trace of Mercy, any hint of the risk the spirit posed, and it would be far better for the elves to learn of it from him.

Better for whom? Adam wondered. The mountainside faded away. *For Annie or you?*

4

The sword's weight became heavier, more tangible, as Adam willed himself east. It felt like the blade was homesick, like a horse racing for the gate.

The link between them grew every time Adam held it, which was why he so rarely did.

Then he was at the Watchtower of the North. Adam sank into the sheer force of the magic surrounding the King of Swords's seat of power.

The night shone green beyond the brightness coming from the tower and its many incandescent bulbs. The pale glow drove back the moonlight and lent the old Ferris wheel and roller coasters a nimbus that washed the world to black and white.

All of it was beautiful, though the gates and fence were new.

Forged of a bright metal that reminded him of chrome, the barrier stood shaped in delicate whorls and spirals. Adam could have squeezed between the bars, but he knew better. The fence marked a line of magic, thick and deep. This was merely the circumference of a sphere. Nothing could approach the tower from any direction unless the king willed it.

Adam narrowed his gaze as he stared upward.

In the past the tower's shine had chased away the emerald moonshade. Now it encroached in threads of vibrant green.

Tensions ran high among the immortals, and trouble was brewing.

Adam thought he heard music, a wisp of violin strings. His senses tried to follow the sound but couldn't locate its source.

He took it as a sign of the spirit realm's recent volatility. He didn't know why, not exactly, but suspected it was a sign of the limits to Silver's influence. The old King of Swords had been a terror and an absolute bastard, but he'd also been an absolute power.

His son's rule was marked by tolerance, open-mindedness, and a willingness to do things differently, but that meant plenty of other beings thought they had a chance to climb to the top of the ladder. It also meant the Guardians had their hands full with all sorts of magical crimes, and it meant Adam never went anywhere without the sword.

Despite his love of fantasy heroes, he was starting to not like carrying the blade all the time. It meant it was always there, and he could use it anytime.

The open-carry crowd was like that. They wore their guns everywhere, always looking for trouble. One of magic's first rules was that like draws like. Walking around constantly armed meant he had a greater chance of stepping into a fight.

Still, it marked him as a servant of the elven throne. There was protection in that, but it also meant he wasn't as welcome in some places as he'd once been, which made his job harder.

He didn't need to brandish the blade for the guards to recognize him, but elves loved their pageantry. It sang free of the scabbard and gleamed when he lifted it. There was no doubt now. The sword was happy to be home.

It was a simple-looking thing, at least for a sword forged

by elves, with two rings on the cross guard and silver threaded into the steel.

The gates swung open, and Adam stepped inside.

More than ever, this place felt like a blend of two worlds. Attractions long gone in the mortal world went gracefully through their motions, giving the place an old-fashioned allure.

The plants were new.

Blue flowers rained from graceful, forking trees. They danced along the ground, swept by the spirit realm's breeze. Adam did not know what they were called, but they'd sprung into being three years ago and had grown steadily, month by month, ever since.

Elves were everywhere, as always. Adam had learned more than a few of their names. He knew which ones to avoid and which ones would snub him in turn. Silver's court was not unlike high school, and Adam wished he could drop out of this too. It was some comfort to know the king often felt the same.

The first time Adam had visited the northern watchtower, he'd seen only elves strolling through the park or enjoying the attractions. Now that Silver was king, visitors came from across the planes.

Adam spied dwarves and gnomes, along with several things that, while they acted friendly enough, seemed the stuff of nightmares, like the trio of creatures who carried their heads in their hands. An elegantly dressed cat man walked beside a dapper bird, and he hoped that ended well.

As always, it was tempting to stare. The realms held life in an array of forms, from lanky tree people with bark skin to multi-armed, winged insectoids. Many of the races were beautiful, like a trio of naked, crystalline women, each a slightly different shade of pink. Some were harder to look at, their bodies a mass of worms or serpents. He fought the need to flinch when a group of hairy spiders, their eyes swiveling at him in equal curiosity, scurried past.

Some were petitioners, some supplicants, others ambassadors or merely tourists. Even at this hour, figures moved along the park paths or took in the view from the Ferris wheel.

The crowds meant guards were everywhere too.

They stood on the roofs, guns in hand, fedoras tilted to give them a view of anyone approaching the tower.

Adam didn't need to salute them or make any gesture. They could count the hairs on his head if they wanted. They knew he belonged here, as much as any mortal could.

He reached the ballroom near the tower's base, a long hall with a polished wooden floor and delicate, scrolling decorations no longer accessible in the mortal realm.

Silver used to play the piano here, in his days as a prince and the Knight of Swords.

Now he almost sprawled on a throne of milky ice that Adam could not imagine was comfortable.

The king looked nothing like he had a few hours ago. He wore a perfect pinstripe suit and a fedora like his guards. A ring of embroidered blades in the ribbon at the hat's base made the only concession to a crown. His sword rested in its scabbard across his lap.

A black strap crossed his chest, and Adam knew it was connected to a holster. Silver had brought firearms into the elven world, into their traditions, and forever changed both.

Bowing was required. Adam bent at the waist with one hand held across his belly. He hated it, partly because he didn't like treating anyone with that sort of deference, and partly because it made him feel as though Silver were a stranger. They were friends now, and had once been much more. The differences in their position had always been clear, but the throne and crown put a distance between them that he didn't know how to bridge.

Straightening, he scanned the king's face for any sign of the youth he'd loved but found none. Perak, the name Adam had known him by, was gone, if he ever truly had been.

"It is late in your world, Page," Silver said without moving. He didn't straighten or show surprise at Adam's approach. "What brings you here at such an hour?"

Adam swallowed. He had to tell Silver, but he'd rather not spill the beans on Annie to all the court and whoever might be listening.

"I ask an audience in private, if you will."

There wasn't anyone hovering near the throne, but privacy was never guaranteed unless requested and granted.

Silver cocked his head. When he didn't say anything, Adam added, "I fear a change in the world, and came to you first, as is my duty."

He knew the game, how to speak and stand. The first year of his new role had mostly been spent learning court protocol and rules.

And still Silver didn't say anything.

Finally, he steepled his fingers together.

"Not just yet. I've a task for you first."

Adam blinked.

The rejection didn't sting, but it did confuse him.

He needed to tell them about Annie. Silver wasn't stupid nor was he as arrogant as he pretended. If he didn't want to hear what Adam had to say it meant he had reasons, and it might be that he already knew.

"Of course."

"Our efforts this night, to go among the mortals and visit the practitioners, were fruitless. We were rebuffed. Their numbers have grown, but they keep their distance from us, from the Guardians and the throne. I wish to know why."

"You want me to go talk to them for you?"

"Yes. There are concerns that their goals are not aligned with our own."

Adam wasn't certain if Silver was using the royal "we" or if he meant the Guardians or the elves. The lines were blurry, though Silver was taking steps to clarify them. The school he'd started was a good start. He'd also put Argent in charge of the Guardians in an attempt to separate them from the throne.

"What are you looking for? What do you want me to do?"

"I had hoped that the tradition and its whimsy would soften their perceptions, but they would not open their doors. You must learn why they distrust us so."

"I'll do what I can."

He almost added, *whatever you need*, which was something he might have said to Jesse, his other boss, but he had to be careful with how he phrased things. Words had power among the immortals. Offering them *anything* might be taken literally.

He turned to go.

"And Adam," Silver said, turning him back around. "Go to them soon, and take Dautre with you."

Adam hoped he managed to not grimace as he nodded. Including Dautre meant he'd have a harder time convincing the mortal witches that Silver was friendly.

The elf was young, but still one of the old-timers, the sort who didn't seem happy with the changes Silver had made. He was also the squire to the new Knight of Swords, who was an old-timer in every sense of the word. Silver had appointed her to appease the more conservative factions, but Adam wasn't certain if it was working or not. He avoided the knight as best he could, and so far, she'd done the same.

Adam could will himself home, back to his body, at any moment, but he walked to the edge of the amusement park, giving Silver the chance to sneak off to talk to him more directly or to send a message, but no one came.

Closing his eyes, he willed himself back to his body and the basement.

"Hey," Vic said as Adam stirred.

He'd stretched out next to Adam, but the lamp on the end table was on, and Vic remained dressed.

"Keeping an eye on me?"

"Keeping watch, yeah."

Adam reached to take his hand.

"Any luck?" Vic asked.

"No. Just more work. I didn't even get the chance to tell them about Annie. How are things here?"

"Bobby offered her the guest room."

Adam thought about their conversation before his spirit walk. "He's worried."

"He should be." Vic squeezed his hand. "His wife just came back from the dead."

"I didn't go to Sara's. I don't want to tell her until we have to."

"It's not going to be pretty when she finds out, and it'll be worse if we don't tell her ourselves."

Wasn't that close to what Adam had said to Bobby about the elves?

"I just don't understand how Annie can be here? You reaped her."

"I reaped Mercy." Vic focused on the wall for a moment, the way he always did when he talked about the Reaper.

"But not Annie?"

Vic shrugged. "I don't know. It was like eating something really spicy. You can't taste the other flavors. Whatever Mercy was, it overpowered the sense of anything else, at least as far as I can remember."

Adam swallowed.

"Still, I don't want Sara doing whatever she's going to do to Annie until we know more."

"I don't know if you can hide it from her." Vic nodded to the foot of the bed where Spider lay curled up in a ball of black fur.

Sensing their attention, the cat lifted his head and slowly blinked green eyes at Adam. Adam returned the cat's gesture of trust.

"Spider's good. He might be a psychopomp but he's not a narc."

"Didn't you just go to tell the elves?"

"That's different," Adam hedged.

"How?"

"I trust Silver."

"Valid," Vic conceded. "We still don't know exactly how the Reaper works. She may already know whatever I do."

Vic wasn't wrong.

Sara—Death—was Vic's boss in a less direct way than Silver was Adam's. The difference was that time stopped when Vic was sent to claim a soul. He'd described it to Adam. The Reaper came over him like a shadow. He touched the corpse and absorbed the soul. It was a regular occurrence, and it never cost Vic his job at the kitchen, at least in any way that anyone else noticed.

Adam hadn't been around for one of these calls, and wished he had. The first time he'd seen a Reaper, when he'd met and saved Vic, he'd been able to talk to it. He wanted to know if that was part of him having magic or if it had been Sara's will. She'd wanted them to meet, to become entangled, so she could use them as tools.

So much of Adam's life, it turned out, had been guided by her, working behind the scenes for her own ends. He'd avoided her since their last exchange.

A confrontation felt inevitable now. She might obliterate Annie for breaking the rules, and Adam could not shake the little spark of hope he'd seen in Bobby's eye. If someone were messing with them Adam was going to be extremely pissed off about it. Scratch that, someone was definitely messing with them. It was just a matter of finding out who and why.

Vic yawned.

"Sleep on it," he said. "But maybe go brush your teeth first."

He gave Adam a little shove.

Adam laughed and rolled to his feet.

5

Adam woke up early, which felt unfair after the night he'd had, but at least he could enjoy the sight of dark hair and golden skin tangled up in charcoal-colored sheets and one of Sue's old crocheted blankets. Vic slept deeply, comfortably, and the sight of him eased Adam back against his pillow.

Spider had skulked off to chase birds or escort wayward souls.

"Hey," Vic murmured, eyes open to a crack.

"Hey. Did you get the license plate number on the limo?"

"Good morning to you too."

"Sorry."

Vic gave a sleepy chuckle.

"Yeah. I'll bounce it off Dale later. I didn't want to send it to her last night. Halloween is a big night for cops."

Vic still had one friend on the force, though most of them had been done with him once he'd quit. He said he didn't know if it was leaving the force, coming out as bi, or some combination of the two. He also said he didn't worry about it, but Adam wasn't sure how true that was.

Dale was good people. She and her wife had invited them over for dinner when lockdown had lifted. They had a small house on the southeast side of town. Everything had been tastefully decorated and clean. They kept chickens in a coop in the backyard. They seemed like grown-ups, adults, the sort Adam sometimes wished he was and felt lightyears away from being.

"You said Silver gave you some work?"

"Yeah. He wants me to talk to the local covens. I guess I'll start with Jodi."

"That's a good idea." Vic nodded at the ceiling. "Think it's related to the situation upstairs?"

"I don't know. It was weird. He didn't even want to hear what I had to say."

"Did you try Argent?"

"I didn't look for her. She's so busy with the school and the Guardians. I was surprised she took the time to come by last night. I'll get this thing done for Silver and see if that earns me some face time."

One thing Adam had learned over the last few years was that to get something, you needed to bring something, usually results. The elven court ran on favors and patronage.

"I wonder if he's protecting her." Vic stretched.

Adam blinked.

"Annie?"

"Yeah."

"I hadn't thought of that."

Silver might very well know what was going on. Not letting Adam announce her return at court might have been a way of keeping her safe.

"Maybe."

Vic reached to wrap an arm around Adam. He let himself be pulled closer. This was one of the best parts, one of his favorite things about them, how they fit together. It amazed him every time, and he was grateful for it every day.

When his therapist had asked him to list all the good stuff in his life, Vic had been the first thing he'd written down.

"What time do you have to be at the kitchen?"

"Noon."

Plenty of time then. Adam didn't have to be at the garage until ten. Then he remembered that they had a possible zombie situation.

"Bobby's got work too. What are we supposed to do with her?"

"Leave her here," Vic said. "Unless there's anything valuable that you're worried about."

"Not really."

The family grimoire was in a plastic box under Adam's bed, but he'd scanned and uploaded it to the cloud a while ago. He'd only translated part of it, and knew he'd have to study German for a long time before he had it all in English.

"Then we've got an hour," Vic said. "Shower before or after?"

Adam pretended to consider the question.

"Third option. During."

Vic grinned.

They made their way upstairs a while later. Dressed and happy, Adam almost didn't mind that he hadn't had any caffeine. He was used to the kitchen being quiet at this time of day.

The smell hit him first: eggs, toast, and coffee—usual breakfast smells, only not so usual to Adam. His taste ran to cereal. Vic's cooking was so much better than anything he could make that he didn't even try to compete.

Annie looked at home in the kitchen. Sitting at the table with a plate before him, Bobby looked a little less comfortable.

It struck Adam that this was a scene from their marriage long before Bobby called Adam and asked him for help. This was how they were supposed to be, who they were supposed to be—before Mercy, before Annie had died.

Adam exchanged a glance with Vic, who gave a half shrug.

"Oh, Adam," Annie said, spotting him. "I fed your cat. I hope that's okay."

"Yeah. Thanks."

"He wanted to go outside. I let him. Is that all right?"

"He comes and goes."

"You really should get him a collar. What's his name?"

"Spider."

"That's fun."

He couldn't decide if she was mocking him or being nice. He went with nice and smiled at her.

"And I, um, made breakfast." She waved a hand at the table.

"It smells delicious," Vic said.

Adam followed his lead and took a seat.

Food was food, after all.

Annie put plates on the table.

Adam took some eggs and toast but ignored the bacon.

Vic ate everything and they both said their thank-yous.

Bobby chewed slowly, looking stunned and more than a bit off guard.

"It's awkward, isn't it?" Annie looked past her fork to the three of them.

Adam waited for Bobby to say something, but when he didn't, Adam said, "It's, uh . . . yeah."

Annie gave a nervous smile.

"It's just different," Adam hedged. "And you really don't have to serve us or cook or anything."

"I don't have anything else to do. It's not like I have a job. My license is expired."

"You were a nurse at the hospital, right?" Vic asked, looking between her and Bobby. "That's where you two met."

"Yeah." She beamed.

"They could use you now," Bobby said. "Everywhere is short-handed."

"I'm sure. It was so strange waking up in Chicago instead of here."

Her cheerful air dimmed.

"That's where we met too, you know." Vic reached over to squeeze Adam's hand. "At Mercy."

"Really? That's neat," Annie said.

Adam tried again to read her, for magic or insincerity, and found neither. His therapist encouraged him to assume the best in people's words, not because it was always true, but because it helped him be less anxious about interactions. He tried, he really did, but it wasn't easy when literal cosmic forces wanted to fuck with his life on a regular basis.

"What did you do in Chicago? After you woke up, I mean."

"Tons and tons of physical therapy. I read a lot, and probably watched way too much television."

"You never called," Bobby said quietly. "Your parents never told me you were even alive."

Annie's eyes sank toward her plate.

"They didn't want me to. It wasn't like they were keeping me prisoner . . . but they weren't happy when I told them I'd made up my mind to come home."

Adam got the sense she was holding back, and this time he decided to push a little.

"Why?"

"That's just how they are. They wanted me to stay near them, with them, be like them."

Bobby nodded, and Adam could see how that might be something they'd had in common, something they'd connected over.

Bobby had felt trapped in Oklahoma. He'd done everything he could to get away, to become Doctor Robert Binder. Annie's possession and death had shown him that the past never went away, not completely, and he'd done his best to reconcile his old life with the new.

"I'm really happy that you two made up," Annie said to Bobby. "I know it hurt you to not have Adam in your life."

Talk about opening old wounds, Adam thought, but they could weather it.

He and Bobby had literally been to hell together, and after that he doubted there was anything that would put them completely on the outs again.

Adam gave his brother an encouraging smile, though he couldn't answer the question in Bobby's eyes. He still did not know if this was Annie, and if it was, he still didn't know how it was possible.

"I have to get to work." Standing, Bobby took his plate to the sink to rinse it.

"Me too," Adam said. "Thank you for breakfast."

"There's extra coffee if you want some to go. Robert said you drink a lot of it."

Adam smiled and rinsed his plate, put it in the dishwasher, and reached for the pans on the stove.

"You can leave those," she said.

Adam paused, unable to tell if he was balking at her motherly tone or if it was more that he was used to cleaning up after himself.

"Okay." He reached for a travel cup.

"Drop you at the garage?" Vic asked.

"That would be great," Adam said.

Unfortunately, Adam's role as the Page of Swords had not come with an employee vehicle, which seemed a little unfair as Argent had more cars than she could count. It didn't even come with a paycheck.

Thankfully, the pandemic hadn't hurt the business at Jesse's garage. If anything, with the shortage of used cars, it had meant that people wanted to maintain what they had and even get some older vehicles running again.

Jesse was savvy. He'd seen the shortage and quickly responded by finding vehicles that needed repairs and selling them.

Adam spent his time on the bus studying German or translating pages from the grimoire. The main issue was that the bus took forever, which cut into his time with Vic, especially when his night job required extra hours.

He also missed driving to relax, letting his mind wander as he took in the city. He occasionally looked at vintage Cutlass Supremes online, but even if he could have afforded one, the mileage would have been hell and the car wouldn't feel the same.

It was like the tarot deck. Adam had gone to all the local bookstores. He'd tried decks of every sort. Vic had been sweet enough to buy him one, before Adam had to explain that it just didn't feel right. It was too impersonal. He'd even tried sleeping with them under his pillow, but it hadn't helped.

Vic drove north, heading for Jesse's garage. He'd drop Adam off and then swing by his mom's for a change of clothes before he went to work at the ghost kitchen. He liked his shifts there. He got to make a lot of different food, all for various delivery services. It was good practice but too little pay. Adam didn't know how they'd ever afford for Vic to open a place of his own, but that was his dream, what he wanted more than anything, so Adam had vowed to find a way to make it happen.

But first, Adam needed a car, and they needed an apartment, especially if Annie really was back. Bobby's house would be way too crowded if their marriage worked out and they started trying for kids again.

That thought brought a spikey green twinge of concern.

"Nickel for your thoughts?" Vic asked.

"I thought it was a penny."

Vic shrugged. "Inflation."

"I was just wondering what's going to happen, you know, with Annie coming home."

"Hopefully good things," Vic said. "Bobby never moved on. He still loves her."

"That's what I'm worried about. If she's some horrible *thing*, then I don't want to see him go through that. I don't want him to get hurt."

And he didn't want Bobby to have to watch if Adam was forced to put his sword through her.

"Have you considered that she's not? What if she's exactly who and what she appears to be?"

"I just don't know how that's possible."

"That doesn't mean it isn't." Vic pulled into the garage's small lot. "Good things can happen too."

He wasn't wrong. They were proof of it.

Adam unbuckled his seatbelt, paused, and made sure he looked Vic in the eye when he said, "I love you."

"I love you too."

Vic leaned in for a quick kiss, and Adam climbed out.

He made sure he said it every day. He made sure Vic knew he meant it.

Adam had lost him once. He'd take nothing for granted after that.

6

Thinking about Dautre made Adam's head hurt. The elf was prickly, but Silver had given him a task, and Adam would do his best to complete it.

He sent the text on his break at work.

> Hey. I was wondering if I could come to your next coven meeting.

The response came pretty quickly.

> They're called Sabbats and why?

> I want to check it out.

> Sure.

> Can I bring a friend?

Adam could picture Jodi's eye roll.

> Samhain ends at sunset.
>
> Cheesman Park.

His cousin might be new and improved, but she was still Jodi. He also couldn't argue that she had a better in with the local witches than he did.

Dautre would be a bigger problem. He had no tact. If Silver hadn't commanded him to include the elf, Adam would have left him out of it.

He toyed with the idea of not telling Dautre until the last minute, but his therapist would say that was passive-aggressive, so he called a number. A polite attendant with a faintly British accent took a message for Dautre with the relevant details.

The elves were slowly catching on to mortal technology, which meant they were up to answering services. They might get the idea of voicemail in another century or two.

He didn't have time to go home before sunset, and with the added bus commute he'd barely make the sabbat in time. He hoped Jodi's crew didn't mind if he smelled of motor oil. At least he'd worn his coat.

Colorado winters weren't like Oklahoma's. It got about the same degree of cold most of the time, but it was dry here. It didn't have that constant humidity that worked its way under your clothes, which was a plus. Still, it snowed more, and both states shared enough flatland that the wind came quick, growling and harsh, from time to time.

Cheesman Park didn't allow cars, but buses still crossed the north end. He got off there and stepped toward the trees.

Dautre walked out of the shadows. The elf had chosen a glamour that made him look human, around twenty-five, though his clothes still set him apart, like he'd stepped out of the 1930s.

At least the wool coat and pork pie hat weren't entirely out of place with the weather. Adam had to give Dautre points for the quality of the glamour. It looked seamless, and he was better than most at seeing through magical disguises.

"Let's get this over with quickly if we can," Dautre said.

"Hello to you too. We're here at the king's request, remember? I'm sorry if that means you have to wear a costume for a few hours so you don't incinerate anyone."

Dautre scoffed.

"A costume? Is that what you think a glamour is?"

Adam lifted a shoulder in a half shrug.

"What is it then?" He probably didn't have to ask. Dautre adored lecturing him on every little thing.

"Imagine taking all of you and putting it into a box one size too small. It is more than a disguise, warlock. It is a *lessening*."

Despite the patronizing tone, Dautre's words put something blue and red in Adam's chest.

Silver had ordered all of his people to wear glamours at court, to avoid harming the humans who might be in their presence, humans who were ignoring the invitation to work with the immortals.

Adam knew what that felt like. He'd been through it with a few of his customer interactions and sometimes, despite how great Jesse was, with some of the crew at the shop.

Yes, it was better here. This wasn't Oklahoma, but even when he felt fully comfortable, being out and about, he looked over his shoulder before letting Vic take his hand in public.

Nothing was ever simple, one-sided, or easily handled. If there had been easy problems, someone else had been lucky enough to deal with them.

"I didn't know that," he said. "I'm sorry."

Dautre didn't respond as they started walking. He likely assumed it was Adam's fault, and considering Adam's history with the Court of Swords, it probably sort of was.

"I think that's them over there." Adam pointed in the direction of a group of people huddled around a barbecue grill.

Dautre rolled his eyes as if to say "*obviously*," but Adam didn't think that was very fair of him. There were hippies in the marble pavilion at the top of the hill. Some were dancing to the music of a drumming circle. The sun had nearly disappeared behind the mountains, and the pavilion's lights were already on. The music echoed off the stone.

Adam followed the traces of magic toward the group at the grill.

His cousin Jodi stood over it, holding out her bare hands to warm them. It smelled good, and he suspected they'd added incense and herbs for their ritual to close the sabbat.

Jodi, like Adam once upon a time, had a fondness for wearing black, though she'd gained a little style since she'd come to Denver. Her hair was longer and neatly cut, dyed the shade of glossy midnight with purple streaks.

College suited her, as did life in Denver. As far as he knew, she was sober and a good student, well on her way to fulfilling her dream of becoming a teacher. That didn't mean they were friends. He'd always remember what she'd put him, Bobby, and Vic through in Guthrie.

She didn't quite smile when she saw him, but she scowled when she saw Dautre.

"He's one of them, isn't he?" Her accent had faded, but she still had a bit of an Oklahoma drawl.

"Yes. This is Dautre."

She looked the elf over, shoe to hat, and said, "I liked Vran better."

A lot of things had surprised Adam when he'd moved to Denver, but the way Jodi and Vran had gotten along had been one of the biggest. She'd taken to the elf much like Adam had, treating him like a mascot or a little brother and he, in typical Vran fashion, hadn't put up with any of her crap.

She turned to Adam.

"You're late. We did the ritual already."

"I couldn't help it. I had to work."

Without giving Dautre a chance to introduce himself, Jodi nodded to another woman with long brown hair.

"This is Nicole. She's one of my roommates. Nic, this is my cousin Adam."

Adam tried to get a read on Nicole and the other witches gathering around the fire.

He knew most of them would be dabblers or hobbyists. They didn't have much, if any, Sight.

"Does that sword on your back get heavy?" Nicole asked.

Adam squirmed. Okay, so some of them had more Sight than others.

Jodi smirked.

"That's Emily, and Cole," she said, indicating the nearest members of the group.

Emily, a round-faced blonde, eyed Adam warily and Dautre with open curiosity. She wore a patchwork coat that looked something like one of Sue's crocheted blankets. She had a little power. Adam could feel the magic woven into the garment.

Cole was a larger guy with hair dyed emerald green and black nail polish. He wore a *Magneto Was Right* T-shirt under his open leather jacket.

"Well, this is it, Adam," Jodi said, waving to indicate those she'd introduced and the others who gathered in little clusters, talking among themselves and drifting off into the night.

"I thought there were more of you."

"There are, but most of us stayed up late for Samhain last night," Nicole said.

"Or already left," Cole added.

"Sorry to have missed it," Adam said.

"What do you want?" Jodi asked.

He looked around the little circle of witches.

"They know everything I know," she said. "About the Other Side, I mean."

He took her meaning and appreciated it. Jodi knew he was a warlock, something that wasn't adored among practitioners, and a few other things that he didn't want getting out.

Besides keeping his own secrets, he decided honesty was the best policy.

"Silver, the King of Swords, sent me. He's trying to build bridges between his people and us."

"But you're not like us," Jodi said. "You're not Wiccan. You're not even pagan."

"No, but we're all witches of a sort. We're all practitioners."

"And the king wants us to bend the knee?" Emily asked.

"Not at all. He wants cooperation."

"That's not what I've heard about elves and mortals," Cole said.

"He's a new king," Adam said. "I know him. He's trying to change things for the better."

"You can't reform a broken system," Nicole said. "You can only tear it down and build a new one."

"One king's the same as another," Cole said.

A murmur of assent passed through the group. He tried not to scowl at the hostility, but something must have come through in his expression.

"Times are hard, Adam," Jodi said gently. "Everyone is struggling, especially those of us on the outskirts."

"I know." He gestured to his clothes. "Do I look like a trust fund baby?"

"You look like someone who got his," Cole said. "You're hanging out with royalty. They gave you a sword. Where's ours? Where's this king of yours while we struggle?"

Dautre stiffened and the temperature around him dropped a degree or two.

"He's trying to make a difference. That's why he sent us here."

"And he had nothing to do with all the witches who went missing three years ago?" Nicole crossed her arms over her chest.

Some of the witches who'd been drifting away had wandered back, intrigued by the exchange.

"The sacrifice they made was not in vain," Dautre said.

"Says the elf," Nicole snapped. "You're going to live forever."

"Many of my people died in that conflict," Dautre said icily.

Adam held up a hand and tried to explain.

"A spirit attacked the city three years ago. It killed the practitioners, a few other people, and some of the elves too."

"What happened to it?" Emily asked.

Adam took a breath. Two days ago he might have mentioned Annie and the part she'd played, the sacrifice he'd made, turning himself into a warlock, to bind the spirit in her body.

"It died," he said. "We stopped it, elves and humans working together."

He didn't need to tell them that he'd been the one to kill it. It had been the hardest thing he'd ever done. It haunted him, and damn it was tempting to think that his sin might be erased, that he'd been forgiven for an act that he could not forgive himself for, no matter who said it wasn't his fault, that she'd already been dead, or whatever else they told him.

"So it's gone?" Nicole asked.

"Yes," Adam said.

Jodi and her friends exchanged a glance.

"Then who's responsible for the witches who've gone missing lately?" Jodi asked.

"Jodi!" Emily snapped. "That's none of their business."

"What is she talking about?" Adam asked. "If something's happening, then the Guardians should know about it."

"You want to bring the cops into it?" Emily asked.

"If they can help, then yeah," Adam said. "That's their job."

"All cops are bastards," Cole muttered.

Emily shook her head.

"How do you know they're not behind it?" she asked.

"They wouldn't do that. I trust them."

Jodi's expression said that the conversation wasn't going well. Adam couldn't tell if the sour expression on Dautre's face was aimed at him, the witches, or mortals in general.

"Wait . . . " Cole said. "I've heard of you. You're the warlock. It figures you'd be working with them."

He drew himself up to his full height and balled his fists. He gathered what power he had, and Adam braced to defend himself.

"I think you should leave," Cole said.

Nicole and several of the others nodded agreement.

"It's not what you think," Adam said. "Tell them, Jodi. Please."

"Adam's okay, but Cole's right. You should probably go. I'll walk you to the bus stop."

They kept quiet until they were away from the group.

"Silver is trying to help," Adam said.

"I know. I saw what he did for you back in Oklahoma, but this group isn't exactly big on authority figures."

"The Guardians aren't exactly cops."

Jodi sighed.

"I know you've got a soft spot for a man in uniform, but that's exactly what they are."

"Vic isn't a cop anymore."

"That doesn't matter." Jodi nodded back toward the witches. "They're suspicious of the Guardians, and you can't say they don't have reasons to be."

They reached the bus stop. Dautre had vanished without saying goodbye. It figured. He probably couldn't wait to tell Silver how badly it had gone.

"Are witches really going missing?"

"I don't know," Jodi said. "There are rumors. Some people left the group without saying goodbye, but people flake out, you know?"

"Still, I want to look into it. Can you get me their names?"

Jodi looked over her shoulder.

"I'll try."

"Just, be careful, okay?"

He meant it. Jodi finally had her life on track. He didn't want some new menace pulling her back into the gutter.

She gave him a little nod and started back toward her friends.

Getting home would take forever. Maria's house was closer, and Adam toyed with the idea of trying to sneak in to spend the night.

Maria liked him, and she was happy that he was with Vic, but she didn't want them sleeping together under her roof unless they were married. As progressive as she was, that was the line she'd drawn. Vic complained that it made him feel like a teenager, and while Adam just wanted to crash, he didn't push his luck.

He was almost downtown when Jodi texted him three names.

Adam started searching through social media and for news

articles as the bus rumbled along, starting and stopping to pick up or disgorge passengers.

All three were ghosts, at least as far as the internet was concerned.

Social media profiles, pictures, even résumés, none existed.

Vic had suggested that Adam get his PI license before the state had done away with them.

He could probably pay for access to databases and search tools the general public lacked, but being the Page of Swords came with some perks. Adam got off the bus when it reached downtown and started walking away from the stop.

7

It wasn't like Silver hadn't made mistakes. Adam didn't know if sending the mortal practitioners against Mercy had been his decision or his father's. Either way, they'd died. Dautre wasn't wrong, fighting Mercy had cost the elves too, but the price was often far higher for people like Adam when they played games usually best left to the immortals.

Of all the efforts Silver was making to bridge their worlds, Rogue Community College was the king's biggest show that he intended to correct the mistakes of the past. Sure, the name was strange, but that was what they got for letting the students choose it. Vran had made the suggestion. The students had voted, and the name stuck.

It was also a watchtower.

The downtown clock tower that served as its anchor in the mortal world was an easy walk from the bus stop.

Adam yawned. He'd been up too late, worked a full day at the garage, and still had a long bus ride home. He was tempted to put this off, but if people were missing, he needed to suck it up and get it done.

The clock tower had offices on its upper floors in the

mortal world, but Adam had never seen them.

He stepped into the elevator and let the doors close.

"Hey," he said gently. "It's me. I need to go to the school, to see Jack."

The elevator didn't rise, but it dinged.

The doors opened, and Adam wasn't in Denver anymore. He wasn't even on the mortal plane.

RCC was like a lot of places in the spirit realm, a mix of modern and ancient. The school's exterior resembled a castle built of stone blocks mortared together with emerald light. All of it pulsed with slightly unstable magic.

This part of the interior, the entrance hall, with its vaulted ceilings and iron chandeliers, echoed the medieval feeling. He didn't know the layout well, but the library was close enough that he could find his way.

"Thanks," he said, patting the wooden door before starting off in search of Jack.

The librarian kept odd hours, or at least ones that aligned with Adam's work for the court. Made of wire, copper, and gold, he favored bow ties and sweater vests, having a general adorkable look that Adam never could have pulled off.

"Hi," Adam said, approaching the long metal counter that served as a desk beneath the sign that read *Absolutely No Magic in the Library.*

Jack cocked his head to the side. The whites of his eyes were golden, the irises green.

"Adam. Do you need help with something?" Jack sounded hopeful. While he seemed to like his job, Adam suspected he craved a bit of excitement now and again.

"Yeah." Adam leaned in.

"Is it for the court?"

Adam reached to scratch the back of his head.

"Kind of. It's tangential. I need to find someone, or someones. I've got some missing witches."

"Well, we can't have that."

Jack stood and led Adam to one of the steel tables set around the room. Like all of them, it sported some very sleek-looking computers.

The library was mostly metal, with journals and books organized on clean steel shelves in a manner so neat that Bobby would have wept tears of envy.

Adam preferred paperbacks and fantasy novels. He bought them used from the little shops that somehow managed to stay afloat here and there around town. There was a book mall on Broadway, and a new-used store in the Highlands that felt like a charming maze, but most of his reading materials came from the library.

That was one advantage of having moved from Guthrie to the big city—Denver's library system had a lot more in stock, and he was able to get just about anything he wanted via interlibrary loan without having to drive to Oklahoma City.

Jack, on the other hand, had linked RCC's network to all sorts of databases, and Adam's status as the Page of Swords meant he had access even though he wasn't a student.

"Here you go." Jack waved at a computer and it lit up, the search screen already open.

"Thank you."

Adam took a seat. He didn't try to hide his search. The librarian was a technopath. He'd know what Adam looked for.

That must be fun with the students, knowing they were likely to get up to all sorts of things with the type of access Jack could provide.

Adam ran the same searches he'd put through his phone and got the same results. There were a lot of similar names, but nothing in Colorado, and no one connected to Nicole, Emily, or Jodi.

"Can you show me if they had accounts that were deleted?" he asked. "I need to see their history."

"Probably." Jack concentrated, and the screen flashed. "How far back do you need to go?"

"Just a month or two before they got deleted."

"Hang on," Jack said. "It may not all be there, but there are usually echoes, caches around the 'net."

Jack sat next to Adam and pulled the keyboard toward himself.

He rested his hands on the keys without typing.

The results came up a moment later.

"Sorry that took so long."

Adam laughed.

"Dude, that was like two minutes."

Adam went through them, one by one, carefully skimming.

Each of the missing witches had been active in some way. Lauren had posted lots of flower pics. Lisa had been very vocal about her interest in the craft and how it connected to global politics, especially climate change and women's rights. Amber had been really into dogs, though an occasional cat meme snuck in.

Then they'd vanished, deleting their accounts—or they'd been deleted for them.

Adam looked at the dates of the last posts that Jack could find and confirmed they'd all been removed at the same time.

"Can you check for bank accounts, stuff like that?" he asked. "See if those are gone too?"

"Sure."

This one took Jack a little longer. Adam's screen lit with new information.

"All closed," Jack said. "But there were transfers first."

Adam narrowed his eyes.

"Are you hacked into the banks themselves?"

"Cracked, but basically."

"Um, isn't that super illegal?"

"If they can find me, they can arrest me." Jack lifted his hands in a *whatever* gesture.

"Does Argent know about this?"

The Queen of Swords had a "don't ask, don't tell" policy when it came to mortal laws. She drove at ungodly speeds through the spirit realm in whatever car she felt like boosting. He'd never seen her in the same ride twice.

"I don't know," Jack admitted. "Are you going to tell her?"

"Not if you don't tell her that I asked you to do it."

"You have a deal, Mr. Binder."

Adam looked back at the screens.

"Some of these are money transfers, right?"

"Yes." Jack squinted. "But they do all go to the same place."

"Who is it?"

"Not a who. I think it's a shell company. Give me another moment." It was only a handful of seconds before Jack said, "Got it. The parent company is called Rubrum, Inc."

"Rubrum?"

"It means *red* in Latin."

"That doesn't sound ominous at all."

"Not in the least," Jack agreed. "The weird thing is none of the information is public. I don't see a list of board members or officers, anything like that."

"But that's where the money went?"

"Eventually."

"Can you email me the chain of companies?" Adam asked. "And pictures of the missing witches?"

"Sure."

"I really appreciate your help, Jack."

"Anytime."

Adam left the library, his mind whirring.

It couldn't be Mercy, which was a relief. What would a primeval spirit need with money?

Still, there weren't any traces of the missing witches. He'd been fearing the worst, that someone was targeting them for their magic, but this felt far more mundane, like a scam.

So where were they?

He didn't even know if they were dead. Sara, Death, might be able to tell Adam if the witches had been reaped, but he wasn't ready to approach her, especially until he'd solved the mystery of Annie's return.

Silver had given him a simple task, and he'd fulfilled it. He could report back and call it done, but he kept seeing the images of the missing women. It wasn't his job, not officially. He could and probably should take it to the Guardians, but the money hinted at a mundane crime, not a magical one—and it was Adam's job to bridge the two.

He found a door in the main hall. Too tired to be certain if it was the same one, he leaned his forehead against it.

"I need to go back now. I'm sorry I don't come by more. I'll work on that."

He stepped through, expecting to find himself back downtown.

Instead, it was the closet door in his bedroom at Bobby's house.

"Thank you," he said, meaning it.

8

Adam knew it was a dream, but he didn't mind when he opened his eyes and saw Vran sitting on the edge of his bed.

The sea elf looked as he had when he'd lived at the house. He wore black jeans with strategic holes and one of Adam's old T-shirts that said FML. His hair, a cloud of ink, curled around his ears. His skin, tinted just slightly blue, blended to the shadows as he stroked Spider's inky fur.

Vran put a finger to his lips, gesturing for silence. Adam nodded and stood when Vran waved for him to follow.

They went upstairs, which looked as it did in the waking world, but the windows and blinds were wide open in the living room, letting in a night too dark and rich for the waking world. It made Adam think of space, of nebulae and stars, not empty darkness. He walked that way to get a closer look, and when he turned back, Vran had vanished.

Adam felt a pang in his chest, but he smiled. That was how Vran had lived, and he supposed it was how he was now.

Outside, he caught sight of something, a cat. It wasn't Spider. This was a rough street cat. It had a nasty notch on one ear and a limp. Adam didn't know the breed but it was the grayish sort with black stripes. Across the street, in another house, two other cats watched. They stood side by side in the window, eyes shining as they watched the one outside.

Mist tinged with red swept over the scene.

It erased the cat, the houses—the entire world—until Adam stood alone, an island in a sea of gray.

He felt suddenly cold, sprayed with droplets like the ocean in the early morning.

The sound of music, a violin, played, brief but long enough to snap him awake.

"So much for sleeping," he said aloud.

It hadn't been a nightmare, not exactly, but it had felt important, portentous. What had Vran wanted, for Adam to see a cat? To see all three cats? Or had the mist and music been what mattered?

Spider was a psychopomp, an escort for the dead.

Were these the same? Three cats. Three missing witches.

Maybe it was something he could sort through in therapy. His next session was coming up.

He still went, twice a month, though it wasn't cheap. He wasn't even entirely certain he still needed it. Dr. Cahill told him that she'd let him know when she thought he was done, and he could admit that he still had a lot to unpack.

Adam showered and shaved. He couldn't have grown much of a beard if he tried, but it got a little scratchy once a week, so he kept it clean, though he had to admit that he liked the feeling of a little scruff on Vic's jawline.

Making his way upstairs, he hoped that Annie hadn't put together another big breakfast. He could use some quiet time with his coffee and a piece of toast.

He was halfway through his second piece when his phone pinged with an email. He straightened when he saw it was from Vic. He'd forwarded the results of Dale's search. The limo that had dropped Annie off had been from one of the local rental companies.

Adam quickly typed up an email to Jack with the date and information, asking if he could track down who had paid for it. He expected to find Annie's parents on the other end, but it wouldn't hurt to trace it.

He was on his second cup of coffee when Bobby came downstairs.

"Hey," he said.

"Hey."

Adam's brother must have had the day off too because he wasn't dressed for work but in a pair of jeans and a red OU sweatshirt.

Bobby poured a cup of coffee and inched toward the table. He eyed a chair nervously, as if asking permission.

"It's your house, you know."

Bobby pulled out a chair.

For a while, when it had been the four of them, Jodi and Vran, Adam and Bobby, with Vic making regular appearances, the place had felt warmer. Now it was just him and Bobby, or it had been.

"She's out for a walk," Bobby said, sensing the direction of Adam's thoughts.

Adam never knew if those little moments were a side effect of his brother's analytical nature, or the vestiges of Bobby's Sight. He certainly had some magic. All Binders did, and while he'd once shown some interest in honing it, that had gone by the wayside. Adam was okay with that.

It was enough that Bobby no longer pushed him or what he was away, that his brother accepted his magic and the role it played in his life.

"I haven't found out anything," Adam admitted. "But I've been careful. I can't ask Sara without tipping her off."

"It's okay." Bobby sipped his coffee. "I'm not sure I want to know any more. I'm just glad she's back. Does that make sense?"

"Bobby . . . are you sleeping with her?"

His brother didn't quite sputter, but he did look offended.

"It's been two nights, Adam," he said, sounding older than ever. "And no. We've just been talking. There's no way it's not her, Adam. It's Annie. She's here. She's alive."

Adam used a sip from his mug to buy a moment.

"Even if that's true, that it is her—we still need to know how she's here, not to mention what you're going to tell Mom."

Bobby blinked.

"Shit. You're right."

"She's still coming out for Christmas, isn't she?" Adam asked.

"Yeah, and she's bringing Early."

"Oh good, let's add some law enforcement to the holiday."

So far their mother's sheriff boyfriend hadn't been a problem, but that was before a dead woman had come back to life.

Adam's phone buzzed with another email.

He swiped and saw that Jack had responded.

Adam's Sight told him what he would find even before he read it.

"What is it?" Bobby asked.

"How much do you know about Annie's parents?" Adam asked.

"Why?"

"Because they paid for the limo that brought her here from the airport on a company card, and that company is one of the ones associated with three missing girls."

"What?"

Adam explained what had happened to the witches in Jodi's circle.

"We need to talk to Annie," Adam said.

"About what?" she asked from the doorway.

She took off her coat and came into the kitchen.

Adam forced a smile.

"I want to ask about your parents."

"Okay." Annie poured a cup of coffee and sat. "Ask me anything."

Bobby had the grace to look a tiny bit guilty.

"Do you know any of these women?" Adam held up his phone to show Annie the pictures of the missing witches.

"No. What do they have to do with my parents?" Annie genuinely looked confused.

"All three disappeared recently. Any money they had was transferred to a company owned by your family."

"I don't understand. What are you saying?"

"I'm not saying anything, because I don't know what it means yet, but can you tell me what they do?"

"Real estate investment, commercial mostly. My grandfather started it in New York, but he got wiped out in the nineties. That's when they moved to Chicago. They've never really been happy there. You don't think they have anything to do with these women, do you?"

"The money thing is strange," Adam said.

Annie cocked her head to the side. "Why are you looking into this?"

"My cousin was friends with them."

"I'll admit that it's a weird coincidence," she conceded.

Adam's aunt Sue had told him that there were no coincidences in magic, only connections. He had the sensation that he'd stepped in something, or tripped over it, like a thread in a spider web. That wasn't good. You never wanted to alert the hunter to your presence before you knew what or where they were.

"You'll let us know what you find out?" Bobby asked, exchanging a look with Annie.

She nodded.

"Please."

"I will," Adam said, mostly because he had the feeling that whatever was going on with Annie's return was related, even if she wasn't aware of it.

He had too many questions, but so far it was all tying back to Annie.

He knew he had to see Silver, to report on his meeting with the coven. Maybe, just maybe, he'd get some answers too.

"I'm going to go take a nap," he said.

"Didn't you just get up?" Annie eyed his coffee cup.

"It was a long day yesterday."

"Adam works hard," Bobby said as Adam headed to the basement stairs.

He missed his tarot deck. A reading might provide answers.

Restless, he retrieved the deck Vic had given him from the drawer in the nightstand.

The cards had a Día de los Muertos theme, with lots of colorful skulls and dark-cloaked—but not always ominous—figures. They were beautiful, and he tried to focus as he shuffled them, but his magic wouldn't sync with the deck. It bounced right off, possibly because he felt strange reading with cards from a culture that wasn't his own.

To the tower then. He needed to tell Silver what he'd learned.

Lying down, he stretched out his hands as if to grasp a pole. He imagined a boat full of swords, and with a mental shove, pushed off from the shores of consciousness.

He imagined himself stepping off the boat, and in a wash of pale light, he came to the Watchtower of the North. The amusement park included a lake. On this side, the docks were intact, still white and gleaming, unlike the closed and mostly demolished edifice in the amusement park's modern self. He'd gone with Vic the prior summer, exploring it entirely in the mundane. It had filled him with a deep, golden sadness, like a final sunset. He knew how beautiful the place had been, but probably never would be again.

He usually came by night, and it was always twilight here, but by day the moon shone a little stronger, and the grounds were more alive. The rides were fuller. The groups of elves and other races were larger, and they gathered in tighter groups. Their cliques reminded him of Jodi's coven, how everyone had their people and how, so often, he did not.

"You're getting very good at that, Adam," Argent said. She sat on the dock in a retro one-piece swimsuit. The black-and-white stripes went with the pair of cat-eye sunglasses propped on her head.

"Thank you." He nodded at the oversized parasol shielding her from the moonlight. "Do you need that?"

"Not in the least, but it completes the look." Setting aside her copy of *Car and Driver*, she patted the deck chair next to hers.

"And looks are important," he said, accepting her invitation.

"Of course they are, especially here." She waved and smiled at a pair of passing deer who walked on two legs. "But you know that, or you wouldn't have arrived in style."

"I get the sense you're trying to tell me something, Your Majesty."

"Perhaps."

She leaned back in her chair.

"I think you're forgetting how dense I can be about these things," he said.

"Never." She smiled.

"You're worried about appearances."

"Not me. *I* don't mind if things get shaken up a bit."

"Silver, then?"

"Among others."

"You know, don't you, what it is I need to tell him?"

"I know that whether you mean to or not, you shake things up," replied Argent.

"They've been quiet for a while," Adam argued.

"On the surface, perhaps, but things are changing, Adam. Be cautious."

"You met me here to warn me?"

"I met you here to ask you to look deeper. That is what you do best."

She lifted her magazine, dismissing him.

He stood up and gave a slight bow, then walked away, wondering at her intent and more than a little frustrated by the cryptic request.

The guards stepped aside in a single, fluid motion when he reached the ballroom.

There were courtiers by the dozen.

Silver looked up from his throne of ice.

"You have come to make your report?"

"I have," Adam said. "Has Dautre made his?"

"He came to us immediately."

Silver looked pissed, which wasn't good. Adam needed to talk to him, and an angry elven king meant his access would be limited.

"Walk with me, Adam." Silver rose from the throne. "We will speak of your delay."

Adam obeyed.

Following his king, he couldn't help but remember when he'd first come to Denver, and first met Silver, not knowing that he'd once been Perak. He'd changed again when he'd taken his crown. He was bulkier, broader of shoulder and chest, but the shift was more than physical. King Silver was colder, less playful, but it made sense. The weight and eyes of entire worlds rested on his shoulders.

Silver led him to the Ferris wheel. They took a seat in one of the buckets and the wheel lifted them into the sky. Adam wasn't certain how these things were ever legal. The bucket hung precariously, tipping as the star-shaped wheel slowly revolved. Silver did not seem concerned, and Adam trusted that he had magic enough to save their lives should they fall.

Below, the blue flowers spread like a lake. Their silvery leaves rippled in gentle waves, like placid water in a breeze.

"What are those?" Adam asked before remembering that Silver was angry with him.

"King's Blood. They sprang into being when my father died."

The world went silent, telling Adam that Silver had drawn a spell over them. More warmly, he said, "I want them to think you are being chastised. Look afraid, please."

Conjuring the memory of disappointed teachers, Adam hunched his shoulders. Head bowed, but eyes raised, he asked, "Am I?"

"No, but I need you to convince them."

"Why?"

"Because I do not want anyone to know what we're discussing. The news you bring could cause a panic."

"You know that Annie's back."

"Yes. Have you found any trace of Mercy?"

"None. The only signs of magic I've seen are a network of spells, healing, I suspect, cast by a coven. It's too—well, it feels mortal, human, but I don't know its type."

Silver let out a little sigh of relief, though his expression remained stern.

"Then I see no reason to interfere, not at this time."

"There's more to it."

"Tell me."

Adam explained about the companies, the missing witches, and the connection to Annie's parents.

Silver let out a breath.

"We have been so focused on conflicts in our world that we've ignored what trouble might be brewing in yours. I'm going to have to ask more of you, Adam."

"Like what?"

"I need you to keep looking into this matter, but be careful. We are stretched thinner than I like. You may not have backup if it comes to a fight."

"What about other resources?"

"Such as?" Silver's tone was amused even if it clashed with his expression. Adam had to remember that he wasn't supposed to smile.

"I, um, may have already asked Jack for some help."

"So my sister tells me."

It wasn't really a surprise. Silver wouldn't have lasted even this long as the King of Swords if he didn't keep on top of things. The school was his pet project. They trained Guardians there, and Argent was in charge of them.

"Are you okay with it?"

"You have access to the school. I would not deny you that, but be careful to bring no danger there. The students and faculty have enough to deal with."

"Thank you."

"Take care, Adam. I cannot say what, but something is coming. Have you sensed it?"

"I think so. I've heard music, like a violin, and Argent is worried."

Silver lifted an eyebrow.

"She didn't say it that way, but she is, isn't she?"

Silver cocked his head to the side in consideration.

"She is. We have all heard the music."

"Is it connected to Annie?"

"I don't think so, but perhaps."

It was not easy to read Silver's moods. Looking at him, Adam understood the term *schooled his expression*, but Adam felt certain the king was also worried.

Is he safe? Argent, in her usual style, hadn't given him a clear answer.

Adam wondered how worried he should be for his ex.

"The music, do you know what it's coming from?"

"No, but I suspect it is coming from a crack, or something that slipped out of one."

"What do you mean?"

"We are preservationists because we know that cracks can become fissures. We are environmentalists because we know that to remove one piece of a system threatens it all. Yes, that means we become mired in the past and trapped in our ways, but we are slow to change out of caution. If things change too quickly, it can crack the worlds or the lines between them." Silver nodded to the lake of flowers. "I fear I acted rashly."

"You're worried this is your fault, because you killed your father?"

"Yes."

"You saved the world. You saved *my* world. I can't imagine what that cost you."

And he really couldn't. When the time had come to take a life, Adam had not been able to do it. Silver had saved him from that weight.

"I know it was a necessary action, but also a rash one."

"Do you think what's happening with Annie is connected to your father's death?"

"No, but I want to caution you, Adam, to not act recklessly. I broke something that day. It may heal, with time, but should something strike us sooner, all may be swept away."

"It's just for the day," Adam said as Vic drove them toward his work.

"I'm not worried, though I still think you should have asked Argent if you could borrow the Challenger."

"I didn't want anything too flashy, plus I can't afford the speeding tickets."

"That's okay, I'd drive it while you use my car."

"Oh, now I see what you're up to."

"You *are* supposed to be psychic."

Vic was dressed for work in chef pants and a jacket.

He'd spend the day cooking for one of the shops at the ghost kitchen. He rotated between them to get the hours he needed. It could make for long days, but he was learning to cook almost anything.

"How's the investigation going?"

Adam brought Vic up to speed on what he'd learned about Annie's parents and the missing witches.

"I just don't know the next move," Adam said as Vic pulled into the kitchen's parking lot.

"You'll figure it out. You always do."

Vic bent in for a quick kiss. He passed Adam the keys before they got out.

Vic walked toward the kitchen, which looked weirdly like an office building. He turned to shoot Adam a smile over his shoulder, because he knew Adam would be watching him go.

Adam warmed as he climbed behind the wheel of the Civic and opened his phone.

Jack had sent Adam the last known addresses of the missing witches, so he'd start there. Maybe he could get Vic's cop connection to find out if anyone had reported them as missing. He had to be cautious about how often and how deeply he tapped that well. He didn't want to hurt Vic's friendship with Dale. Vic didn't have a lot of friends, and Adam worried that coming out and the pandemic had narrowed the circle.

The dream of the cats kept coming back to him. More and more he felt like his Sight had been trying to tell him something. Maybe two of the witches were safe and one was not? He needed a new focus for his Sight, but without one it would be best to stick to the practical side.

Adam brought up the first address and drove that way, letting his phone give directions in its slightly feminine robotic voice.

He wasn't surprised to find that Lauren's last apartment was near the Botanic Gardens. The four-story, if you counted the garden level, brick building with lots of windows, looked comfortable. She'd probably walked to the coven's rituals in the park as it lay just on the other side of the gardens.

He parked Vic's Civic and went to the front door.

Luckily, there was an option for the manager when he scrolled through the names on the little digital screen.

"Hello?" a creaky voice called when Adam punched the button.

"I'm looking for Lauren Baker."

"She moved."

"I know. I'm looking for her. Can you tell me anything?"

"Hang on."

The little box made a sound like a phone disconnecting. Adam took a step back.

He waited long enough that he considered calling again.

The big wooden door swung open and a woman with long, frizzy hair and sun-worked skin stepped into the tiny lobby.

She stood in the doorway, holding it open just wide enough to talk to him.

"What do you want?"

"I'm trying to find Lauren. Do you know where she went?"

"Nope. Broke her lease and moved out. Left everything nice and tidy."

"Did she leave a forwarding address?"

"Not with me." The manager shrugged. "The unit's still available if you need an apartment."

"I do actually. Can I see it?"

"Sure." She pushed the door open for him.

Adam followed her inside and up the stairs.

It was the sort of building Vic would like, with wooden floors and thick, plastered walls.

The manager stopped at a door on the second floor, took a ring of keys from her pocket, and opened the broad wooden door.

Plenty of windows, freshly polished hardwood floors, and toothpaste-white walls made for a bright interior. A radiator sat beneath one window. He'd never lived with one, but Maria had them at her house.

Apartment shopping wasn't the reason for his visit, but he could imagine living in this space. One bedroom, though, which wouldn't work. Vic wanted two.

He wasn't surprised it hadn't been leased yet. Prices were high in this part of town. There was plenty of inventory but the rent was too much for most people, including them.

Buildings were going up. Cranes dotted the city skyline, but anytime Adam priced a condo he had to wonder who could afford them. Not everyone in the city was making a hundred grand a year.

"Do you take pets?" he asked the manager, still feigning interest. "I have a cat."

"Yeah. We charge pet rent and an extra deposit."

"It's nice," he said, even if the pet rent and extra deposit seemed excessive.

The bathroom had been fixed up and was big enough that he and Vic wouldn't be tripping over each other.

The kitchen would be a deal-breaker, though. It was too small for Vic to be happy cooking there.

"She had it full of plants." the manager said. "It was like a jungle in here, but she didn't hurt the floors."

"She really didn't say anything about why she left?"

"It's not like we were friends. She paid her rent. She didn't make trouble. The movers came and took everything. Very professional."

"Did you get the name of the moving company?"

The woman narrowed her eyes at him and he made a show of looking in the kitchen cabinets.

Movers meant money enough to pay for them, and hopefully that meant a trail Adam, or Jack, could follow.

It also meant Lauren hadn't just vanished. She'd purposefully gone, or been taken.

He couldn't exactly spirit walk with the manager hovering, but he extended his senses.

Old traces, very faint, came from the apartment. He caught

a whiff of lilac and lavender. She'd liked her herbs. It was a part of the craft Adam was woefully ignorant of. The strongest scent was sage. Lauren had used a lot of it, and likely last.

He knew that it was burned to purify or for protection. When he reached, he could feel the barest trace of her wards, now extinguished. This wasn't the same sort of magic he possessed, the same flavor, but she'd had some.

"How much is it?" Adam asked, feeling he could guess but wanting to keep up the pretense.

"Thirteen hundred and seven a month."

"Do you have any two bedrooms?"

"Nope."

It wasn't perfect, but they could afford it if they split it evenly and neither of them lost their job.

"Does it come with a parking space?"

"In this neighborhood?" She huffed.

"Thanks. I'll think about it."

She gave him a shrug and locked up behind them before following him downstairs.

Strike one, he thought before driving to Lisa's last known address.

Her apartment manager wouldn't even talk to him. The guy gruffly told Adam to go away. No, there weren't any available units, and no, he wouldn't say what had happened to her.

Amber's last address was an old house that hadn't been divided into apartments. Hopefully she had roommates who'd be more forthcoming than building managers.

Set back from the street, the place needed painting. The yard was mostly dirt, with scraggly junipers growing beneath the windows.

The bins were lined up for trash day, including a green one for compost.

Adam sensed the wards before he stepped inside them. They were woven into the fence lining the front. It was a metal frame with nets of woven twine stretching between them. The artful patterns were earthy, depicting leaves and trees.

A witch lived here, perhaps more than one.

That gave him hope. Maybe Amber was here. Maybe he could actually talk to her or someone who knew what was going on.

Adam rang the doorbell and rocked on his heels. He was getting hungry. He'd head home after this, eat, and maybe go another round with Annie to see if she had anything new to tell him.

The door opened and Emily poked her head out. She didn't look any more friendly than she had at the coven meeting in the park.

"Oh," she said. "What do *you* want?"

"I was wondering if Amber was home. She lives here, doesn't she?"

"Not anymore." Emily still had one hand on the door. She eyed it, clearly considering whether or not to slam it in his face.

"I'm not with the Guardians. I'm just trying to find Amber and the others."

"Why?"

"To make sure they're okay. All three of them vanished. Lauren broke her lease and disappeared. Lisa, too, as far as I can tell. I'm worried that someone's after them."

Emily's eyes dipped downward. She sighed and opened the door.

"Come in."

Adam followed her into a living room that rivaled Bobby's in size. The furniture was far more worn, with two mismatched couches and a coffee table covered in rings. The surface was so rough that he could spy bare wood through the polish. Someone had painted a wall bright purple and hung a colorful tapestry that reminded him of Emily's coat from the park.

He could sense the spell worked into the piece. It filled the room with an air of tranquility that went well with the bohemian vibe.

"That's good work," he said.

Emily scoffed.

"I don't need a warlock's approval."

"Did Jodi tell you how I became one?"

She narrowed her eyes.

"I cut out a bit of my heart to cast the binding that stopped that spirit, the one that killed the Denver witches." Adam put a hand to his chest. It was a reflex at this point, to prod the hole he'd put in his soul.

"Why would you do that?"

"So we could kill it."

It felt odd to say it aloud, especially when what he'd been doing was killing Annie.

"No, I mean why would you do that to yourself?" She took a step closer.

"Because someone had to stop it, and binding it like that was the only way."

He could feel her looking at him with her Sight, trying to probe the hole in his chest. It didn't feel exactly comfortable, but he didn't push her away. The wound stirred. It often did, sometimes acting like a living thing, but he willed it to calm and let her See him.

"Maybe I misjudged you," she conceded. "But I still don't understand why you're asking about Amber."

"Did you know she closed her bank accounts and deleted all of her social media?"

"Can you at least tell me if she's alive?"

Emily shook her head.

"All right. I'll go, but if you hear from her, will you at least tell her I'm looking for her?"

"Why do you care?" There was something in her eyes, a tell. She was worried too.

"I'm not sure she's with good people."

It wasn't entirely true. He had no proof that there was anything amiss, but the idea that the three of them had gone completely no contact with their lives didn't sit right.

Adam turned toward the door.

Something cracked. Like silent thunder, it rippled through the house, through the ether.

"What the hell was that?"

"It wasn't me," Emily said, looking alarmed.

Outside, the compost bin exploded in a whirlwind. Leaves and twigs melded around a trio of half-rotten, squirrel-chewed jack-o-lanterns.

Adam barely registered Emily following him out onto the porch.

"Get back inside!"

"Like hell."

The pumpkins lumped together into a triple head as the thing took on a shape like an octopus made of garbage.

As tall as two of Adam, it pulled itself along, bits of the broken bin stuck among the leaves and branches. A shard with the label *No Basura* poked out of its side.

"What is it?" Emily asked.

Adam could see something at its core, a spiraling mix of energy. It was a spirit, but not any kind he'd seen before.

"I don't know, but we can't let it wander around. It could hurt someone."

Adam drew the sword.

It chilled his hands as the blade turned white with frost.

"Hey!" he shouted.

Two of the pumpkin heads turned to face them.

"Brilliant," Emily sneered as it charged.

The thing wasn't fast, just big, but Adam could imagine the harm it could do. He ran at it, blade extended, and hoped it liked the cold even less than he did.

He came at it from the side, swinging with both hands. The thing made no sound as the blade chopped through the branches making up its belly.

It swept out an arm, knocking him aside.

It was like being hit by a bush. Scratched, but unbroken, Adam staggered back. He readied another strike when the thing ripped off one of its heads and tossed it at him.

The pumpkin collided with Adam's chest, exploding and knocking him to the ground.

The thing turned toward Emily. She dashed away from it as he got to his feet and hit it again, driving the edge of the blade into its back, over and over. Leaves and rotten leftovers flew and fluttered, but the thing didn't stop. It still didn't make a sound.

"I'm not getting anywhere here!"

"No shit," Emily called back. "Catch!"

Holding onto the end of the string, she tossed Adam a ball of yarn. He felt the charge of her magic in the thread as she ran off the porch.

"Hold tight!" she said.

Adam dropped the sword and did as she said.

He saw her intent and together they cut the thing off at the knees. He didn't expect the string to hold the thing's weight, but it did.

The creature twisted toward Emily, tripped, and fell. She hurried to Adam and took the ball from him.

"I bind you," she said, breath heaving. "I bind you. I bind you."

The spell went off and the thing stopped moving. The hold wasn't complete. The creature shivered like she'd wrapped it in a net.

It shed its makeshift body as it writhed, and he could see the spirit in the center, a mass of barbed tentacles. A wide mouth, lined in jagged teeth, opened at the center of it all.

"What is it?" Emily asked.

"I don't know."

The thing strained against Emily's binding, coiling and stretching.

Adam retrieved his sword and drove the point down into the center of the thing. Ice spread through it until it froze. With a single crack, it shattered, dissolving into a pile of snow.

"I need to wear gloves," Adam said, letting go of the sword long enough to rub his hands together. "Nice spell."

"Nice sword."

"Thanks." Adam took in the pile of debris. He wiped what he could off his shirt and jacket. He'd be smelling rotten pumpkin for days. "You're going to need a new compost bin."

Adam put the sword away. Emily went to get a pair of snow shovels, and together they dumped the mess into the intact trash bin.

Emily apologized to a couple walking past when their dog went crazy for the smell.

"Thanks for helping," Emily said, shaking her head.

"Are you ready to tell me about Amber now?"

"I don't even know what that thing was!"

"I don't either, but I think it was here for you." It was a

bit of a lie. The thing had looked like it wanted to wander off. He felt bad about using Emily's fear, but he didn't know how else to pressure her. "Why? What would it want with me?"

"Because you know where Amber is."

10

"I don't know where she is," Emily said. "Not exactly, but I told her not to go."

"Go where?"

They were back inside on the couch. Adam had left a message with the elves' answering service. To his surprise Dautre had come almost immediately. He looked like a reject from the 1940s again, but Adam couldn't complain as he was currently laying fresh wards to keep Emily safe.

Emily's eyes darted back and forth.

"Emily . . ."

"Fine. She joined a new coven."

"That's it?"

"Not exactly." Emily took the ball of yarn from the fight and started nervously working it with her fingers, weaving it into a cat's cradle. "They wanted her to move out, give up all her worldly possessions, that sort of thing. They sent movers guys in coveralls who packed everything up. I told her I didn't like it, that it seemed controlling. It sounded more like a cult than the craft, you know?"

"What did she say?"

"She said I was wrong, that I wouldn't understand, but they were going to make things better, for all of us."

"That does sound pretty culty."

Emily gave a little nod.

"But she was really excited about it. They taught her these old spells, rituals. I didn't like the feel of them. I asked her not to cast them in the house."

"Let me guess, she cast them outside, in the yard?"

"You think she called that thing up?"

"Did it feel anything like the rituals she was using?"

Emily's face crinkled. "I don't know."

"Did she leave anything behind, anything at all?"

"Nothing."

It made sense. Any personal trace might have left a chance for sympathetic magic or a tracking spell.

"How about the name of the moving company?" he asked.

"No. They were just a bunch of guys with a big truck."

"You have other roommates, right? Can you ask them?"

"Sure."

"I am finished," Dautre announced from the doorway. "That should keep any spell or being less powerful than myself out for a good while."

Adam expected Emily to make some crack but she said, "Thank you."

Adam's stomach grumbled.

"I'll get out of your hair," he said, standing.

"Leave me your number. I'll let you know if I think of anything else or if Cole and Jessica know the name of the company."

"Cole, the guy from the other night?"

"Yeah. He lives here too." Emily went to the kitchen and came back with a pad of sticky notes and a pen.

"I appreciate it," Adam said, writing down his number and email.

Dautre followed him out.

"They are truly vulnerable, aren't they?" he asked, looking back at the house. "She's fortunate you were here."

"Not as much as you think," Adam said. "She bound that thing, whatever it was, pretty quickly."

"Show me the remains."

Adam walked Dautre to the dumpster and opened the lid on the mess inside.

Dautre's face bent with disgust, probably at the meatier bits that had come out of the compost.

"Never thought I'd see an elf lose their lunch." Adam let the lid drop.

"You said there was a spirit at its core?"

"Yeah." Adam described it. "Sorry, I couldn't take a picture. Do you know what it was?"

"No, but it does not sound native to this plane."

"If it's not from here, then how did it cross over?"

Dautre stared at the curb where the bin had exploded.

"That is a very good question. I wish you had not destroyed it."

"It didn't really leave me a choice."

Adam's stomach grumbled.

"I will stay and keep looking for traces of its crossing."

"Thank you, Dautre, and thank you for coming."

The elf didn't respond. Adam took that as his cue to leave.

Vic's car hadn't been ticketed, booted, or destroyed in the fight, so maybe his luck was turning.

He drove back to the ghost kitchen and parked with enough time to think before Vic's shift ended.

He wasn't much of an artist, but maybe he could try to draw the thing and run it by Jack.

Vic tapped on the glass a moment later.

Adam started.

"Hey."

"You okay?" Vic asked as Adam rolled down the window.

"Yeah, just had some excitement. You want to drive?"

"Nah, not if you're up for it. It's been a long day."

"Cool."

Adam hoped he didn't have any thawed monster guts on his shoes as Vic circled the car to climb into the passenger seat. He set a paper bag in the back.

"Where to, sir?" Adam asked.

"Home, Jeeves. I wish to survey the estate."

"Very good, sir. Shall I draw you a bath?"

"Not unless you want my mom freaking out."

"Good point."

Vic reached out and put a hand atop Adam's leg, probably to let him know it wasn't a rejection. It hadn't taken Adam long to understand that touch was Vic's second love language.

It was harder, being together without being able to just instantly read each other like they had in the beginning, but it was also better in many ways, like savoring a piece of cake instead of gulping it down, something else Vic was trying to teach Adam. He wasn't in survival mode now, not always on the edge of starving. Food didn't have to be an exercise in eating all at once because there would be more.

Vic was like a favorite book that always had new chapters, new things to learn and discover.

He sniffed.

"Is that . . . pumpkin?"

"Yeah. I need a shower."

Adam told him about the incident at Emily's.

"That's new, right, the hermit crab thing?"

"Yeah. I don't know if it was trying to make a body for itself or some kind of armor."

They drove a while.

"What's in the bag?" Adam asked when the smell made his stomach grumble.

"I had a shift at the Indian place today, Naan of Your Business, so mushroom masala for you and meaty stuff for the rest of us."

"Does that mean I'm invited for dinner?"

"If you want. I mean, if you have time."

"Always."

Adam wished he could steal a kiss, even to peck Vic's cheek, but Vic had leaned his seat back and closed his eyes.

The sun had almost fully set when Adam pulled up in front of the Martinez house.

It hadn't changed since he'd first come here, following his connection to Vic to see how he was recovering from the attack that had bonded them, but the rest of the street had experienced some gentrification. A few of the homes had been scraped and replaced with modern boxes that ate up most of the backyards.

Maria, Vic's mother, complained about the noise from the construction, but said she was staying put. It lit a warm amber glow in Adam's chest.

He'd enjoyed the summer nights on the patio with Vic, here and at Bobby's. He hated the idea of not having any green space and attributed that to the Binders' history as Druids, a tradition the family grimoire was annoyingly vague about.

It did have a lot of spells, and more than a little history or personal notes. He made a mental note to search it for entries on tentacle garbage monsters.

"Jesse's not home yet?" Adam asked, noting the missing SUV.

"He's been gone a lot lately," Vic said. "Mom thinks he's got a girlfriend."

"He hasn't said anything at the shop. Then again, the guys would tease him mercilessly."

Maria was already at the table, reading through some student papers with a glass of wine beside her and a red pen at the ready.

"Hello, you two," she said, looking up as they came through the door. "Are you staying for dinner, Adam?"

"If you'll have me."

"Always."

Maria stood to accept Vic's kiss on the cheek and move her work to the coffee table.

She liked dinner to be something they did as a family, for it to count. Vic said she'd always been that way, but it had been even truer once his dad died.

The Martinez house always felt warm and inviting, and almost never cramped, despite the small size. Adam felt welcome there.

"You can borrow one of my shirts," Vic said. "I'm going to go shower."

Adam felt less like a leftover pumpkin pie after changing.

"Sit, please," Maria said when he'd returned to the little dining room.

He obeyed and managed to avoid saying *yes, ma'am.*

"Have you thought any more about going back to school?"

Education was important to her. She taught history at the local state university. She never said she wasn't happy that neither of her sons had gone to college, but Adam knew she'd had mixed feelings when Vic had joined the police academy.

"Sometimes. I'm not sure."

"Why not? You got your GED, didn't you?"

"Yes, but, well, money is one thing."

"I told you that I'd help you apply for grants."

"I know, but I don't know if I have the time, and it's a long commitment."

"School isn't for everyone," she conceded. "But you should think about your future. It comes on quickly, faster than you can imagine. And it's not like you have to have a big wedding. Not to mention that men's rings cost less than women's."

Adam blanched.

"Mama," Vic scolded her from the doorway. His hair was wet from a quick washing. He'd tugged on old jeans and a red T-shirt that was just the right amount of tight on his shoulders. "Leave Adam alone. He had a long day."

Maria blushed a little.

"That's your brother," she said as a car pulled up. "I'll set the table."

"Uh, I've got it," Adam said. "If that's okay."

"That's sweet of you," Maria said.

Vic followed Adam into the kitchen.

When they were out of sight he wrapped his arms around Adam's waist. Adam turned in the embrace and pressed a kiss to Vic's neck. He tasted of clean skin and bit of lingering body wash, something gingery with black pepper.

"It's okay to set boundaries with her you know," Vic whispered into Adam's hair. "You already have a mom."

"I know, but I want her to like me."

"She already likes you, which is why she badgers you about your future. That's not going to stop if you ask her, politely, to back off."

"It's more like fussing." Adam could admit, at least to himself, that he sort of liked it. Maria worried about him, about his future. He hadn't had that for a while. It felt good.

"Either way, welcome to the family."

The noise in the outer room died down, telling Adam that Jesse and Chaos had arrived.

"We'd better get to work," Adam said.

Vic made a disappointed sound and tightened his grip.

Adam spied a little hole in Vic's shirt. It would be so easy to hook a finger into it and tear. It would be even easier to give in and stay in Vic's arms.

He was saved by a bundle of dark, muscled energy. Jesse's pit bull bolted into the kitchen and almost knocked the pair of them over. Laughing, Adam pet Chaos while Vic plated dinner on Maria's mustard-yellow dishes.

11

His best dreams were always of Sue.

Tonight they were in her kitchen. Adam chopped potatoes while his great-aunt showed him how to fry them, just right in a thin layer of oil.

The oil bubbled in the cast iron skillet, glossy and crackling when he used the knife to slide the potatoes in. He sprinkled in the salt and pepper, then stirred it all with a spatula.

The oil popped and the potatoes sizzled, filling the trailer with the smell.

Sue laid out a plate with two paper towels on it to soak up the grease when Adam spooned them out.

She hummed a song he didn't know. It sounded familiar, though.

He wanted to ask her about it. He wanted to tell her how much he loved her and how grateful he was for all she'd done for him.

She smiled, telling him she knew. Then she stiffened and looked to the trailer door.

Nothing knocked. Nothing burst through, but it opened, letting in a crack of icy blue light.

Adam woke with a prickling feeling. It brushed over his skin like needles, softly scraping, not quite piercing.

Something was at the wards, touching them, but not pushing or breaking through.

Remembering the spirit from Emily's house, Adam rolled out of bed and jerked his clothes on.

Hurrying upstairs, he tried to move quietly as he opened the front door. He didn't want to alert Annie and Bobby until he had to.

The street in front of the house was full of mist, but as he watched, pink slowly filled it until it turned a bloody red.

The fog curled and crept but stopped at the curb. It pooled against the line of his meager defenses.

The wind cut through his worn T-shirt but didn't disperse the mist. He wished he'd grabbed his coat.

Whatever was out there didn't seem to want in. It didn't press harder but just kept circling to send that spider step feeling across his shoulders and the back of his neck.

The mist thickened and a figure strode forward, stepping dramatically into view.

Not fully there, he stood transparent in a crisp tuxedo and a carved wooden mask shaped like a wolf's head. It was painted an uneven, ruddy red. The figure cocked its head to the side as if to ask a question.

Adam didn't draw the sword. The figure hadn't threatened him, not yet.

"What do you want?" he demanded, trying to sound imposing though he knew he was shivering and had to look ridiculous standing there without a coat.

Adam studied the figure. He obviously had magic, but was strangely blank to Adam's Sight, almost as lifeless as an image on a TV screen, like some sort of projection.

"Who are you?" It didn't earn him any better of a response than the first question.

They stared at each other for a long while. Then the wolf man righted his head, nodded, and stepped back into the mist.

The street cleared a moment later.

Adam waited, senses extended, but the unknown figure had gone.

He gave it another moment to make sure, then went inside.

There was no way he'd be able to go back to sleep.

Crouching beside the bed, he dragged out the plastic case he kept tucked next to the old shoes he should, but couldn't, bring himself to throw away.

The Binder family grimoire still smelled faintly of the rattlesnake den Adam had rescued it from. He laid it on the small writing desk he'd picked up at a thrift store, turned on the lamp, and began flipping through its pages, looking for signs of *der rote wolf* or *roter wolf*—the red wolf. Nothing popped out, but the book was hard to read. At some point his ancestors had run out of pages, so they'd begun using a technique he'd learned from Maria called crosshatching, where they'd turn the page to the side and write diagonally before turning it the other way and doing it again. It made trying to find a single phrase nearly impossible.

Adam hoped to get the whole thing translated and put into some kind of software where he could search it, but knew that was years away.

He could ask Jack to do it, and the technopath would likely have it uploaded in minutes, but Adam felt this was something he should do himself, that the slow unlocking of the language was part of learning the magic and history hidden in the pages.

He found nothing but admitted that he was too tired to focus. He wished Vic were there, if only to curl against his chest and listen to his heart. Even Spider was gone, off doing whatever psychopomps did in the wee hours.

Adam's therapist recommended he keep a journal, which he sometimes did. He didn't want to write in the family grimoire, but a black leatherbound notebook had called to him in Mexico when he'd gone to the ocean with Vic.

The memory was golden, perfect. They'd walked the beach at night, hand in hand. The ocean had been a wonder, bright and glittering by day, dark and roiling by night.

He sniffed the journal's cover. Any trace of sea salt was probably his imagination, but it still eased some of the needling.

The journal served as his personal book of shadows. Not that he'd written any spell recipes or, frankly, anything he thought future generations of Binders would find useful. It was mostly an account of what he'd encountered in case he needed notes later. He sometimes imagined it falling into mundane hands and decided the reader would just think they'd stumbled upon someone's fan fiction for an overly complicated anime.

Opening it now, he wrote down everything he could remember about the figure in the street.

12

Adam forgot about breakfast. He didn't even try to get up. He'd left another voicemail for the elves, detailing the incident in the yard. He'd likely need to spirit walk to the tower and talk to Silver again, but what he needed most was time to think, so he lay drifting, too awake to sleep, too drowsy to rise.

He had three missing witches. They'd joined a new coven, or a cult. If Emily was right about Amber, then there was a good chance they were together, dead or alive.

Regardless, all of their money had gone to a company owned by Annie's parents. A spirit of some unknown sort had appeared at Emily's. Why? To silence her? That didn't make any sense. She hadn't really told Adam anything. Were they trying to hide the connection between the company and the cult? No, his first impression was the right one. The spirit had appeared on Emily's lawn but it hadn't come for her specifically.

The biggest question was the motive. What was the cult after?

Power was the usual answer, but the transfer of funds indicated money could be another factor. The three women hadn't had much of it, but someone had wanted it all the same.

They were young, all around a certain age. He needed to know more about their craft and beliefs. Maybe there was something that made them lean toward the cult's philosophy, which he knew nothing about.

Adam groaned.

It didn't feel like they'd been taken. It was more like they'd been recruited and the cost of their admission had been their mortal possessions.

Was it some sort of magical pyramid scheme, or was it about control, making certain they didn't have the resources to run away?

The doorbell brought him more fully awake, but he didn't move quickly. It was Annie's house. He'd let her deal with it.

Something brushed against his senses. Nothing like what he'd felt the night before. It wasn't a threat, but his Sight was still warning him.

Pulling on jeans and a shirt, he moved upstairs.

He froze when he reached the kitchen and saw Annie escorting two people into the living room.

They didn't look like cultists. He'd expected robes, maybe those wavy daggers that reminded him of snakes. They looked like a pair of middle-aged white people with slightly upscale, albeit old-fashioned taste in clothing.

They weren't smiling, but didn't seem hostile. It was Annie's behavior that made Adam move into the room. Her movements were too careful, like they'd chase her if she bolted.

"Oh, Adam," she said, spying him. "These are my parents, Patrick and Edwina Wilcox."

She sounded so formal and yet, younger. The cheer that he'd seen since she'd walked through the door on Halloween had vanished.

"This is Robert's younger brother, Adam."

"Is he a doctor too?" Edwina asked, and it was just shy of, well, his mother would have called it catty. His therapist would have called it passive-aggressive.

"No. I'm an auto mechanic," he said, choosing to go with aggressive-aggressive. "Oil changes, that kind of thing."

But then again, she already knew that. Annie had said they'd had PIs watching the house, watching him and Vic. A flare of something hot and orange stabbed through him, but he forced it down. He needed to make sure Annie was okay.

Patrick said nothing during the exchange. He didn't react to Adam or Annie's introduction, as though acknowledging Adam was beneath him.

Maybe Silver and Annie should form a support group for people with icy dads, Adam thought.

The polite thing to do would be to excuse himself, to say something nice and leave the room. He opted to play the barefoot hick, too ignorant of manners to do the polite thing. He wouldn't leave Annie alone with these people. He took a seat in the puffy armchair as Annie and her parents settled onto the couch.

Annie flicked her eyes to him and he thought he read gratitude there.

"I'm confused," she said, facing her father. "Why are you here?"

"We wanted to check in on you, dear," Edwina said. "We hadn't heard from you, and you left so suddenly."

"It's only been a few days. You didn't have to fly out."

"It's only the jet, dear," Edwina said.

"I think you should come home now," Patrick announced. He looked around the room but didn't seem to really see it. "Like we discussed. Have you packed whatever you wanted here?"

Like her husband? Adam barely managed to contain the thought.

"No, Daddy," Annie said. "I said I was coming back here to stay, and I meant it."

Another flick of her eyes to Adam.

How could Bobby have missed this? How had he not seen what Annie had dealt with when it came to her family?

Probably because he hadn't wanted to. Bobby had been so busy running from his own history, his own family, that he'd been blind to Annie's past.

A little of the old resentment for his brother resurfaced.

Still, Adam wished Bobby was there, if only so they'd outnumber Annie's imperious parents. Gods, he needed coffee, but he wasn't moving until they did.

"This is college all over again," Edwina said. "We never should have let you go to that school. We should have picked for you."

"Annie's staying," Adam said. "As long as that's what she wants."

"We are speaking to our daughter," Patrick snapped. His anger put a crack in his glamour and the warlock wound growled at the brush of his magic. "Not some—"

Patrick froze mid insult, and Adam knew they knew.

Their magic was well hidden, but Adam had its number now. He could follow the line of it to both of their uninvited guests.

The wound rose on its haunches, snarling gleefully, like it wanted out to play, begging Annie's parents to try their luck.

And yet he still felt nothing from her. She had no clue who her parents were, what they were involved in, or what they were.

"Auto mechanic?" Adam finished when the silence had lasted too long.

"Some . . . *auto mechanic*," Patrick sneered.

"You're going to have to do better than that," Adam said. "I don't scare easily."

He reached as if to scratch his shoulder, and watched Patrick's eyes when he touched the sword, bringing it just out of its sheath so that anyone with Sight would see it.

"I think you should go." Adam dropped the blade and let it slide back out of sight.

Patrick took a moment. He remained stiff-backed and braced for a fight. He could have one, if that's what he wanted.

This might be Annie's house, but it was Adam's home. They were in his place of power, within his wards, and any hesitation about using the sword's magic vanished when he thought about them threatening their daughter.

Edwina put a hand to her husband's arm and sniffed. "When you come to your senses, we're staying in Cherry Creek."

"Of course you are," Adam said.

He decided he did not like these people, that he wouldn't have liked them, even if they weren't possible cultists connected to the missing witches. He would have disliked them for being snobs who were jerks to their daughter.

Edwina followed Patrick out the door to where a town car waited at the curb.

"I guess a limo was just a bit too much this time," Adam said. "You know, since they took the jet."

Annie closed the door and locked it.

She sank, like her bones had gone soft.

"Come on," he offered. "I'll make you some tea."

"Why?"

"Because that's what Vic would do."

The electric kettle was easy and the coffee pot was soon gurgling. Neither of them spoke until they were halfway into their cups. Chamomile for Annie, and freshly ground Kenya AA with two shots of almond milk for Adam. This encounter called for the good stuff.

"You lied to us, didn't you?" he asked. "When you said they hadn't kept you locked up?"

"It's not like they chained me to the bed." Annie looked to the front door, like her parents were on the other side, like they could bust through at any moment and drag her away.

"It was more like that." She waved toward the living room.

"I'm sorry."

She muttered a quiet thank you.

"They're not good people, are they?" Adam asked.

"No. I don't suppose they are." Annie shook her head. "Thank you for not leaving me alone with them."

"You're welcome."

"How did you know to stay?"

Adam swallowed a chuckle.

"How much has Bobby told you about our dad?"

"Not a lot. He doesn't like to talk about him. There aren't even any pictures in the house."

Oh boy, that was a can of worms.

Adam had learned the truth about their father's murder only after Annie had died. Bobby's confession had started the healing between them, but it had also rocked his world and driven a wedge between him and Vic when Adam had kept the secret, something that hadn't been easy to do when they were psychically linked.

Just because you were done with the past doesn't mean it was done with you.

"Let's just say that we didn't have a sitcom kind of childhood."

He wondered how much of Bobby's blindness to Annie's situation was because Patrick and Edwina had the life he aspired to—the clothes, the car. The jet. They clearly had money. Adam wondered how much of it had come from witches like the three missing women.

Why would you ever want to be like that?

Bobby should have seen what Annie had been dealing with, but maybe he could now. He'd been so far up his own ass when he'd met her, but he was better now. They had some work to do, a lot of it, if they were going to be okay. In the meantime, Adam knew that Annie wasn't part of her parents' mischief.

The way they'd spoken to her said that they clearly saw her as a possession, something they owned. The way they'd just marched in and demanded she go with them . . . He wrapped his hands around his mug and applied a little pressure, squeezing to let some of the red out of his chest.

He could see it now. Of course they'd put her back together, brought her back, but it wasn't out of love.

He'd originally thought Bobby had seen her that way too, just a pretty thing. Then she'd died, and he'd fallen apart too completely for it to be anything but love. If any doubts had remained, Bobby's moping around unshaven and in terrible need of a shower had put them to rest.

"I can't believe you got my father to leave," she said. "He never backs down when he wants something, and they came all this way. How did you do that?"

"How much has Bobby told you about me, about what I am?"

"I know you're gay, Adam. It doesn't bother me."

"No, not that."

"What are you saying?"

"I'm saying that when Bobby gets home, we're going to have a long talk, the three of us, as a family."

Annie looked nervous.

"It's nothing bad. Well, okay, some of it's bad," he said. "But I think it's time you both knew everything."

Adam read until then. He'd gotten the latest Shaun David

Hutchinson book, and it, along with the coffee, had settled his nerves enough to push the circling questions aside for a while.

Bobby came through the door at last.

"What?" he asked, meeting their gazes.

"We need to talk," Adam said. "All of us."

Adam started at the beginning, what had happened when he'd first arrived in Denver, why he'd come when Bobby had asked for his help.

Annie took it better than Adam expected. She sat, wide-eyed for a moment, before asking, "I *died*?"

They were around the kitchen table. No one used the small formal dining room on the other side of the kitchen, though maybe it would have been more appropriate for this talk.

"Yeah," Adam said. "I was there."

"Then how am I here?"

Bobby took her hand.

"That's what we've—I've—been trying to find out."

"And you're like, Buffy or something?"

Adam chuckled.

"Something. Just without the clothing budget or a theme song."

"Does that mean vampires are real?"

"Not as far as we know," Bobby said. "Wait, they're not, are they? You never said for sure."

"We're getting off track," Adam said. "Do you remember the accident at all, the one that put you in the coma?"

"No." Annie stared into her tea. Adam had made her another cup, because again, that's what Vic would have done. "But the doctors said that's normal, a trauma response."

Adam looked to his brother.

"That could be it," Bobby hedged.

"But you don't think so?" Annie asked.

"I . . . no. I think Adam's right. He saw you die. I believe him, and I saw something too."

Bobby explained his own coma experience, how Annie had come to him in the hospital and given him her magic, her life, to bring him back from the brink.

"I don't remember any of that," she said. "I don't remember dying. You say I did, but—then how am I here and how did I get to Chicago?"

"And why?" Bobby asked.

"I know why," Adam said. "Your parents weren't willing to let you go. Not because they love you, but because they see you as an extension of themselves."

"Adam," Bobby scolded.

"No, Robert, he's right. It's why I got a nursing degree and took the job here. I wanted to get away from them. I wanted to escape, to run away."

Adam heard the unsaid, *It's why I married you.*

From his expression, Bobby heard it too.

That had to hurt, but Adam hoped they could work through it.

"If you guys need a good therapist, mine works on a sliding scale."

Bobby looked affronted.

"Maybe," Annie said.

"I want to take you to the hospital," Bobby told her. "X-rays, MRIs, that kind of thing. I want to make sure you're really okay."

Annie looked uncomfortable. She'd probably had way too much experience with hospitals at this point.

"I'll leave you two to talk," Adam said.

"Where are you going?" Bobby asked.

"Back to bed. Wake me if there's an apocalypse."

"Isn't Vic coming over tonight?" Bobby asked as Adam reached the basement stairs.

"Okay, Vic can wake me up."

Maybe he didn't have a theme song, but he'd scored big in the supernatural boyfriend department.

Adam had always been a reader. His parents hadn't done a lot of things right, but they'd made certain their sons had books. The shelf in the trailer had always been full. His mom would buy them used, take them to the library, or get one of those subscriptions that sent a new kids' book every month.

High school dropout or not, Adam liked libraries. He liked research and often wondered what he would major in if he did go back to school. History, probably. Some of his best conversations with Maria happened when she'd go on for a while about some historical event. Vic feigned interest, because he'd had a lifetime of it, but for Adam it was a wonder to spend time with a parent who wanted to talk about that sort of thing, who had something to say about a world greater than her corner of Oklahoma.

He didn't know how to convey to Vic the sense of peace that the Martinez home brought him. They could be loud, and yes, they didn't always agree on things, but when there was anger, it passed quickly. There weren't days of walking on eggshells. The place wasn't infused with the barbed wire red feeling he'd grown up with.

He'd never understand what his parents had fought so much

about, or why his father raged so much and so often at him. He had vowed to never live like that.

The library at Rogue Community College didn't have the same feeling as the Martinez house or even one of the public libraries. It was more clinical, but he could admit that the blue weight in his chest didn't come from it, just his associations with the school.

He headed there after work. It had been nice to wake up with Vic. They hadn't even been cuddling, but just having him beside him in the bed left a lingering warmth Adam could feel all day. He wanted that every day.

If he had one note, it would be that the library held too few books, too few quiet nooks to sit and read. That and it didn't smell like a library should. It felt too clean.

A few of the students were working at a table in the corner while Adam scrolled through page after page of digitized and translated text. He didn't know them, and they didn't bother him. One, a boy with hair the color of the sea, occasionally looked at him, probably trying to place him or figure out what he was doing there.

"Anything?" Jack asked, wandering over to look over Adam's shoulder.

"Not really. It's pretty much what I suspected. True resurrection doesn't come up outside of fiction and fairytales. Dead is dead, even when magic is concerned."

"You might find more in the library at the elven academy, but it would take the king's permission for an interlibrary loan, and he's only granted it once. Or I could try the Archive Infinite."

"The what?"

"They're an enclave of scholars," Jack said. "A bit stuffy, but they collect a lot of knowledge. They might know something."

"I don't think it would make much difference," Adam said. "If you could bring a person back to life, it would be a big deal. Someone would have written it down. They'd want people to know."

"Are you sure?"

"I'd brag about it."

"Unless Death buried the truth of it," Jack considered.

That was a thought. Sara liked her rules, and she'd done horrible things to innocent people to enforce them. The elves and Guardians weren't above altering mortal records. It wasn't much of a leap from that to editing the immortal accounts. Still, he didn't think so.

Beings like the King of Swords would make contingencies. So if dead was dead, then that left the idea that Annie hadn't crossed over, not completely.

The spirit realm remembers.

Aunt Sue had first told him that. He'd seen it constantly in his spirit walks, signs of places and things long forgotten in the mortal realm. Maybe it had remembered Annie as alive. Maybe there'd been a spark that someone had been able to fan.

But who? How? And why?

Her parents were the obvious choice, but what he'd sensed in them hadn't been strong enough to knit a body back together. The trace of spells across her skin might have told him more if they hadn't been so faded from the casting.

"I'm looking at the wrong thing," he muttered.

"How so?" Jack pushed his glasses up.

"I need to look at healing magic instead. If Annie was as bad off as I remember, and someone healed her." Emily had said the cult was teaching Amber rituals. "I need to look at group castings—stuff like that."

"Some of the professors or Hex could help you with advanced magical theory, but healing is a very specific application. We don't have anyone working on it directly. Do you have any details?"

"It was a cooperative approach," Adam said, remembering how the spells had intertwined. "A complicated ritual that took at least a dozen people."

"Probably thirteen," Jack said. "Most covens like their themes."

He turned to the shelves of paper volumes and came back with a plain-looking book.

"It's a reprint." He set it down and began flipping through it. "What we had before was mostly fragments."

Adam peered at the pages.

It was a spell book, a grimoire, or had been. This was in far worse condition than the Binder family tome.

"Is this old English?"

"It's modern, but Elizabethan spelling could get pretty creative."

Adam squinted. Lots of spakes and thines and thous. It made his head hurt, but he could read it. He supposed he should thank his mother for all the Bible readings he'd endured in his childhood.

"It's from a matriarchal British coven," Jack said. "They did a lot of healing work."

Adam's eyes traced the details of the spells, piecing them together. It was a ritual casting, where the full coven of thirteen contributed various parts. Not a resurrection, but a revival.

"This is it, or something like it. Thank you."

Jack smiled and went to check on the table of students in the corner.

Adam read on.

This ritual, or one like it, could mend a body—for a price. The coven would have to use some of their life force in order for it to work. The worse the damage, the more they'd have to spend.

How many witches had cast the spell, he wondered, *and how much did it cost them?*

"Can I borrow this?"

For the first time since Adam had met Jack, he looked uncomfortable.

"It's okay," Adam said.

"It's not that I don't want to help, but we don't have the original images on file. I can't print another. I'll scan this one and send you a digital copy once we've captured it."

"That would be great."

Adam turned to his other mystery, the Red Wolf, but found nothing. The creature was a ghost.

"What about this?" Adam asked, gesturing at his search results.

Jack laid a finger to the mouse and stared at the screen.

"Nothing," he said. "I mean, really . . . nothing. Want me to put out some feelers?"

"If you can, but be careful, okay? I don't know what he is, or what we're dealing with. I don't want you drawing its attention."

Jack nodded.

Adam thanked the school for taking him home and opening a door into his bedroom again.

It was odd to have the house to himself. Bobby and Annie must still be at the hospital, running all the tests that Bobby could come up with. Vic wasn't coming over.

Adam made a cup of coffee and settled into a chair on the back porch.

He'd made a little progress in the garden in his time here. Annie had laid out some flowerbeds lined in bricks before she'd died, but she hadn't planted anything.

Adam had put in some bulbs, irises mostly.

They were asleep for the year, but the last of their blades still stuck out, brown and green, like irregular teeth, from the mulch.

His mom would never know that they'd been the greatest gift she could give him. She'd trekked over to Sue's old trailer lot and dug up a few bulbs. Adam could imagine the conversation between her and whoever lived there now. Hardened in the Oklahoma clay, they thrived in Denver, and Adam had already divided them to gift a few bulbs to Maria.

He loved the idea of them spreading and bringing people joy wherever they went. In a way, it was a legacy, a way to remember Sue.

His phone pinged with an email and a large file. Jack worked quickly.

Looking through the fragments of the ritual again, zooming in and out to parse the details, Adam circled back to the coven that had saved Annie. Her sacrifice, giving her life to bring Bobby back from the brink made sense, especially now that he could see how much she loved him. He'd have done the same for Sue.

But who had these witches been to Annie?

He was holding the questions too tight. If he relaxed his grip, the answers might come.

Adam put down the Elizabethan word puzzle and let the sounds of the suburbs drift over him.

If he reached, he could feel the ground, the soil, and the things that never truly slept.

Sensitive, that was the word they'd always used for him.

Adam is so sensitive.

Sometimes his teachers or mother had meant it in a kind way—he was empathic. He did not like to hurt others and did not like to see them hurt.

Sometimes they meant it another way, that he should be

tougher, harder, more of what they thought a boy should be.

Moments like these, when he remembered, came less often now.

He was more interested in what he could do, what sensitivity brought him.

Reaching downward, he felt more. There were seeds in the earth, grass and weeds, roots. They slept, waiting for spring. A hive of green sweat bees had taken to ground. They huddled for warmth, shivering to protect their queen.

This side of his magic was hereditary. Natural druids, they'd lived to strike a balance between nature and survival. They'd lived on the edge of civilization, at the border where people met nature. The more he studied the family grimoire, and magic in general, the more that path called to him, and he could understand why his father had wanted to live in the woods, why he'd planted his rough little garden at the top of their property, where he'd wanted to build a house but never had. Adam got it, a little, though most of him balked at the idea of going back to that life.

He knew a lot of it was the state of things. The future should feel full of promise, but the world had been struck a blow. He could not ignore the pandemic and the people who'd died. He'd seen firsthand the toll it had taken on Bobby, who in the early days had secluded himself from the rest of them in case he brought home a virus they hadn't understood.

Things felt broken, harder, even as Adam's life had settled into something better. Jodi and her friends weren't wrong to be upset. He'd been lucky, and very few things felt fair these days.

He was weathering it. Vic was weathering it, but he had to look up at Bobby's fancy house and wonder if Cole hadn't been right: Had he gotten out? Was he trying to pull the ladder up behind him? Adam thought about the missing witches and their social media posts. They'd wanted a better world, or at least a fairer one. Had they wanted it badly enough to run into the arms of a cult?

Yes, things were broken. It felt like people no longer had any sense of connection to each other, any sense of community, but even then, there was magic in the world.

He'd been looking for something ominous in Annie's return, but what if it was a gift, a miracle?

It felt too close to faith for him to embrace it.

Jodi had been right about that too. He wasn't a pagan, nor did he believe in what his mother did, with her whispered prayers and ragged Bible. He didn't pray to any god, but still, there were times he had to think there was something out there, something kind. He knew it wasn't Life. Life was cruel, chaotic. Death could be merciful, but he knew from personal experience that she wasn't good, no matter how nice she could be at times. She only played for keeps.

The thing he felt was rare and pale, like candlelight. It flickered in his chest, a mix of gratitude and hope.

Adam closed his eyes and said a quiet thank-you.

14

He was cleaning up in the kitchen when Annie and Bobby returned.

"How did it go?"

Bobby looked to Annie, and she nodded, giving her permission.

"Lots of scars, lots of broken bones, all expertly set," Bobby said with grudging approval.

Annie sank into herself, deflating.

"But no chance of children." She rubbed at the corner of her eye with her sleeve. "They couldn't fix that."

Adam didn't know how to react. He knew how much Bobby had wanted to be a father, and he could see how hard it was for Annie. It had been their dream. This had to be the worst kind of haunting, like breaking the same bone in the same place, over and over again.

"I'm so sorry."

His first instinct was to leave them alone, to flee the scene, but he'd learned a long time ago that those instincts could be wrong, that he'd learned to do everything wrong from his parents.

Telling the part of him that said he could only make a

bad situation worse to shut it, he wrapped Annie in a hug.

Adam could feel the weight of it, the loss, seeping out of her. It wanted to pull her to the ground. She was fighting it, forcing herself to stay on her feet. This was, for her, perhaps the hardest thing she'd faced—worse than fighting her way back from death.

He didn't get it. He'd never wanted to be a parent.

But it wasn't about him.

Adam held on for a moment longer, letting her feelings seep through his defenses, the walls he'd learned to put up so long ago when his Sight had threatened to overwhelm his sanity.

It brought one thing into perfect clarity.

This was Annie.

Any doubts about her identity were erased.

"It's okay." Forcing a smile he knew she didn't feel, she took a step back. "I mean, it wasn't working out before, anyway."

He'd done this. He'd cost her, both of them, this thing they wanted more than anything else. He'd killed her, and while she'd come back, it wasn't whole. Something vital, at least to her, had stayed behind.

"I'm so sorry," he repeated.

He felt tears well in his eyes and knew he'd probably flushed red with feeling.

"Adam . . ." Bobby said, knowing what he was thinking. "This isn't your fault. It was Mercy's."

"I'm, uh, going to go for a walk."

The sun had set, and the streets were quiet. Adam watched for the neighbors, especially the speed-walking woman. There had been two of them, usually in matching track suits, and then, recently, just one. He didn't know their names, didn't have the heart to ask what had happened. They'd been a part of his landscape since he'd first come to Denver, and now that had changed too.

He needed to separate what was his from what was Annie's. His guilt. Her sorrow.

He'd almost untangled it all when a surge of magic hit his senses. Adam's nose wrinkled at the flavor, but he didn't draw his sword. It wouldn't have helped against her. She could slice off his arm before he'd gotten it out of the scabbard.

The street filled with a gust of cold, a sharp bite of wind just a bit too icy and too early for the season.

It sent leaves skittering along the sidewalk and a shiver up Adam's spine. Snow swirled in the streetlamp, and the Knight of Swords stepped into view.

She wore a glamour, as all elves did now, but it was barely an attempt at a disguise. Magic leaked out of her, especially the joints in her plated armor. Her arrival alone was an announcement that something otherworldly was afoot.

Silver had worn the title as a moniker. She took it literally.

The bands of silvery steel fit her body at sharp angles. Forged of blades, it gleamed in the streetlight.

This wasn't the feminine terror of Argent in her aspect of the Queen of Swords.

The knight always looked ready for war.

Hopefully any spying neighbors would just assume that she was the vestige of a late Halloween party or an escapee from a LARP party.

"I really have to get you people to use the backyard," Adam muttered.

"You people?"

Adam bowed, to just the amount he was supposed to. He had to kiss her ass, but he didn't have to like it.

"My apologies, Lady Knight. I meant to say that visiting dignitaries would find it more accommodating than arriving in the street."

Her eyes narrowed, telling him she wasn't buying it.

"You are far too familiar, Page."

"I mean no disrespect," he said, keeping his back bent but raising his eyes.

Silver had taught him how to speak to elves, and she had a point. He was a long way from the fear he'd felt when he'd first met Argent or approached Silver at his court.

Building bridges went both ways, and the new Knight of Swords remained staunchly to one side, inflexible and unwilling to meet anyone in the middle.

Adam knew Silver had chosen her to appease the hardliners among his people, to counter their anger that he'd been willing to appoint a mere human the Page of Swords.

"You drew your blade in battle," she said, almost casually, which told Adam that Dautre's report to the court hadn't been only for Silver's ears.

Had that been what Argent had been trying to tell him, that he was being watched?

If so, the knight might have spies watching him. She didn't seem the sneaky type. That was more Argent's style, but the Court of Swords was full of intrigue. He couldn't blame her if she had eyes on him, but if so, an assist against the pumpkin monster would have been appreciated.

"Yes, against a spirit," he said. "A kind I didn't recognize."

She'd probably consider that a failing. He almost mentioned that Dautre hadn't seemed to have heard of it either but decided not to throw him under the bus too.

"And how did you fare?"

"I destroyed it."

He was careful with his language. The elves could be funny about death. They wielded weapons, which meant they had to have some amount of comfort with the idea of taking a life, yet he suspected that she'd be the first to call for his head if he broke a rule or protocol.

He wanted to ask her what she wanted. It had been a rough night, learning what he had about Annie. His heart ached for her and Bobby. His brother had been making peace with everything that had happened—losing his wife, not being a father. All of this had to be ripping the wounds open again. And Annie, to come back when she could have gone anywhere. That took strength and guts, especially now that he knew what she faced back in Chicago.

"Show me your blade." The knight extended a mailed hand.

Adam drew it and held it toward her, balanced flat atop his palms. She took it gingerly, as if she feared she'd cut him, which was almost kind of her.

It was laughable to think he could hurt her.

She had to resent him, his race, his rank.

He could feel the magic seeping out of her in ways he never could with Silver or Argent. Her glamour was too tight, like it could not contain all of her. He thought about what Dautre had told him and tried to conjure some sympathy for her.

She gave the sword an experimental wave, then held it out straight to run her eye over the blade.

"Your hesitation to draw your weapon shows wisdom."

"Thank you."

"You are no warrior."

"Oh, I know. I'm just a mechanic."

"And yet you have been given a place among us. Many would exploit such a gift. They would attempt to drink too deeply from the well of our power, and thus destroy themselves. You show knowledge of your limits."

Adam blinked. He wasn't certain, but that had come close to being an actual compliment.

"Yet you have much to learn."

There it is.

Adam suppressed a smile.

"Yes, ma'am."

She passed the blade back to him, hilt first.

"I will petition the king to assume responsibility for your training."

"Lady?"

"The blade tells me that you struck many ineffective blows. Such a mistake would have killed you had you fought anything with greater will or speed."

"The sword talks to you?"

"As it does you, only you are not attuned to its voice. If you were, as you should be, you could command it, and were you elven, His Majesty would have ensured you trained for a century before you were brought into his court. I would have dedicated decades to ensuring that you knew your forms before you fought so much as a target made of sticks."

"But I don't have a century."

She seemed a bit angry then.

Adam didn't know exactly what he'd stepped in, which appeared to be his luck lately, but stepped in something he had. What the hell had Silver gotten him into now?

"As it is, the court cannot suffer weakness, and incompetence is weakness."

Adam swallowed.

"You are aware, Lady, that I am not like you? I mean to say that I cannot train as an elf can."

"I am," she said. "You are not the first human I have met."

He barely managed to keep from asking if her experience had been to eat them.

She vanished in another slight flurry of snow.

Hopefully Silver would tell her no.

"Great," he muttered. "Can't wait to start."

The problem with bridges, he considered, turning back toward the house, was that they sometimes collapsed.

15

At least whatever the Knight of Swords had planned for him didn't start right away, and the next day was one where Vic would stay over.

Adam spent the morning comparing the fragments of the spell book Jack had sent him to the Binder grimoire.

There wasn't much overlap, but one principle remained clear. Magic had a certain sort of conservation of energy. You couldn't undertake some big act like healing wounds on the scale of Annie's without getting the power from somewhere else or without risking death.

That was why covens worked rituals, to share the burden and avoid burning out.

Annie didn't make breakfast, and he didn't blame her, but he also hoped it wasn't a sign of the same depression that had left her bedridden and open to Mercy's possession.

He wanted to help and considered trying to cook, but decided he was probably the last person she'd want to see. He walked the boundary of the property instead, pouring his will into his wards, strengthening them, in case another hungry spirit came looking for a snack.

The casting was not hard, just a matter of calling up his power and charging the lines he walked. He thought of Annie the entire time and hoped he could keep her safe.

No matter what Bobby said, Adam had killed her. He'd shot her with arrows, she'd almost died, and the experience had cost her something precious.

The garage was open but he wasn't working today. He considered going in anyway, if only to work on another of Jesse's reclamation projects.

His hands itched with the need for activity, but neither work nor the commute to get there appealed to him.

This wasn't boredom, not exactly. That felt gray, flat, a little bit like hunger, but in his brain. It lay in his chest too, lower than his heart, but higher than his stomach. It felt slightly purple.

Restless, he decided to call it. He was restless, and there were too many things circling.

Night was too far away. Vic always settled him, no matter how tense things got or how many mysteries begged him to solve them.

Not having much else to do, Adam walked to the bus stop and grabbed the zero, the bus running the length of Broadway from Highlands Ranch to downtown.

He got off around Yale and dropped into the occult bookstore.

"Adam!" the woman at the register called. "Here for another tarot deck?"

He almost blushed.

"I thought I'd look," he said, trying to conjure some hope.

She waved as he approached the shelf with display copies of the decks and their books laid out atop a glass case.

Adam ran his hands over them, letting his Sight try to feel the cards and see if any spoke to him. He'd done the same with much of the shop's contents during prior visits, trying to sense a connection to crystals, wands, or statues of various deities. Some of the stones were pretty, and he could admit that he'd love to have them around just to look at, but none really clicked with his magic.

The statues, too, brought nothing. He liked the one of Herne, muscle god of nature, but it didn't click with his magic.

Never one for tools, he walked right past the wands and singing bowls. The closest he came were the tarot-based invocations he used for spirit walking.

"Nothing?" she asked, coming over to observe his progress.

Adam shook his head.

"They really do work better when they're a gift," she said with a bit of hope.

He'd bought a book last time, a volume about druids, just to feel like he wasn't wasting the shop's time with his endless browsing. It had proven useful, giving him some context for his family's role in things.

She was right about the gift thing and he wished the deck Vic had given him had worked.

He knew giving Sue's deck to Jodi had been the right thing to do, but part of him wished he hadn't. So much Binder history, and so much of Sue, was wrapped up in those cards.

"I'll just take some incense," he said, picking up boxes and sniffing until he found one he liked. Dragon's Blood.

She nodded with understanding.

"That's a good choice, especially if you're dealing with negative energy or need inner healing."

"I always do," he said, thinking of the Knight of Swords and what felt like his never-ending delve into therapy and his past.

"Do you want a bag?"

"My pocket's fine."

"Got to help Mother Earth," she said, smiling.

The day was pleasant enough so he walked a few miles in the wrong direction, just to feel the city.

It seemed like construction was everywhere, condos and apartments. He hadn't lived here long but he could feel an older Denver trying to poke through. Sometimes it failed, sometimes it succeeded. Change was burying that city, erasing it, forcing it into the past. He'd see it in the spirit realm, eventually, when the 1970s caught the realm's attention.

Wandering by foot wasn't like driving. The sensations came slowly. He eased up against them, against the city. He could take it in sips rather than a rolling slam of sensations. Downtown lay straight ahead, due north.

One thing he'd read about were ley lines, bands of magic wrapping the earth. He didn't feel anything like that, but Broadway had something like a flow, a sense of life, from all the people passing to and from their houses. Colfax Avenue was that way too. It flowed east to west and formed the city's other axis.

Maybe he was another kind of druid, something different than his ancestors. Maybe he was attuned to roads and highways, wherever tires rolled and headlights ran like rivers.

His thoughts drifted through that idea as he walked north, pulled along by the city's energy.

At least walking spared him having to deal with the city's traffic.

Magic would be a factor when he and Vic chose a place. He'd need to set wards, sure, but he also needed to feel safe there, to know they could tune the city out. Maybe he'd get lucky and the apartment building would have a courtyard, someplace he could plant a few of Sue's irises and continue to try to cultivate that bit of his craft and history.

On a whim, Adam took the bus north, got out at Speer, and walked along the canal toward Cherry Creek.

Tents and tarp-covered shopping carts, homeless camps, peeked out of the shrubs.

Then the vibe shifted and he was somewhere the unsheltered would never be welcome.

This was the part of the city he liked least. It was too rich, too expensive. It thrummed with steel and glass and overpriced food. Parking on the street meant feeding a meter. Even the mall didn't feel like somewhere he belonged, though he and Vic had caught a movie there over the summer.

He didn't like the wealthy. He knew that. He didn't trust them. Maybe that was another topic for therapy, or maybe it was a prejudice he'd be okay with keeping. He hiked on, past the country club and into the shopping district, keenly aware of the kind of money that poured in and out of it.

With Annie's parents staying there, the neighborhood felt even more like enemy territory.

They'd be at one of the hotels.

There were a few, all upscale, all stylish, and just overdone enough to tell him that he'd never be able to afford to stay there.

Adam didn't sense anything as he went eastward. Beyond was a neighborhood, and past that, the city would start again, feeling more like a place he could breathe, though the traffic along Colorado Boulevard was arguably the worst in the city.

The last hotel in that direction pinged his senses. He felt it as soon as it came into view. Thirteen stories, which could not be a coincidence. The front wore a tacky facade of white stone that reminded him of a Greek temple, which fit the name, the Erythraean. It clashed hard with the glass and steel that made up the rest of the edifice. There were windows, but he doubted they opened, and no balconies. There were doormen in black suits, and heavy, heavy wards. The magic's flavor felt instantly familiar.

The protections were woven much like the spell that had

knit Annie back together, a layering tangle of various magics. Some got along better than others, but there were gaps. If he was careful, he could slip inside, especially if he came in spirit.

A single, thick thread ran through all the layers of protection, like a master rope the others linked to. He'd felt that flavor of power at the house.

Adam didn't go any closer. He didn't want to be detected if he could avoid it.

Letting his Sight glide over the invisible boundary, he carefully scanned for gaps or breaks.

As if they functioned like a singular unit, the doormen's heads swiveled toward him, staring coldly, their senses extended. Adam gave a little wave and backed away. He didn't show them his back. They didn't move, but kept their gaze fixed in his direction, their noses pointed like a pair of Dobermans that had caught his scent.

Annie's parents weren't just staying here. They owned the place. This wasn't a hotel. It was a fortress, a place of power. They weren't visiting Denver. This was an invasion, and the city was occupied.

16

Adam had settled into the basement with Vic when a knock sounded at the door to his room.

He opened it to find Bobby, looking serious, on the other side.

"Will you come upstairs, please?"

"Just me or both of us?"

"You should both come."

Adam and Vic exchanged a look, but Adam could only shrug.

"Your guess is as good as mine," he said as they padded their way upward to find Bobby and Annie at the kitchen table.

"Adam, I want to hire you," she announced.

Adam blinked.

"Um, for what?"

"To get to the bottom of what's going on with me and my parents."

"I'm already trying to do that." He took a seat. "But you know I'm not a private eye, right?"

"Maybe not, but you're the closest thing we have to an expert, and something's not right—hasn't sat right, since I came back. I don't remember so much—dying, what happened after, and I need to know."

"Okay," he said. "But you don't have to pay me. You're family."

She sat with that for a moment, then said, "Okay. Will you at least let me cover the expenses?"

Adam shrugged. "There aren't any so far."

"There will be if we go to Chicago."

Adam and Vic exchanged a look.

"My parents are here. They won't expect us to sneak off and try to find out what's going on behind their backs."

It was sort of brilliant, and she was right. They wouldn't see a move like that coming. He liked that they'd have the upper hand in surprises for once.

"When do you want to go?"

"As soon as we can."

"That's going to cost you a lot," Vic said.

"I won't be paying." Annie laid a black credit card on the table. "My father will."

"You can use that?" Vic asked.

Annie shrugged.

"It's how I got here and rented the limo from the airport. It's still active. I checked a minute ago."

"You said your parents paid for the limo."

"They did. They just don't know about it."

Adam smiled.

"Will he know?" Adam asked. "If we go to Chicago?"

"Not for a month or two when the statement comes in, and if his accountants bother to tell him. If he has a problem with it, then I'll deal with him then."

Adam didn't enjoy the idea of putting her into further conflict with Patrick, but he liked that she was willing to stand up to him.

"I think I can get the time off from the garage," Adam said.

"Me too," Vic said.

Adam opened his mouth to say something, but Vic cut him off.

"I'm coming. I want to be there to watch your backs."

Adam couldn't argue with that.

They looked at Bobby.

"I can't go with you. They need me at the hospital, but I trust you, Adam."

He leveled his gaze at his younger brother.

Adam got it. He really did.

Bobby had just gotten Annie back. For all the pain he'd gone through and the confusing tide of emotions he was feeling now, he couldn't bear to lose her again.

Adam would do everything he could to protect her. He tried to convey that to Bobby silently.

"Okay," Bobby said.

Annie didn't sigh, but Adam read something in her eyes that he took to be relief. For whatever reason, she didn't want Bobby there.

Adam took a breath.

"All right," he said. "Let's go to Chicago."

The drive from Highlands Ranch to the airport was long enough for Adam to steel himself for the experience of flying. Bobby dropped them at the check-in and got out long enough to give Annie a hug.

The longest part of the process was checking Vic's gun. Adam had packed light, with a backpack containing a change of underwear and socks. He spent the time waiting trying to find the art that had spawned so many conspiracy theories, but other than a gargoyle springing from a suitcase most of it seemed to have been removed by the ongoing construction.

Annie led them down the escalator to snake their way through the long security lines.

"You okay?" Vic asked as Adam watched the occasional trapped bird fly beneath the giant tent that acted as the terminal's roof.

"Yeah. Just . . . crowds, you know?"

Vic put an arm around him and it helped to still some of the buzzing-bee feeling of anxiety leaking in from the people around them.

Adam exhaled and willed himself to stay calm as they passed through the scanners and took another escalator down to the train.

They had time to kill, so they checked out the little bookstore in their concourse before they boarded.

"Do you want some coffee?" Vic asked, eyeing the shop on the upper level, but for once, Adam said no.

Adam could handle the plane. Annie had booked them seats together. She wanted the aisle and Vic gave Adam the window seat.

A family boarded and Adam could not miss Annie's expression as they carefully steered their toddlers toward their row. She smiled, but it was heavy.

He didn't know what to say.

Having kids wasn't something he thought about, nor had he and Vic really talked about it. Neither of them seemed to strongly want them or feel repulsed by the idea, but Annie and Bobby were people who wanted, more than anything, to be parents.

Adam didn't get it, but he could understand wanting

something you couldn't have. He turned to stare out the window before Annie caught him watching her.

He pressed himself against the wall through the safety presentation and the mandatory commercials that followed. Vic entwined their fingers as they took off.

Slow walking his way through the city allowed him to let his Sight relax, but flying did the opposite. The spirit realm flew by outside the window and he had to shut it down, despite the slow glide of the cloud-dwelling creatures that looked like manta rays or the floating islands of the blue-skinned cloud giants.

Their trip to Mexico had been his first flight, and he'd been so excited to go with Vic that he'd managed to not let the experience of being on a plane rattle him, but now it crept in.

It let the landscape rush by too fast. He couldn't watch the spirit realm slowly pass by, couldn't soak up the changes to the watchtowers or the boundaries. He could barely tell the spirits and creatures around them that he meant no harm, that he was just passing through.

The plane winged over Lake Michigan, and he marveled at the blue expanse, something Colorado lacked. It didn't even have all the lakes and reservoirs of Oklahoma. It was green here, so much greener than Denver and its arid plains.

Then they landed, and it felt almost like a jolt, being dropped elsewhere, into a new place. His senses had to recalibrate, to learn the rhythm of the magic here. It felt like breathing different air, which it was.

Chicago tasted old in a way that Denver or Oklahoma didn't. It was already chilly compared to Colorado. Adam wished he'd brought more than a leather jacket, but the air had a bit of the kind of dampness he was used to from back home. That felt familiar, comfortable, though the slightly dizzy feeling of someplace new remained while they collected Vic's locked case and picked up the rental car.

"Gray?" Adam asked when Vic chose a boring sedan.

"We're kind of undercover, right?" Vic asked them.

"Yeah," Annie said.

"Gray is boring. Cops don't look for gray."

"Never tell Argent you said it's boring," Adam warned as he took the backseat.

Vic followed Annie's directions out of the city and toward the suburbs as Adam felt his way through the changes in the magic.

He'd expected a city, the kind of skyscrapers he'd seen in movies, but the airport wasn't near downtown.

Denver flowed toward the mountains in one direction and the plains in another, but Chicago sprawled, flat and low. It felt like Oklahoma City in a lot of ways, how the skyscrapers clustered together and the suburbs ran toward them. Only here there was the lake, bigger than any they had back home, bigger than any inland body of water he'd seen.

"How far out are they?" Vic asked.

"Suburbs . . . exurbs really," Annie said.

They drove for another half hour.

When they stopped it was pretty much at the kind of house Adam expected, though it wasn't as big as he'd thought it would be.

"They really like that whole column theme, don't they?" he asked as Vic parked in front of a manor where an army of men with muskets and red coats would look right at home.

"Yeah." Annie unbuckled her seatbelt with a deep breath.

The house was mostly brick, two stories, and wide. The curving driveway made a half circle around a lawn that Adam could only call manicured.

"Let's get in and get out," Vic said. "We want any clues as to what they're up to."

"Will anyone be home?" Adam asked.

"It's the maid's day off, so no, not if my parents are still in Denver."

"What are you getting?" Vic asked Adam.

"Magic. Wards . . . nothing scary. It's not like the hotel in Denver."

"Can you get us inside?"

"I have a key, and the alarm code," Annie said.

"He means magically," Adam said. "I don't want them knowing we were here if we can help it. There might also be a booby trap or two."

The wards were what he expected, another weave of many colors, all bound around the central thread of Patrick's magic. He wondered for a moment how Edwina fit in, if she had any power of her own or if she just followed her husband's course.

It took Adam a moment, then he had it, a little gap in the spells, probably a spot where one of the casters hadn't been as focused, or maybe they just weren't as powerful.

He picked carefully at the thread with his senses and lifted it like a curtain.

"Step where I step," he said to Vic.

"What about me?" Annie asked.

"You don't have any magic and the place knows you, so you won't set off any traps or warnings."

Annie considered Vic.

"What about him?"

"I'll explain later," he said.

Once they were across, he nodded to Annie.

She unlocked the front door and immediately stepped to a keypad to disable an alarm.

Vic closed the door behind them

"My father's study is probably the best place to start."

Adam swallowed a comment about anyone having a room named that as she led them toward the broad stairs. The foyer and wide living room felt more like a high-end antique store than anywhere genuinely livable.

They followed Annie upstairs and into a room that looked like it belonged on the *Titanic*. Everything was wood paneling. A desk bigger than Vic's car stood in the middle.

Vic produced a few sets of hospital gloves and they began to search. Annie went through the desk drawers while Vic looked through the bookshelf and filing cabinets.

Adam searched in his own way, letting his senses brush across the place.

A lot of spells had been cast here.

They weren't the sort of sky-shaking power an elf wielded, but closer to his level. It became instantly clear that Patrick wasn't a heavyweight. He likely worked all of his magic like the wards at the hotel, through a coven who'd bound their power around his castings.

There were other traces, faded but tactile, like the impressions of heavy furniture left in carpet. Adam ran his senses in that direction.

This was Patrick's magic, but he couldn't discern the purpose. It wasn't defensive.

His Sight caught on something, a painting, and he stepped to it.

Annie straightened.

"That's my great-grandfather, Silas."

Adam stared at the portrait, which was the sort of thing he'd walk right by in a museum. The white-haired man struck an imperious pose, his chin jutting toward the artist as if to challenge him to a duel or a fistfight. Annie had his eyes, but it was the background that caught Adam's attention.

Silas had a shadow, one painted with a tinge of crimson. It blended with the golden details behind him, the rich room of statues and drapery. Adam could just pick out the ears and a tail. He felt himself moving toward it, even if he didn't want to.

"Adam," Annie said. "You shouldn't touch—"

But he'd already pressed a hand to the canvas.

17

The world went liquid and greasy. Adam felt stretched for a moment, then compressed. This wasn't the spirit realm, though it had some of the same surreal quality.

The light around him came from everywhere and nowhere.

He knew the scene—the painting of old wealth he'd been examining.

Behind the borders of the room was only mist, crimson and swirling.

He could breathe, but the floor beneath him didn't feel exactly solid. He didn't feel solid.

An old record player, a Victrola if he remembered the name correctly, played a familiar tune: the violin music he'd heard before. The sound came and went in waves, inconstant, like the space he'd been pulled into.

Booby trap, he thought. *And I'm the booby.*

Adam pulled his will around him, shoring up his defenses. It was instinct now to guard himself from outside energy.

External to him, the sword hadn't come along for the ride. He had only his magic and the warlock wound, the hungry scar upon his heart.

If this was the painting, where was Silas? The leather upholstered chair sat empty.

"Adam," a voice said behind him. "This is a surprise. I didn't expect to see you here, at least, not yet."

The Wolf stepped into the room.

"So you can speak."

"When I want to."

"And where exactly is this?" Adam waved to indicate the room.

"You're inside the painting, Silas's painting."

"It's a trap?" Adam asked.

"More of a vault, of a sort. Wilcox uses it to commune with me, just as his forefathers did. It's a channel, much as I suspect your tarot cards would be, if you still had them."

A tool, then, one Adam did not know how to use.

"You seem to know a lot about me."

The Wolf's blue eyes narrowed behind his mask.

"Oh, I know all about you, Adam Lee Binder."

"Wish I could say the same. Why did you come to see me outside the house?"

"Why do you assume it was to see you? Why do you assume it was me?"

Adam looked closer. The tuxedo was the same, he thought. They all looked alike to him. This one was worn, a bit dusty at the edges.

They had the same eyes, or at least the same color of eyes, but this wolf seemed harder. The ear of the wooden mask was notched, like someone had chipped it with a bullet, and there was more gray in the brown hair.

"I don't suppose you'd take off your mask?"

"Your supposition would be correct."

"You said Wilcox was communing with you. I'm guessing you give him advice?"

"Another good guess."

Was it divination magic then? It made sense. A businessman who could see a bit of the future would have an advantage. No. Adam had plenty of Sight and he'd been around Jodi, lived with Sue. This was something else.

"My turn. Do you miss your sword?"

Adam shrugged.

"I don't use it much."

"You destroyed the boggin with it."

"Is that what it was?"

"It's the name I gave them. I'm surprised you killed it. You're usually such a bleeding heart about these things."

"I didn't enjoy it, but I couldn't let it roam around."

"Such a hero," the Wolf snarled.

"Did you summon it, send it to hurt Emily?"

"Me?" The Wolf shook his head. "No. It was merely a side effect of Amber's practice. She's quite strong."

"Is that why Wilcox wants her?"

"Yes. She and the others are the cream of the current crop."

So there had been others, or would be more.

Adam narrowed his eyes.

"Who are you?"

"I'm not ready to tell you, and you're not ready to hear the answer."

His voice wasn't familiar. He didn't sound like an elf, or any other immortal Adam had met.

"Is that why you're wearing a mask?"

"Well, you'd see through a glamour, wouldn't you? The important thing is that I am not your enemy. At least, not yet. Nor do I have to be. We could even be friends."

"And what would that take?"

"Just stay out of my way."

There was little chance of that, especially if whatever the Wolf was up to could harm others, but this was no place for a fight.

"I'll think about it."

Adam turned toward the wall of mist behind him. He reached toward it with his senses and knew immediately that he'd find no escape that way.

"Isn't that what got you here in the first place?" the Wolf asked. "Poking at things you don't understand?"

"I never said I was the smartest warlock."

"Just the most dogged?" The Wolf head tilted in amusement, then gestured to the padded chair. "You might as well sit. You're going to be here a while. It's too bad your Reaper isn't connected to you anymore. Then he could probably pull you out. That kind of connection would let you open a door."

"Is this the part where you make me a deal? You tell me what you want and you'll show me the way out?"

"What makes you think I want anything from you?"

"You came to the house. You tested my wards. You've clearly been doing your homework."

"Like I said, that wasn't me."

"So someone is stealing your act?"

"Let's just say that we're at cross purposes when it comes to you. He's in a different place. I only came here because I felt you enter the painting."

"Then how about you tell me the way out, you know, since we don't have to be enemies and all that?"

"Because watching you squirm is fun." The Wolf took the seat Adam had refused.

Adam pushed at the edges of the spell, feeling for weaknesses. He'd been trapped before, but that had been a living thing, something he could kill, something the warlock wound could consume.

He'd broken other spells, but this wasn't targeting him. He'd simply fallen into it. It was old, but mortal. Given time he could pick it apart, find a breakpoint; but he didn't know what would happen to him if the painting dissolved. He didn't know what lay beyond. Hopefully Vic didn't panic and burn it or something.

"What's out there?" Adam pointed to the misty nothing.

"The Between, and trust me, you don't want to go there. Not yet."

Something in the Wolf's voice, his sincerity, made Adam shudder. He'd been outside reality once, in the nothing there, and it hadn't been pleasant.

He thought about the tornadoes back in Oklahoma, and the people who'd once survived by going into their bank's vault and setting a timed release. When they'd opened the door, the vault had been the only thing left standing in the town.

Maybe that was the case here. The room in the painting was all that stood between him and oblivion.

"It's going to get pretty boring for you if I'm stuck in here forever," Adam said.

"I can leave whenever I want. There's a trick to it, you see."

"It's a neat bit of spellwork." Adam tapped the floor with his foot. "Yours?"

"Let's just say that I consulted. There are a lot of lost things in the Between. Time runs long there, and I've had plenty of years to study the magics I've found."

"And how about you, are you a lost thing?"

"We all are. Every one of us." The Wolf tried to sound playful, but Adam heard real bitterness in the question.

The more he prodded, the more Adam felt the spell was something like a clock or mechanism. There were a lot of moving parts, all of them energized by magic. It almost felt magnetic, the way it pulled and pushed at him at the same time, holding him there like a fist closed around an egg.

He had to convince it to let him go.

It had drawn him to it the moment he'd shown his magic, sucked him into its grasp. The painting was the fist. His defenses were the eggshell.

"Oh, there it is," the Wolf hummed. "You never were as stupid as you pretended to be."

Adam took a breath and lowered his defenses.

"See you soon, Adam."

The misty world of the painting faded.

"Adam!" Vic was saying. "Can you hear me?"

"Yeah."

He was lying on the study floor.

"What happened?"

"You touched the painting," Annie said. She pulled her fingers off his neck and stopped timing his pulse. "And then you collapsed. We didn't know what to do."

"It's okay."

Adam struggled to sit up.

"Are you all right?" Vic asked.

"Yes. It's just been a while since I was that disconnected from my body."

Adam felt around inside himself, made sure he was intact. The sword was back in place. It hummed a bit, like a pet who'd been worried about its owner's absence.

He glared at the painting.

"I've always hated that thing," Annie said. "Is it cursed?"

"Not exactly. It's more like a private room and I didn't have the key."

"Should we do anything about it?" Vic asked.

"Not if we don't want Patrick knowing we were here."

Adam wasn't certain the Wolf would tell him. Whoever, or whatever, he was, he didn't talk like an immortal or feel like a spirit. He seemed bored, and he seemed to have known about Adam for a long time. He spoke like they were old— well, not friends, but something, even though they'd never met.

He'd explain about the Wolf later. They couldn't stay here forever.

"Let's finish with the study."

They got back to work.

Annie came up with a list of properties and investments. Vic took pictures of everything while he and Annie moved through the rest of the house.

They didn't find anything nefarious or magical. There wasn't a shady basement with a hidden dungeon or a secret ritual room, no large space for a coven or cult to meet.

The house felt sterile. The bedrooms with their perfectly made beds and spotless bathrooms gave some semblance of domesticity, but living here would have been like living at a bank.

Still, the furniture was impressive, old-world wood, leather, and thick fabrics, but none of it seemed like it would be comfortable. The art was too vague and generic to be called pretty. So much of it was beige and colorless. Adam had to peer into other paintings to find detail, and he was careful not to fall into any more of them, but the rest were mundane.

He could see now why Annie preferred the floral prints and pastel colors she'd decorated her and Bobby's house in. It wasn't to his taste, but it had a lot more style than this lifeless showroom.

"I don't think there's anything else here," Annie announced.

She'd saved her room for last. It matched the rest of the house, and had nothing of her style or vibrancy.

"Is this where you recovered?" Adam asked.

She perched on the edge of the bed, like a bird ready to take flight at the first sign of a cat.

"Once I got out of the hospital."

"Do you remember which one?" Vic asked from the doorway. "Maybe there's someone there who could tell us something?"

Annie blinked.

"No . . . I don't remember. That's odd, right?"

"It is," Adam said.

Annie took in the room, her shoulders slumped.

"I hate this house. I'd burn it down if I could."

"I don't blame you, and not just because it's so ugly."

He'd hoped to coax a smile from her but failed.

"I always told myself that I'd do it all differently, that I'd be a completely different kind of parent."

"There's always adoption."

"I know. Maybe that's what we'll do."

Adam exchanged a glance with Vic. They didn't need a magical connection for him to know that Vic wanted to remind him not to linger. Even if they had forever, he wouldn't want to keep Annie here. She seemed so reduced, so much less, in this place.

"Let's get out of here," he suggested.

"Yeah," she agreed. "Let's."

An hour later they were in a diner, huddled together in a booth with empty plates pushed to the side as they went through their phones, scanning through the records Vic had photographed.

Adam was having a veggie Chicago dog. The mustard and onions he liked, but the pickle spear, sliced peppers, and relish so green that it could have come from the spirit realm were all a bit of a shock. He didn't hate it, but probably wouldn't make it a regular meal. Vic had gone for baked mostaccioli, a pasta neither of them had heard of.

The food was fine but the decor made the place. They'd done it up like a little street or boardwalk, with colorful signs and classic posters from the World's Fair.

"Go back. What's that one?" Adam asked, looking up the map location of one of the Wilcox properties. "A church?"

"Yeah," Vic said. "That's weird, right?"

Annie hummed.

"Most of dad's investments are boutique hotels or office buildings. He must have bought it to redevelop the land."

"I don't think so," Adam pointed to the date of the last sale on a realty site. "He's had it since 2008."

Vic scrolled through the photos on his phone. He reached over to zoom out on the church on Adam's phone and click on the buildings and houses around it.

"It's not just the church. They bought the whole neighborhood, piece by piece."

Adam pulled up the street photos and held his phone up for them to see. The place was boarded up, with a tall, chain link fence around the perimeter.

"It's not too far away. I think we should check it out."

Vic considered the pictures.

"We'll need tools, flashlights, that kind of thing," he said. "We should be careful, go early in the morning, a few hours before sunrise."

"I like that plan." Adam didn't admit it, but he could use a long nap.

"I'll get us some hotel rooms," Annie said.

18

"It's been a weird day," Adam said. He pulled off his T-shirt and laid down once Vic had pulled back the comforter.

"But you can't say it's been boring." Wearing just his jeans, Vic settled crossways onto the bed, the back of his head on Adam's stomach. Reaching, he ran the tip of his thumb over Adam's chest, idly tracing a bit of the scar that crossed it. The sensation wasn't uncomfortable, not exactly.

"Will you visit me in prison if we get busted?"

"That's not funny."

"Hey, what's the point of you being an ex-cop if you can't help with breaking and entering?"

"We have to be careful," Vic said. "Me especially so. You and Annie might get a warning. I'd probably get shot."

Adam winced.

"Sorry."

"I know."

They didn't talk about it that often, the difference in their skin. Mostly it came up in culture, the way Vic's extended family handled religion and weddings: Catholic versus rural Protestant made for some sharp contrasts.

Adam knew he could never understand Vic's experience, but he hoped he could at least learn not to say stupid shit.

They lay there for a moment, the rhythm of their breathing syncing until he felt more at peace than he had the entire trip.

Adam was glad that Annie's idea of quick accommodations meant a proper hotel with a king-sized bed.

"I wish Vran was still around," he said.

"Me too."

The sea elf had never had a problem with skirting the law or helping Adam into places he shouldn't go.

Adam combed his fingers through Vic's hair.

Vic closed his eyes. "You're going to turn it gray, you know."

"At least you'll look hot if you go all salt-and-pepper."

"Uh-huh."

"I guess I could ask Isaac for help with this stuff," Adam suggested.

"You don't like Isaac."

"Yeah, but that's not his fault."

It was true. Isaac Frost wasn't Adam's favorite person, but he hadn't really done anything to earn it. It was all tied together: losing Vran, the school. Adam would work on it, eventually. His brain only had so much space. He couldn't unpack any more trauma boxes right now.

"Did you see Annie in that room?" Adam asked. "Or on the plane? She's so torn up about the babies."

"Yeah."

"Do you ever think about it?" Vic asked after a long pause.

"About what? Having kids?"

"Yeah."

"Sometimes. I don't think I'd be very good at it."

"At what, being a dad?"

"Yeah."

"Why not?"

"I didn't exactly grow up with a positive example, and I'd want them to get to go to college, travel . . . stuff like that. Bobby and me, we were always worried about money, you know? If I had kids I'd want them to be free of that." Adam tried not to shift. He didn't want Vic to move, to stop resting his head on Adam's belly. He didn't want to know Vic's answer, not exactly, because it could be the thing that drove them apart if they felt differently. "How about you?"

"Sometimes." Vic's weight pressed down on Adam as he shrugged. "But then I think that's just what was expected of me. That's been a lot of it, you know, coming out, changing jobs—I keep unpacking what my future looks like. I keep picturing it and questioning if it's what I really want, or if it's just what I was taught to. Does that make any sense?"

Adam nodded and tried not to fold in on himself. If Vic was questioning everything, then how long until he questioned—Vic reached and gave a tug at the patch of hair at the center of Adam's chest.

"Oww. Why?"

"Stop it."

"What?"

"You know what. I'm asking questions about what I want, but I know you're a part of it. You're my future, okay?"

"Okay."

They napped, or Adam tried to.

The Wolf and the painting kept rising in his thoughts.

Whatever the spirit was, he didn't feel malevolent, at least not completely. He'd known Adam, but it could have been just what he'd learned from Wilcox's people.

You never were as stupid as you pretended to be.

That insult felt personal.

They needed more information on the Wolf. He'd dig into Silas Wilcox. That might yield results. He'd looked at the company but not its origins.

Vic's phone beeped, telling them it was time to go.

"Be right back," he said, rolling out of bed to pull on his shirt and shoes. "You get ready and get Annie. I'll pick you up in twenty minutes."

"Where are you going?"

"You'll see."

Adam dressed and pulled on his leather jacket. It was lined enough to keep the wind off, and he'd brought gloves so he didn't leave any fingerprints or in case he needed to use the sword again.

Annie didn't answer her door. Adam texted her.

Where are you?

Outside.

He found her around the corner from the hotel's entrance. He recognized the acrid, slightly sweet taste as she rubbed a cigarette against the wall to snuff it out.

"Please don't tell Robert."

"That you smoke?"

"I quit, but . . . It's just one, half of it, really, and it doesn't matter now."

She tucked it into a pack in her purse.

"You're going through a lot," Adam said.

She nodded but still looked guilty as they walked toward the entrance.

"Are you sure you want to come?" he asked. "We can go without you."

"I need to know. Besides, my family owns the building. If we get caught I might be able to get us out of trouble."

Adam winced, remembering his conversation with Vic, and said, "Hopefully it won't come to that."

They stood there, almost shivering.

"Why didn't you want Bobby to come with us?" Adam hadn't quite meant to ask it aloud, but the question popped out.

She let out a long breath.

"I don't like who I am around my family. I don't like who I am here. I don't want him to see me that way. I know that doesn't make any sense."

Adam laughed.

"It makes plenty of sense. You should see me around my mother and her boyfriend."

Annie gave a little nod but she looked lost in thought.

Vic pulled up at the front of the hotel. He liked to be punctual, and Adam tried; Denver's public transportation made a lot of stops, so taking the bus sometimes meant arriving very early or very late.

They'd found their rhythm eventually, once Vic had explained that he felt like promptness was a sign of respect for his time and Adam had accepted that arriving early just meant more time with Vic.

The warm flow of the heater chased away the damp trying to wrap around Adam's skin as he shut the car door.

Vic handed them each a warm paper cup.

"Coffee?" Adam asked, trying to keep the hope out of his voice.

Vic smiled. "I know the way to your heart."

"Have I ever told you how much I appreciate that your love language is food?"

"You can show me when we're in lockup together."

"I thought you said it wasn't funny?" Adam took a sip. Vic had gotten it perfect. Just the right amount of cream and sugar.

"It's not funny when you say it."

In the rearview mirror, Annie buried her grin in her cup as Vic drove.

Even at this hour, Chicago lit the horizon with a glowing arc. It reminded Adam of Oklahoma City, how you could see the light pollution at any hour as you drove toward it. There weren't a lot of open spaces here. One town flowed into the next, highway to street. Magic pooled like islands in a sea, covens and spirits marking their territory. Adam kept his senses wrapped tight around himself. He ignored the temptation to see the local anchors for the watchtowers. He did not want to broadcast his presence, not here, not when he didn't know the territorial lines and alliances.

Vic's phone gave directions on their way to the church.

"What exactly are we getting into?" Adam asked.

"Most of the businesses around it are closed or quiet now," Vic said. "Most of the houses are empty. The church has been abandoned for years."

"But they'll have security, won't they?" Annie asked.

"Yeah," Adam said. "And I think we can expect wards or trap spells too."

The building, with its lightless steeple, came into sight.

"Then we'll be extra careful," Vic said.

The fence walled off the dull brick building, marking it as slated for demolition, but as far as Adam could tell, there were no plans for it. Its little yard had gone to the weeds long ago.

The steeple and dormer atop the gabled roof were the only indication that the place had ever been more than a simple office building. Still, it was big.

Sheets of plywood covered every window. A thick chain held the front doors sealed.

They weren't the first ones to come here. Graffiti tags covered the plywood but not the bricks, like some bit of reverence had remained in the back of the taggers' minds.

Vic leaned forward to eye the eaves and corners. "I don't see any security cameras. You?"

"No," Adam said. "Maybe they'd look suspicious on an abandoned building?"

They parked a few blocks away.

Many of the street lamps were out, and none of the houses had their porchlights on. The industrial buildings across the road showed some signs of life, with their loading docks illuminated, but it didn't push away the sense that they'd driven into a ghost town.

"Let me get some things from the trunk," Vic said as they climbed out.

Adam tried to act normal, to look like they belonged here, but he still closed the door quietly and tiptoed as he circled the car.

Vic handed Adam and Annie flashlights. He tucked a short crowbar and a pair of bolt cutters into his jacket pocket.

They circled for a bit, checking again for signs of cameras or guards.

Satisfied, Vic walked around to find the same gap in the fence that the graffiti artists had used.

"Wait," Adam said as prickles ran across his skin. "There are wards."

"Can we get through?"

"Yeah, they're old. Fading. Let me find a hole."

It helped that he knew the pattern. They were the same as the hotel in Denver and the house. The wards were loosely wound around each other with loops and spaces. One lay close to the opening in the fence.

"Step where I step."

He led them over the lines of magic.

"Is the door safe to touch?" Vic asked.

"Yeah."

Vic was efficient, and with a little pressure, he popped the padlock off the chain with the crowbar. Drawing his gun, he went first. Annie followed.

Adam breathed in the smell of old carpet and mold as he closed the door behind them.

The flashlight lit on bare walls and rows of pews. The carpet was a battered green. The white columns leading toward the stage were slightly water damaged and time stained. The ceiling plaster rippled and bubbled. There was a balcony and he imagined lurking there, trying to listen to whatever had been preached from the broad wooden pulpit.

"Open the doors . . . there are the people . . ." he muttered.

"This feels like our first date," Vic said, following Adam into the gloom.

"That wasn't a date. You spooked me by leaving me alone in a psych ward, remember?"

"Really?" Annie asked.

"Yeah, the one at Mercy," Adam said.

Annie shuddered.

"I hated that place."

"Me too," Adam said.

"Good times," Vic said.

"Then you got shot."

"Not so good times," Vic admitted, but he caught Adam's hand for a moment to let him know that it was okay now.

Adam still wished he hadn't mentioned it, especially in front of Annie.

It had all worked out, brought them together, but now wasn't the time to remember Vic lying in his arms, bleeding out, or the brains on the wall. Vic had gotten lucky. The other guy hadn't.

Annie turned back and forth, eyes narrowed despite the dark.

"Are you okay?" Adam asked her.

"Yeah. It's not as creepy as I expected."

"Is it familiar?"

"No—Maybe? They bought this place when I was in college. We never really went to church, unless there was someone dad wanted to impress or some business connection he wanted to make."

"What about you?" Vic asked Adam. "Anything spooky?"

"Not here."

"Do we check the rest of the building, the offices and stuff, or the basement?" Annie suggested.

"It will be in the basement." They looked at him. "Because of course it will."

They found stairs behind the baptismal. The moldy smell intensified.

Adam remembered services with his mom and the long drive from the trailer to the church on Seward Road back in Guthrie.

He remembered sermons on sin and hellfire or the few harangues against a president or political candidate or two. He'd tuned it out as much as he could and stopped going when he'd been old enough to refuse.

The stairs ended in a pair of heavy metal doors sporting a deadbolt.

"That looks serious."

"It would be if they'd paid for better hinges," Vic said. "Hold this for me."

He passed Adam his flashlight and got to work. Annie and

Adam exchanged impressed glances while Vic chiseled off the hinges with his crowbar.

"Give me a hand."

Annie held the lights as Adam held the doors up. Vic tugged on the doorknob, tilting the whole thing toward them.

They eased the doors to the side.

Annie spun to shine her light behind them, then into the dark ahead.

Adam took a heaving breath and listened for an alarm or any response, but none came.

Vic led them onward.

The first room held old furniture, stacks of metal chairs, and boxes. Beyond were other rooms. Each open doorway was a passage into darkness, but one or two glowed purple-red in Adam's Sight.

"This way."

He shifted the flashlight to his right hand and opened the left as if to catch the wind.

Adam extended his senses, opening himself to any hint of magic or a trap.

The first room would have fit perfectly into a retirement home. It was outfitted with a bathroom and a sink, anything you needed to house a patient.

The power was out, but it had a TV and a hospital bed.

Adam tried to ignore the straps on the bed, restraints, and flipped through the stack of magazines.

Annie eased into the room. Her face had gone very still.

"I was here," she said. "This is the room I was in."

She folded in on herself, like she didn't want to touch anything.

"I don't understand. Was I ever even in a hospital? Who were the nurses, the doctors?"

"People your parents hired, probably members of their cult."

Annie shook her head.

"How did she get here?" Vic asked. "From Colorado, I mean?"

"Probably on Daddy's jet. I can't believe they never told Robert I was alive."

Adam liked the spark of defiance in her eyes. It told him that she was going to be okay.

"And back from the spirit realm?" Vic asked.

"I don't think the coven has that much power," Adam said. "They'd need help for a crossing."

"What kind of help?" Annie asked.

"A patron, someone like the Wolf."

Annie and Vic looked at him.

"He was in the painting, said he'd made some deal with Silas, your great-grandfather. He's been guiding your family ever since."

"This thing is helping my father? With what?"

"Stock tips?" Adam shrugged.

"A Wolf?"

"He just wears a wolf mask, but he's some sort of spirit, but I can't get a read on him. Have you ever heard them talking about him?"

"I—I don't think so." She seemed uncertain.

"Let's keep going," Vic said, pulling them along in his wake.

They found other rooms, all set up for physical therapy or surgery.

"Did you meet any other patients?"

Annie scoffed. "No. I thought I was in some fancy private wing."

"They were certainly set up for it."

Aside from the lack of daylight, it was nicer than Mercy or any of the other hospitals Adam had been in.

The next set of double doors opened onto a large room. Adam guessed it was half the size of the sanctuary above.

Black paint coated the concrete floor. Dusty velvet draped the walls, adding to the vampire's lair vibe.

The wide circle set into the floor was traced in white.

A lot of candles, all in various states of use, sat outside it. The greasy taste of melted wax and herbs lay heavy on the air, but it did not quite cover the other odor.

"What is that?" Annie asked.

"Death," Vic said in a stony tone.

When Adam looked he knew what he would see. The Reaper lay close to the surface, just beneath Vic's skin.

Adam aimed the flashlight at the floor.

"They burned."

He could just make out the scorch marks, the black soot staining the floor in permanent shadows.

"The coven?" Vic asked.

Adam knelt near the closest of the thirteen marks.

"It has to be."

"Now we know why they're recruiting in Denver," Vic said. "They need to replenish their numbers."

Adam had thought the Wolf had been talking about the witches in Denver, the ones who'd died fighting Mercy, but that wasn't the crop he'd been referring to. He'd meant this coven.

Annie crouched beside Adam.

"I don't understand."

He held a hand above the floor, feeling the last of the spell's resonance. There wasn't much left, but what lingered matched the traces in Annie's scars.

"Mortals can only channel so much magic. The spell was too much for them. They burned out. Literally."

"They died to bring me back?"

"Yeah. I think so."

"Why?" She choked on a sob. "Why would anyone do that?"

"That's one more thing we need to find out."

She broke down, a little bit, not into tears, but a stunned disbelief.

Adam hugged her.

"Guys . . ." Vic said. "We need to go."

Annie wiped her eyes and stood.

Adam followed them upstairs.

They were outside when he felt it, the same silent thunder that rang out before Emily's compost bin exploded.

"What is it?" Vic asked when Adam froze.

"Another boggin, like the thing at Emily's. Maybe more than one."

The air split in two, like a bolt of lightning. Beyond lay only swirling gray. It had to be the Between, the place the Wolf had mentioned.

The thing that squeezed through the crack was far larger than the last one. Diaphanous, so translucent that he had to squint to see it, it moved like the ribbony eels at the aquarium, like a wave of gray flesh.

It spiraled, twisting and coiling, rising until it reached the steeple.

The creature wrapped itself around the cross. Parts of the roof, shingles, and plywood flew toward it, creating a protective form.

"What do we do?" Vic asked. "We can't fight a building."

"We need to go," Adam said, leading them through the wards. "Quickly."

They hurried toward the car. In the distance and throughout the nearly abandoned neighborhood, other shapes rumbled to life. They were made of everything from cardboard boxes to flagstones and broken windows. They converged on the church, whether to fight or welcome their new kin, Adam couldn't say.

"That was what you fought at Emily's?" Vic asked.

"Yeah. Different shape, but same species."

"Did we cause that?" Annie asked.

"No. That one just came through. The others were already here."

"The wards didn't stop them," Vic said. "Did they?"

"No. Whatever they are, they're not the same kind of life, the same kind of magic," Adam said. "They're coming from somewhere else."

"How did they get here?"

"I don't know, but we're not equipped to deal with them. I'll see if the elves want to come have a look."

Annie was quiet as they drove away.

It didn't take any magic to know that she was thinking about the basement and the thirteen burn marks laid out in a circle.

The Wiccan Rede said *An ye harm none, do what ye will.* Did self-harm count? What if it was voluntary?

The cult had twisted the witches away from nature and paganism toward whatever Patrick Wilcox and the Wolf were after.

Whatever it was, Annie was at the heart of it.

19

They made it back to the hotel in time for breakfast, but none of them felt like eating or sleeping. They packed, checked out, and it wasn't long before they were going through the limbo of waiting at the airport gate. Adam napped on the plane, stiff in his seat until Vic tugged his sleeve, pulling him near so he could rest his head on Vic's shoulder.

Adam drifted then, grateful that Annie had managed to at least get two seats together on an otherwise crowded flight.

"What's the plan when we get home?" Vic asked when he stirred.

"I should get some hours in at the garage if Jesse will have me."

"I meant in the case."

"I know, but I need the money and it will let me think. We should probably talk to Jodi and the other witches and warn them not to go near Wilcox. This cult is more dangerous than I thought. They're channeling power they can't handle and they're opening these cracks."

He could imagine how it had felt, to die in that basement. He'd touched magic greater than his own, felt the power of entities like the former King of Swords. Just a brush of Argent's strength could burn him to ash. There would have been a moment when they realized they could not handle the spell they'd cast, and by then it would already have been too late.

Vic turned to make certain that Annie was too far away to hear him when he asked, "Why is she so important? I know you think that they see her as a possession, but to trade thirteen lives for hers? Even if Wilcox doesn't care about human life, those witches were a valuable resource."

"I don't know. I thought it was because she's their daughter, but they don't seem to care about her, not in any real way. If she's the key to it all, why let her leave Chicago in the first place? It doesn't add up."

"Do you want me to look into the deaths? I could ask Dale."

"Let me put Jack on it first."

"Are you sure you should go back to that well?"

"Silver said he was okay with it if I don't endanger the school, and I got the sense that Jack's kind of bored. He likes a challenge."

"I meant the other part." Vic knocked their shoulders together.

Adam nibbled his lip.

"I know I haven't dealt with what happened to Vran. And you were right, it's not Isaac's fault. I shouldn't hold it against him or the school. Vran made his choice."

Adam wished he'd taken the window seat so he could stare at the clouds. He didn't mind tearing up in front of Vic, but the other passengers didn't need to know about the weighted ache, the guilt he carried but hadn't processed. It sat like a rock in his windpipe. Grief, unswallowed.

"I know you're mad at him for leaving." Vic leaned over to press a kiss to the top of Adam's head. "But it's what you would have done. It's what you always do, put others first."

Adam shook his head, not because Vic was wrong, but because it hurt.

"You couldn't have done what he did," Vic continued. "In that moment, he was the only one."

"I know."

They paused to let the flight attendants give them a choice of sugary or salty carbs.

"And don't hate me," Vic said after they'd munched. "But I'm glad you couldn't. I want you here with me."

It hurt to hear, but Adam knew where he was coming from.

"I know, and I don't want to be anywhere else, but . . ."

"But?"

Adam swallowed.

"I feel guilty that I wasn't there for him. He needed me, and I wasn't there."

"He had his own life, baby. He made his own choices."

"I know . . ." Adam trailed off.

He couldn't bring himself to say it, but he felt even worse because part of him was glad it hadn't been him.

Adam emailed Jack, asking for help with the Chicago-based cult members, and went to work on the ancient Chevy that was Jesse's latest reclamation project. It was exactly the kind of car he preferred to fix—no electronics, no computer chips, just an engine, oil, and rust. In some ways it was just easier too. Fewer moving parts meant fewer things to break. It reminded him enough of his old Cutlass Supreme to put a smile on his face when the car fought his attempt to fix whatever was wrong with it this week. The bumper had a curve to it, just enough to remind him of a frown.

Still, he couldn't keep her running. He was starting to think the thing was cursed, or just too old to keep on going. At least Jesse understood that it wasn't his fault. He couldn't find the problem either. Adam asked him why they didn't just give up, find something else to reclaim and sell, but Jesse said he wanted to stick it out.

It did make Adam wonder if there wasn't some breaking point, a place where no amount of repairs or new parts was going to help.

Bobby had talked that way about some patients, ones he'd lost, especially among the old. No matter what they'd tried, they couldn't save the person. It hadn't been a cheerful dinner. After, in bed with Vic, Adam had agreed that neither wanted to go out like that: a zombie in a wheelchair, sustained long past any happy quality of life. He wondered if that would change as they aged, if he'd fight for every scrap of time, no matter how miserable he might become, because life was life, and where there was life, there was hope.

"I can't wait to be a grumpy old man with you," Vic had said.

Adam had laughed, but Vic wasn't the only one thinking about their future. Adam knew he wanted them to be married. He said he was okay with them not having it in the church or the family members who wouldn't come, but Adam wasn't certain. He didn't know if he wanted to cost Vic that, and he wasn't sure he wanted to wear a ring. He wasn't certain about any of it.

They loved each other, he had no doubts about that, but was it white-picket-fence love? He had to find a picture of the future that he wanted. He knew that in many ways he hadn't expected to live this long or to ever find this kind of happiness. Now that he had, it was almost scary. There was more to life, but more to lose. So he questioned, and never seemed to stop questioning.

That was the problem with therapy. It got you digging and you kept going, because no matter how much you learned about yourself or why you did what you did, there was always more to uncover.

Adam forced himself to change gears and mull over the case before he spiraled into a panic about money and his future with Vic.

His phone dinged with an email, providing a welcome change of topic.

Jack had gotten back to him about the cult members.

Scrolling through his librarian's findings, Adam wasn't surprised, but he still squeezed his eyes shut for a moment to consider the implications.

He texted Jodi.

I found something. Can we talk?

Jodi responded quickly.

How's 6 at my place? Should I rally the troops?

Yeah. Anyone you think will listen.

Emily met them at Jodi's. Cole was absent, but Nicole came, though Adam wasn't certain if she trusted him or only sat in on the meeting because she was Jodi's roommate.

They lived like college students, meaning little of the furniture matched and the couch looked like it came from when shag carpet had been all the rage. They'd hung a cloth tapestry depicting the moon tarot card, and there was a little altar with statues of various goddesses where a television would normally be, so the place was witchy enough that Adam felt at home.

He presented his findings. He'd even used the printer in Jesse's office to make paper copies of what Jack had sent him.

"I don't get it," Jodi said, shuffling through the pages. "What does it mean?"

"It means we're definitely dealing with a cult."

Adam passed out the obituaries for the Chicago witches.

All were vague. Cause of death wasn't advertised. Many of them hadn't even had funerals. Jack had to dig into coroner's records to find when they'd died.

"Thirteen people," Emily said. "How did they cover it up?"

"They paid off the families."

Adam pointed to the bank records Jack had included.

Eyes widened at the amounts.

"That's a lot of zeros," Nicole said.

"Where are they getting it all?" Jodi asked.

"I'm still working on that, but some of it comes from the witches themselves. They have to buy in with everything they've got."

"For what?" Nicole asked. She sounded angry. "What could be worth their lives?"

"This one is to Amber's mom," Emily said, pointing to a page. "She had cancer, and a lot of medical debt. Amber said she didn't know if they'd ever pay it off. Her parents were going to lose their house. That's why she got into the craft, to try and learn how to heal people."

Adam pointed to the photos of the Chicago witches. "Some of them were homeless. Others had a lot of debt, student loans. Some had criminal records. Addiction issues, mostly."

"They're targeting the vulnerable," Nicole said.

He could feel her anger, white hot and well stoked. Adam drew his walls up to keep it from leaching into him.

"Some of these are from when they were juveniles," Nicole said, thumbing through the police records. "They should be sealed. Where did you get them?"

"I can't say, but I trust the source."

"We have to get Amber and the others out of there," Nicole said. "They're in danger."

"I don't know if that's a good idea, at least not yet." Adam held up a hand. "These people have a lot of money and power. Give me some more time."

"But they could get hurt," Emily said.

"They did go willingly," Jodi said. "I mean, it's a hotel, not a prison, right?"

"But it's *Amber*," Emily said. She gestured at the pages. "Yes, she left, but she's not the brightest, you know? She doesn't deserve that. No one does. We at least need to warn her."

"Please don't go there," Adam said. "I understand you're worried, but poking the bear isn't a good idea, at least not until we know more about what they're up to."

Adam gave his cousin a pleading look. In the past, Jodi had been . . . well, *impetuous* didn't quite cover it.

"Adam is probably right," Jodi said.

"Okay," Emily conceded.

Nicole crinkled the page she was holding but nodded agreement.

20

Annie and Bobby were out to dinner when he got home. Adam would usually relish a night alone with Vic, but the silence wasn't peaceful. It felt ready to pounce. He waited for the next thing to knock at the door. Tension stained the air. They could have retreated to Maria's, but Adam couldn't stay the night, so they picked up takeout and settled in to eat.

"You're quiet," Vic said. "What's up?"

Adam played with his chopsticks, stirring the rice and veggie bowl. It was good, though not worth the price. Still, it was more complicated than anything Adam liked to cook, and he felt like he relied too much on Vic's skills in the kitchen. It didn't feel fair even if Vic loved doing it.

"I keep thinking about what you said, about the future, and I'm sorry."

"For what?"

"For always jumping into the fire. For not putting you first."

"You don't have to put me first, baby. I don't want you to." Vic reached over to squeeze Adam's leg. "And I don't want you to ever stop being who you are."

"But what if I change?" Adam asked, staring into his bowl. "What if we change?"

Vic smiled.

"We're supposed to. We have to grow, and I can't promise that we won't grow apart, but I can promise to try and grow toward you. Promise me the same and I think we'll be all right."

"Same." Adam leaned over to kiss him. "I promise."

One or two of the screws that had been tightening in his chest loosened.

"Can I say something else?" Vic asked.

The screws paused, ready to drill back in.

"Yeah."

"I want an apartment," Vic said, putting an abrupt stop to Adam's spiraling.

"Huh?"

Vic waved at the kitchen.

"I don't want to do this anymore, creeping into your brother's basement or you having to leave my mom's. I want *us* to have a place. I know you're freaked out about money, but we can afford *something*. We'll make it work. Worst case scenario, we get evicted, go to the courthouse, and move into my mom's, okay?"

"Okay." Adam took a moment to get his heart rate back under control. "And, uh, I actually kind of looked at a few apartments already."

Vic beamed.

"Yeah?"

"Yeah."

Vic leaned over to kiss his forehead.

"Let's go look at some together when we've dealt with the zombie situation."

"Deal."

"Cool." Vic got up to put away Adam's leftovers and rinse his bowl for the recycling. "Let's go to bed."

As nice as having the house to themselves felt, undressing and settling into bed felt better.

"Speaking of the case, what's next?" Vic asked, rolling over to face him and propping himself up on an elbow, giving Adam a view of his chest—Adam's favorite part—and the scar from the bullet wound—his least.

He ran his thumb over it. Vic reached to do the same, tracing the line of the slash Adam had taken from a rusty sickle.

"Things are getting complicated. I need more information, especially about the Wolf, but I haven't had any luck. Neither has Jack."

"So where do we get it?"

"I don't know. Seamus is off the table. I would have gone to Sara, you know, before."

Vic put his hand over Adam's.

"What about Mel?"

Adam considered it. He didn't know Death's daughter, but Vic did.

"Will you come with me?"

"Is this because she knows me, or is it a Reaper thing?"

"Both?" Adam hedged. "It could be trouble. Between the warlock thing and the sword, I'm not exactly everyone's favorite person."

"And you want backup?"

"Boney doesn't hurt," Adam admitted. "I think they'll be less likely to mess with you."

"You're the one with Argent on speed dial."

"Not exactly, at least not lately."

"Okay, how do you want to do this?" Vic asked.

"Spirit walk. I thought I'd try to carry you over."

"Can you do that?"

"I'd like to try."

"What do I do?"

"Just lie back like this." Adam showed Vic how to open his arms and hands to lie flat.

"This is the Lovers, right?" Vic smiled as he stretched out.

"Yeah."

"Then shouldn't we be naked?"

"We can if you want, but we don't have to be."

"After this, then. I like being naked with you."

Adam flushed and lay back. Despite everything they'd done, he still got a little shy about sex.

"Close your eyes."

Vic did and knocked his fingers against Adam's.

At first he tried to dispel the distraction, the feelings Vic's proximity aroused, but he fed them into the spell instead.

For a moment, it was like it had been. They were closer, pulled together by Adam's invocation.

The only time he felt like that, like he had when they'd been linked, was in the moment. Sometimes he'd pause there, drawing it out, just to savor that connection a little longer.

Adam opened his eyes and they were in the spirit realm, their hands still linked. He could feel the drain from having pulled Vic along, but he'd managed it. Practice was paying off.

"Good thing it's not as cold on this side." Vic gestured to his boxers.

"Yeah. Let me try something."

A transformation spell, the kind Argent loved, was beyond Adam's power, but he could manage a glamour.

Adam squeezed Vic's hand and willed a little power through their temporary connection. He could taste blackberries and something bitter, something like vegetation on the edge of rotting. One was his magic, the other the taint of the warlock wound.

"Nice," Vic declared.

"It won't hold for long," Adam said.

"Take the compliment. We look *good*."

Adam couldn't argue.

He'd dressed Vic in a black suit with a fedora to match. The tie and cufflinks sported skulls.

Adam had chosen dark blue for himself, but he'd trimmed the jacket and hat in gray silk, a nod to his rank and allegiance to Silver. The sword on his back clashed with the look but it couldn't be helped. He wouldn't walk the spirit realm without it.

"Where are we going?" Vic asked.

"Union Station."

"Then aren't we going the wrong way?"

"Yep, but I wanted to show you something."

The spirit realm's version of downtown was cast in green and yellow, the light of the old-fashioned light bulbs that spelled out the names of the now demolished buildings. Adam and Vic walked along, passing signs for everything from the Chop Suey restaurant to the Empress or Isis theaters.

Vic squeezed Adam's hand, telling him that he appreciated the view.

"Are those Model Ts?" Vic asked, nodding to the rows of cars parked on either side of the street.

"Probably. How should I know?"

"You're the car guy."

"I bet Argent has one," Adam said.

"Nah, not fast enough for her."

A trolley car, packed with otherworldly beings, passed them. Adam caught glimpses of translucent figures and purple, long-eared goblins. A human woman winked at him, though he did not think he knew her.

There were less cheerful humans here too, more than he was used to seeing. They were Lost Ones, mortals pulled out of time by eating or drinking in the spirit realm. Their clothes were from every era, every style. They all had a certain look to them, a bit of sadness or desperation.

Denver's now vanished Chinatown was nearby. Maria had told Adam how it had been destroyed in a race pogrom. He wanted to see it, but he wasn't certain how long he could keep Vic in the spirit realm.

He picked up the pace, pulling Vic along. They had their jackets to ward away the cold as the wind picked up.

In the mortal world Union Station was somewhere Adam took the light rail to. It had a futuristic mesh of white metal where the trains stopped that made him think of a spaceport or something out of science fiction, while the main building remained historic. Inside, shops and even a bookstore were tucked among the long benches where people waited for their cross-country trains.

This version was older. It sported a tower that would have looked right at home on a vampire's summer castle.

This interior maintained the benches, though here they were crowded with families of every sort.

The lounge on the sweeping balcony above remained, but gone were the clean white surfaces of the present. This place felt more real in some ways, with its gas lamps and smoke-stained, cavernous ceiling.

"Is that it?" Vic asked, nodding upward.

"Yeah."

They found the stairs to the side and climbed.

Green-and-pink lights filled a bar decorated in copper and

bronze. A four-armed, orange-skinned man played the piano, but it was the singer who caught Adam's eye.

She wore a glittering purple dress, and she wore it well. Like everything here it had a certain dated quality, one Adam usually associated with the elves. He'd chosen his glamour well. Their suits fit right in.

She swayed with the music, her hands curved around the microphone stand.

"She's beautiful," Adam said, following Vic's eyes and smile.

"She is."

They watched her sway and listened to her sing about a blue moon leaving her alone.

Adam didn't quite understand the bond she and Vic had formed, along with Jodi, but he fought the surge of sour green trying to fill him when she caught Vic's eye and smiled.

A waiter, an elegant creature that looked like a canary yellow fox, approached their table but Adam waved them off.

They couldn't drink or eat anything here unless it had come from their world, and he wouldn't trust it unless he'd brought it himself. If they did, they'd become Lost Ones. It was the first rule Silver had taught him, and the first he'd taught to Vic in turn.

Mel finished her song and turned to the pianist.

"I'm taking a break, Gary."

He nodded and began playing something alien and complicated that took all four of his hands.

Mel slid into their booth to sit next to Vic.

"No suit tonight?" he asked her.

"I like to switch it up."

"You remember Adam?"

"The Page of Swords himself," Mel said. "Good to see you."

Adam didn't know how to take her. He was not on good

terms with her mother, but knew better than most that family didn't often see eye to eye. He would not blame Death's daughter for her mother's choices and manipulations. Still, while Mel didn't have to be his enemy, that didn't make her his friend.

He also hadn't been there when Vic had met her. She, Vic, and Jodi had gone through some heavy stuff that Adam hadn't, stuff Vic didn't like to talk about.

"How are you, Mel?" Vic asked, tipping his head to look at her from beneath the brim of his hat.

"I'm good." She waved to the waiter.

"You look good."

Mel smiled. "You too, Reaper."

"Thank you for taking the time to sit with us," Adam said.

"Anything for this one." She cocked her head at Vic.

Adam had really done a number with the suit. He imagined what the black silk shirt would feel like as he peeled it off or ran his hands inside it.

Save it, he thought, wishing he hadn't invoked the Lovers to bring them over.

"We've kind of got a situation," Vic said.

"I thought you might," Mel said. "To come all the way downtown."

The waiter brought her a martini glass full of something golden and bubbling. It smelled a bit like pickle brine.

Vic looked to Adam, telling him that it was his decision on how much he wanted to tell her. It was a roll of the dice, but Vic trusted her.

"My sister-in-law came back from the dead," he said.

Mel looked at him over her drink as she sipped.

Adam explained it all, what they'd found in Chicago, what they knew so far, about the boggins and the Wolf.

"Why come to me?" Mel ran a fingertip over the stem of her glass.

"Because you're not your mother."

She took a delicate sip.

"You're not the only ones asking around about your wolf," she said. "Some Lost Ones came by the trailer, wanting to know about him."

"That takes guts," Vic said.

"I don't think they knew who she is," Mel said. "It's out there, but not everyone has caught on."

Adam wondered if that was Silver's work. Death's identity had been a long-held secret. She hadn't exactly rented billboards or put up a neon that read *Come See Death's Airstream, next exit.* Sara, as Adam had known her, had posed as an information broker. It made sense, considering the things she knew, since she knew everyone.

"What did they want to know?" Adam asked.

"How to find him. He's their patron saint or something."

"Of Lost Ones?"

"Have you noticed that there are a lot of them around lately?" Mel nodded to a table at the end of the bar where three mortals who looked like they'd stumbled out of the eighties nursed their drinks. Their hair must have been larger than anything Adam could imagine wearing, but time had beaten it down. Their brightly colored clothes were as much plastic as cloth, but all of them had a dusty, haggard look, like they'd seen too much.

They weren't unlike the homeless or migrants occupying Denver's mortal space. A few of them camped in the alley behind the garage and Jesse had a live-and-let-live mindset toward them. He'd occasionally let them raid the coffee he left out for the customers in the waiting area or use the restroom so long as they didn't trash it.

"What did she tell them?" Vic asked.

"Whatever they paid her to." Mel downed the last of her drink. "But they wanted to know about the wolves."

"Wolves?" Adam asked.

"There is more than one of them."

Adam nodded. The one in the painting had hinted that he wasn't the only one. Adam hadn't been certain how to take it, if he'd been lying or playing games. It was good to have confirmation.

"Adam?" Vic asked.

He shook his head. He didn't know what it meant, or how any of it fit together.

"Now if you boys are done here, I really should get back to my set."

"Thanks, Mel," Vic said, leaning over to hug her. "It's good to see you."

She kissed his cheek and strode over to talk to Gary before heading back to her microphone.

"Stay for one more song?" Vic asked, meeting Adam's gaze across the table.

"Yeah."

"This one's for Adam and Vic," Mel announced before launching into an old tune that Adam knew.

"Want to dance?" Vic asked, nodding to the parquet tiles in front of the stage.

Adam beamed and stood.

They were alone on the floor, huddled close together. Adam didn't really know how to dance. He hadn't had much experience, but it felt right, his hand clasped in Vic's, the two of them turning as Mel belted out lines about stars fading and lingering on.

The spirit realm had its dangers. He had enemies here, but no one would blink about two men dancing together.

Adam kissed Vic as the song ended. He could feel the glamour fading. He closed his eyes and opened them again, pulling them back to his bed in the basement. He'd barely settled into his body before Vic rolled over and pinned him to the mattress.

"So?" Vic grinned. "Where were we?"

21

The firm rap at the door would have told Adam that it was Dautre who'd come to visit even if his wards hadn't alerted him to the elf's approach.

Adam schooled his expression before he opened the door.

"Hi," he said.

The elf was growing on him, but it was still early.

"The Knight of Swords requires your presence for training," Dautre said.

Adam sighed.

"I was hoping she'd forgotten about that."

"She has a long memory. I would not trifle with her."

Adam opened his arms. "She can't be serious about me sparring with her."

"I am not privy to her intentions, but I would not defy her."

Two warnings in as many sentences. Dautre *was* worried.

"All right, what do I need to—"

But the light shifted and they were gone, moving planes so quickly that Adam landed on his ass wherever they ended up.

The floor was cold, but it wasn't ice. The tiles were glassy marble, spotted with blue.

The sweeping, spiraling staircases and high vaulted ceilings reminded him of the palaces you saw in history books. Snow-colored scrollwork covered everything. Nothing about it felt comfortable or warm. Nothing about it said he was welcome here.

The corners of the room and ceiling were marked with blue-and-purple lights. Stepping closer, he realized they were a shifting, silent hive of glowing beetles. They crawled calmly across the walls and ceilings. He'd have found them pretty if one or two didn't occasionally take flight. They reminded him of the june bugs they'd get back in Guthrie, including the occasional swarms that got into everything, including his clothes and hair.

Adam shuddered.

"You could warn a guy," he said to Dautre, picking himself up from the cold floor.

"I could not. I was ordered to maintain secrecy."

"Wait, did we leave the front door open?"

Bobby would kill him over the heating bill, not to mention the risk of robbery.

"I will go check."

Dautre vanished, leaving Adam in what had to be one of Alfheimr's colder sections.

He whirled about, trying to contain the tide of black-and-red panic rising within him. Yes, the elven realm was a pristine paradise, but if he strayed too long from the Shallows, too far into the elven realms, he'd return years or centuries later. Vic would never know what had happened to him—

"I can't be here," he said. "Dautre!"

"Calm yourself, Page." The Knight of Swords descended a sweeping white stairwell.

"It's not safe for me."

"You are far closer to home than you think."

"*This* is Earth?"

"Yes."

His breathing fell back into line, and Adam noticed her appearance.

Her glamour still fit awkwardly, but she looked more mortal than he'd ever seen her. In a padded vest, nylon pants, and hiking boots, she could have just come from the ski slopes or snowshoeing.

He couldn't imagine it was for his sake. She'd probably be pleased if he glimpsed her true form and got blown to atoms.

Adam took several deep breaths, tasting snow.

"Hopefully the Alpine air does not strain your lungs," she said.

"I can handle it. I've been in Colorado for a while."

It was sort of true. Winter sports didn't appeal to him. Vic had tried to take him snowboarding and Adam had crashed out, over and over. He hadn't enjoyed the feeling of ice getting in places it should never go. After that he'd volunteered to read at the lodge while Vic and Jesse hit the slopes.

"That will serve you well as we practice."

"We?" Adam looked around for another partner. It wouldn't be much of a contest. Maybe she just wanted to kick his ass a few times.

He wasn't looking forward to the bruises.

She laughed.

"You will not be sparring with me, Page. As I said before, an elven child would already know what you should. Almost anyone else would prove more than your match, perhaps lethally so."

What he didn't know was why she was even trying. She'd made her point, more than once, that he'd never be able to keep up. He didn't need bruises to convince him.

"So I'm going to fight a kid? That doesn't seem right."

Not to mention humiliating.

At least elves didn't use smartphones. He could only imagine the views if someone uploaded a video.

"You will not be fighting today, merely learning proper form. Are you a warrior, or are you not?"

"I'm not. Like I told you before, I'm a mechanic."

"Yet you carry a weapon of office. In time you will be required to use it."

She was right. He didn't like it, but it had happened before. He'd put bullets into a man, another warlock, to stop him from killing others. It hadn't worked. He'd never killed anyone, but the intent had been there, and it would probably happen again.

Despite his love of fantasy novels, despite how cool he thought the sword on his back looked, it was a weapon. It had one purpose, and not everything he faced would be bound and easily killed.

The knight turned to the stairwell. "North. Come down, please."

A boy descended the stairs. Adam forced himself not to gawk.

He was half-elf, literally. One of his ears was pointed, the other round. His eyes were mismatched, human blue on the left and elven white on the right. He was something like a patchwork of their two people, with splotches of luminous white.

He had magic, that was unmistakable, but it didn't feel like anything Adam had sensed before. Silver and Argent's power was cold and pure. The knight's was steely, harder, but not alien.

This was something else, like a tornado in a fragile bottle. It reminded Adam of Vran, of how he'd been after he'd gone to the Underworld. It took most of Adam's self-control not to flinch away from the crackling feeling, the sense of an impending lightning strike.

"Adam Binder, Page of Swords to the King of the same court, this is North."

It said something that she announced the boy without titles. Elves were big on titles. They liked to drag them out at parties or trade them like Pokémon cards to see who had the most.

"Hi." Adam held up a hand to wave.

"Hi," North said shyly, but he smiled as he ducked his head.

The knight cleared her throat and North straightened.

Haltingly, he said, "I greet you in my home, Page of Swords to the king of the same court. Be welcome and, um, safe in our halls."

"Thank you."

Adam knew the feeling on North's face. That line of something thick and metallic had run through him so many times back in Oklahoma. He could still feel it when he thought of his father.

North wanted the knight to see him, to be proud of him. The resemblance was clear, at least on the boy's elven half.

"Lady . . ."

"North is my son, and by bringing you here, I am trusting you with something few know."

The questions whirled. The Knight of Swords, who he'd always considered so stiff that she'd break if she so much as smiled, had a kid—a half-human kid, which meant that at some point in her long life, at least once, she had not been so stiff.

Adam let the train of his thought stop there. He didn't want to contemplate the mechanics.

"I'm honored, Lady." He meant it. A hardliner like her would struggle with this, with having a child not fully elven. He wondered if Silver knew, and if that was part of why he'd chosen her for her title. "And it's nice to meet you, North."

"We're supposed to fight." He sounded about as enthusiastic as Adam felt.

"Yeah, but not for real. We're just going to practice."

He wondered how old the boy was. Younger than Vran had been when Adam had met him. By then, he'd already been the page of his court, and from everything Adam had learned, he'd been a brutal, accomplished fighter.

Adam could close himself off, let the cold in the room seep in, and refuse to show this mismatched child any affection. He pushed the temptation away.

Yes, it still hurt. Yes, it would hurt again. It probably always would, but he would not be that person. He would not let himself become unfeeling or cold, especially toward a child. North hadn't done anything to deserve that.

"This way," the knight said. "We will practice in the conservatory."

Adam had no idea what that meant, but she led them through a pair of arched doors, the frosted glass in their panes hiding the space beyond until she opened them on an indoor winter garden.

The cold was sharper here, just on the edge of what would make Adam shiver.

The roof was glass, the sky beyond a sparkling blue.

The center of the room was a large circle lined in marble flagstones. The corners sported plants, some he knew from Earth, like the moonglow junipers Bobby had talked about adding to the backyard. Others came from Alfheimr, like the bushes of King's Blood with their icy berries that glowed with wintry light. The pots were all a cobalt blue. The style was cold, but beautiful.

Adam inhaled and found his lungs unstrained. He could breathe better here, no doubt thanks to the extra oxygen in the room.

"I didn't know plants from your plane could grow here."

"Our worlds are not so different, not as separate, as you think."

She wove a hand over some small tree Adam did not know and it sprouted two blade-shaped branches.

"Start with these."

She snapped the swords free.

The blade on Adam's back trembled a bit when he lifted the practice blade, humming as if to show annoyance that he'd lift another weapon.

The knight had said the blade spoke to him. Perhaps in time he'd learn to hear it better.

"We will begin with stances," the knight announced. "Position one."

North lifted his blade and held it in both hands. He set his feet apart and rested the blade near his shoulder. Adam copied him, trying to get his body to mirror the boy's.

It was harder than it should have been.

"Two," the knight barked.

North placed his right leg forward in a lunge and turned his back foot. He brought the blade down so he held it near his belly, pointing it up at an angle. He didn't look at Adam, only ahead, his concentration fixed, though Adam got the sense he watched his mother out of the corner of his eye.

Again, Adam copied him, trying to match his pose.

There were two more positions, and as Adam mirrored North, the knight called them out, again and again.

It edged on boring. There wasn't any fighting, or even a meeting of blades, just lifting the wooden sword and holding it as the knight directed. They should have at least had some music so he could pretend he was in a training montage.

The repetition soon put a pang in Adam's arms.

The knight began to correct them, telling them to bend this or straighten that. She showed North no more gentleness than she did Adam.

If anything, she was sharper with her son.

Adam knew too well how it felt to have your parent resent you. Was that how it was? Who was North's father? Where was he?

On and on it went. When she'd said elves trained for decades, he hadn't thought she'd meant all at once.

Then she started mixing up the numbers, having them go from four to two or backward through the poses.

Adam was sweating and short of breath as the rotation went faster.

He thought he'd adapted to Denver's elevation, but this place must be higher.

He wanted to call for a break, but would not give her the satisfaction. He'd prove himself at least as capable as a kid.

"Enough," she snapped.

She waved and the blades dissolved.

"You are too slow, North, and your form remains terrible."

"Yes, Mother." The kid dimmed further, like a distant star hidden by a cloud.

Something blue and magenta bloomed in Adam's chest.

He took in the room again, the winter garden in a palace that felt too cold and unwelcoming for anyone to actually live here, but North did, probably because he couldn't thrive any better in Alfheimr than Adam would. Did he have any friends? Pets? Or had his mother left him all alone?

"He did better than me," Adam said.

The half-elf had hardly broken a sweat, but Adam knew he'd be sore from using muscles he rarely did.

"As he should. He is more experienced. You are a novice."

Adam opened his mouth to say something he probably shouldn't, but she cut him off.

"You are not of our culture, Page. You have no right to judge it, my son, or me."

Adam wanted to argue that North clearly didn't fit into her idea of elven culture, but held his tongue. Even if he wanted to court suicide and argue with her, he didn't know what a comment like that would mean to North.

He managed to hold his tongue and not shake his head.

Damn, he thought. *I'd almost started to like her.*

Whatever this had been, this playdate with her secret kid, it didn't make her his friend or ally. He seemed to be having that thought a lot lately. He was less trusting than he used to be and supposed the last few years had been responsible.

"I guess it's time for me to go." Adam conjured a smile for North. "It was nice to meet you. I'm glad we got to practice together."

The boy didn't say anything, but he nodded, and perhaps a little light came back into his features when Adam added, "I'll see you next time."

"Practice your forms, Page. The more you use your sword, the more it will become an extension of you. It may even save your life someday."

The knight lifted a hand and snow swirled over Adam's vision, turning the sweat on his skin to something clammy.

He found himself back on the street near Bobby's, where the knight had first approached him. He didn't mind the walk. He needed to think.

She'd given him something, revealed a secret. That sort of trust could be deadly, in or outside the Court of Swords. In a sense she'd trapped him, bound him. North was a weakness to her, and by what little Adam could see, an innocent one. She must have known him well enough to realize he'd never harm a child.

The question of why remained.

She'd wanted Adam and North to train, sure, but that couldn't be her only reason. She was far too tactical for that. He hoped one of them was that she realized how lonely her son must be in his fortress of solitude.

22

Adam was the first to arrive at the garage. He locked the door behind him, started the coffee pot, and pulled on his coveralls. Jesse was easy to work for. Vic's brother paid his crew fairly and kept it large enough to show some flexibility, like when Adam needed to take off to Chicago with little notice.

Adam paid him back by working as hard as he could. He clocked in and got to work on the Toyota a customer had dropped off the night before.

Normally he'd put a playlist on the overhead speaker system, skip the earbuds, and enjoy having the place to himself. The other guys didn't share his taste in music, which was fine. The feeling was mutual.

He was leaning over the open hood when a gray car parked outside.

Adam straightened and waited.

The electronic bell beeped and the door opened.

He didn't know the man who stepped inside. Then again, he probably wouldn't remember him if they'd crossed paths. Dressed in slacks, a polo, and a simple leather jacket, he would have blended into a crowd. A movie's credits would have listed him as something like *generic white guy number three.*

"We're not open yet." Adam waved at the closed sign on the door.

The man eyed the wrench in Adam's hand and the corners of his mouth curled into the start of a sneer.

"I'm not here for this," he said, dismissing the garage with a cock of his head, though he never took his eyes off Adam's. "I am here for you."

Adam didn't sense any magic, but the man moved too fluidly, too smoothly, like a predator on the hunt.

Adam straightened.

"Wilcox was too busy to drop by? I'm hurt. I mean, we're technically family."

"I'm afraid my employer doesn't see it that way."

That or he's too afraid, Adam thought, remembering how Patrick had reacted at the house when he'd realized what Adam was.

Adam knew killers. His ex was one. His brother was one. The only other warlock he'd met had killed others out of fear, terrified of Death and what lay beyond her.

This man wasn't afraid.

He was a killer, and unlike Silver or Bobby, his eyes didn't carry a hint of remorse. He was cold, organized, and contained. If he had any kind of soul, it didn't leak out in the waves of messy feelings most did.

While he might be tripping Adam's sense of danger, his Sight had nothing to say. This monster was utterly mundane.

Adam waved the wrench in a *go on*, gesture.

"Mr. Wilcox would like you to get out of his way and stop interfering in his personal business, especially when it comes to his daughter." The man took a thick envelope from his jacket pocket. He laid it on the tool cart. "This is a one-time offer, Mr. Binder. It's quite generous. I'd take it if I were you."

It took most of Adam's control to keep himself from shaking when he asked, "And if I don't?"

"Then you're going to have a problem. Maybe a series of them." The man swept his eyes over the garage. "Mr. Wilcox might start with this place, for example. Faulty wiring, a gas leak—so many things can go wrong in these old buildings. Or he may simply buy the property and terminate Mr. Martinez's lease. You cannot imagine his reach. The hospital that employs your brother, or the school where your lover's mother teaches. Donations speak loudly, and tenure isn't the shield it used to be. Money can do a lot in this world, and you already know that Mr. Wilcox has plenty of it, or you should after your visit to his residence."

"And what do I call you?" Adam asked.

"You don't, but when you meet with Mr. Wilcox, you can say you had a visit from Mr. White." White nodded at the envelope. "Sign those papers and nothing unpleasant has to happen to you or anyone you care about."

White turned and left.

On Adam's back, the sword thrummed in time with his shaking.

He wanted to tear the envelope up, or set fire to it, but he had to know.

Adam opened it and found the same NDA the cult members had signed, the ones Jack had dug up. He also found several pages of personal information, a dossier on him, Bobby, Vic Jesse, and Maria. There was a page on his mother. There were addresses and schedules. Anything you wanted to know about Adam and his people, both his chosen family and the one he'd been born with.

The shaking grew worse when he read the contract. All he had to do was sign, and legally bind himself not to interfere with or disparage any of the Wilcox family interests, Rubrum, Inc., or any of its many subsidiaries.

If he did that, he'd be compensated. Well compensated.

He had to count the zeros twice.

Now he was shaking for an entirely different reason. Vic could open his restaurant. Adam could have a car. They could put a down payment on a house, or they could invest it and live on the interest for the rest of their lives.

All he had to do was go away and leave Annie to the wolves.

A bark sounded from outside, snapping Adam back to the moment. The door beeped again and Jesse called out, "Hey, Wonder Bread."

He had a pink doughnut box in his hands.

Chaos dashed into the shop, nearly tackling Adam in her signature show of affection.

"Hey, girl," he said, crouching to wrap her in his arms.

"You okay?" Jesse asked. "You look like you saw a ghost."

Adam never knew how much of the spooky stuff Jesse was aware of. Vic and his family were close, but telling Jesse about the case might draw even more attention from White. Adam would not be the one to put Vic's brother in danger, except it seemed he already had.

"Nah, it's just this car, you know?"

Adam waved at the Toyota and hoped Jesse didn't spot the envelope.

"It's not as bad as that beater you used to drive."

"Hey! She was a classic."

"Yeah, a classic hunk of junk."

Jesse laughed and his teasing loosened the tightness in Adam's chest. He liked to tease Adam about the Cutlass, the only car Adam had ever owned, but he'd been impressed when Adam had repaired it after a bit of building fell on it and almost as sad as Adam when he'd lost the car. He knew Jesse missed it almost as much as he did.

You couldn't quite see the resemblance between Vic and Jesse unless you knew them well. Jesse was broader shouldered, barrel-chested, and sported a neatly trimmed beard and mustache. His hair was always just a little more than a buzz cut, while Vic had let his hair grow out a few inches since he'd quit the force. Vic took after Maria, their mother, while Jesse favored Eduardo, their father, at least from what Adam had seen in the pictures at Maria's house.

Jesse opened the door to the office. He set the doughnuts on the low filing cabinet and opened it.

"What's with the doughnuts?"

"Does there have to be a reason?" Jesse filled Chaos's water bowl. She had a bed in the corner and a little space heater.

"You only spring for the fancy stuff when you want something or have bad news," Adam said. "So which is it?"

"It depends on how you take it."

"I've already had one too many cryptic conversations today. Can you just tell me what's up? Are you laying me off?"

"No!" Jesse sat hard into his desk chair and gave it a little spin back and forth. "But I do want you to take some classes at the community college."

He pushed some papers across the desk as Chaos found her bed and settled in for a nap.

"Is this your mother's doing?" Adam narrowed his eyes. "Did she get to you?"

"Nope, this one is all me." Jesse leaned forward. "They're offering a certification on EVs."

Adam flipped through the pages.

Jesse had done his research. The printed sheets showed a steady trend of electric vehicle sales increasing in Colorado. He'd sprung for color ink and pie charts to make his case. Adam thought back to what Vic had said about Jesse having a girlfriend.

"Is this how you've been spending your evenings?" Adam asked.

Jesse didn't blush, not exactly, but he dipped his head.

"Some of them, but this isn't about me. It's about the business, and the future."

"You want me to learn how to fix EVs?"

"I want us all to. They're going to be a big part of the market. I want us to be ready, and I want you to go first."

"Why me? I mean, I'm honored, but it's not like I have seniority."

Jesse squirmed a bit before he settled on his answer.

"The other guys are kind of stuck in their ways, you know? I think you'd be the most open to it."

"Who's going to pay for it?" Adam reached for the list of courses the school was offering and tried not to think of the envelope in the other room.

"I think we can split it, maybe. If you agree to teach the rest of us what you learn. If enough of the crew gets certified, then the shop is too. That's something we can advertise."

Adam had to admit that he was interested. He'd passed his GED, but studying for it had been hard. It all came down to money. Maria had said she'd help him apply for grants. If the shop paid half the tuition, he could make it work, but then there was his impending lease and rent with Vic.

"Can I think about it?"

Jesse shrugged and tapped the paper.

"They're not going anywhere, but I'd like to get ahead of it. Let me know by next week, or I'll take it to Carlos. In the meantime, I'm going to work on adding some charging stations to the parking lot."

"Okay."

The workday ended, and Adam passed the bus ride by bringing up the site for the community college on his phone to see what they offered.

He hadn't been in classes since high school or Liberty House, though he couldn't really count those. Would he be older than the other students? The pictures on the school website said no. They showed a mix of smiling, diverse faces, including some middle-aged students.

The envelope sat in his pocket. It felt like it was on fire.

He knew he couldn't just pretend it hadn't happened, that White hadn't threatened them.

Adam texted Vic.

Hey. We've got a problem. Come over tonight?

A zombie problem or something else?

Zombie adjacent.

Be there after work. Don't let anyone eat your brain before I get there.

23

“Do you know a Mr. White?” Adam asked when he’d assembled Annie, Vic, and Bobby at the kitchen table.

“Frank White?” Annie asked. “Yes. He’s my father’s body man.”

Adam and Vic exchanged a glance.

Annie laughed.

“It’s nothing nefarious. Presidents have body men and my dad is the president of the company. It’s a joke.” Her face wrinkled. “Isn’t it?”

“In this case it might be more literal.”

Adam laid the pages White had dropped off on the table and explained his visit to the garage.

Bobby’s eyes narrowed as he took in the dossiers, but Annie’s face reddened.

“He threatened you?”

“He threatened all of us.”

“You did break into one of his properties,” Bobby said.

He held up his hands in surrender when they glared at him and said, “Just playing devil’s advocate.”

“Yeah, don’t do that,” Adam said. “The devil is an asshole.”

He was glad no one asked if the devil was real.

"Weird that he gave you this kind of evidence," Bobby said.

"I don't think he's very worried about the law," Adam replied. He looked over his shoulder. They were inside the house. He had wards for anything magical, but he still felt exposed.

"He's a fixer," Vic concluded. "He cleans up Wilcox's messes."

"How much did he offer you?" Annie asked quietly.

Adam laid the NDA and the contract on the table.

"Three million."

Bobby let out a breath.

"I wished I'd told him to go to hell."

"No, you don't," Vic said. "This guy could be dangerous. You were by yourself. You were smart not to escalate the situation."

Vic met his eye. He knew Adam was tempted by the money. Anyone would be. He gave a little nod, letting Adam know it was okay. Adam forced a smile, because, yeah, it was damn hard.

"I know what we found in Chicago, and I'm not saying I don't believe you." Annie gestured at the pages with both hands. "But how could they be like this, how could my father be like this, without me noticing?"

"Do you remember anything?" Adam asked. "Any rituals or spells . . . anything like that?"

At the moment he'd take a vanilla candle and an out-of-place dreamcatcher to help understand the Wilcoxes' goals and why Annie was so important that they'd threaten everyone in Adam's life.

"No. I just wish I knew why they'd do any of this. Those people in the church . . . I can't get it out of my head."

"You're their daughter," Bobby said, taking her hand.

"No, Rob—Bobby. They don't love me. Maybe if I'd been a son, but no. That's not why."

"What do you remember?" Vic asked.

"I remember physical therapy, the nurses. They weren't fake.

They knew what they were doing. We talked shop, but I had no idea I was in a basement. It's all so fuzzy."

"Someone might have altered your memory," Adam said.

Everyone turned to him.

"I should have thought of it before. There are spells for it. They're not strictly legal, but they're out there. There's a whole underground market in memories."

"Why?" Annie asked.

"Desperate mortals sell them. Immortals buy them to taste experiences they cannot have."

Bobby stared at the table, into his coffee. Adam got it. They both carried things they'd rather forget.

"If they can take them out, can they put them back?" Vic asked.

"I don't know," Adam said. "We're not even certain your memory has been altered. We need an expert, somebody who moves on the shady side."

Vic's eyes bored into him.

"I know," Adam drawled.

"Call him."

"Who?" Bobby asked.

"Isaac Frost."

"Who's that?" Annie asked.

Adam didn't want to explain, didn't want to get into what happened at RCC.

"A student at the king's school," Vic said.

Isaac was a lot more than that. Adam didn't know his exact job description, but suspected he acted as Silver's eyes and ears in the magical underworld.

Vic leaned over to give his shoulder a squeeze.

"It's not his fault."

"I know, but it's still hard."

Adam unlocked his phone and scrolled through his contacts until he found the one labeled *Murder Boy.*

He typed out a message.

I need a favor. Can we meet?

"I thought you were going to call," Vic said.

"He's like twenty. There's no way he'd pick up."

There was a knock at the closet door a moment later.

"That was quick," Bobby said.

"The school knows where to find me," Adam said.

He opened the door to let Isaac in.

He wasn't that much younger than Adam, but Adam still thought of him as a kid.

Isaac wore a tattered leather coat, jeans with a jagged tear at the knee held closed with dozens of safety pins, and biker boots. His hair was so blond that it looked like spiky cotton. He could almost pass as human.

The sword on his back was very different than Adam's. It hadn't come from Silver. Its blade, a long shard of black sea glass, met a wiry hilt crafted of some greenish metal. Isaac rarely took it, the coat, or the two knives he wore on his belt, off.

Despite his dangerous look, he seemed contrite when he straightened and stepped into the hall.

"Thank you for coming so quickly," Adam said.

"Anything to get out of Lit class."

Isaac didn't quite smile.

Adam led him into the kitchen where Bobby and Annie sat at the table, holding hands and looking nervous.

Isaac took in the space, no doubt reading it for signs of Vran, for hints of the time when he'd lived here while Adam made introductions.

"What do you need?" he asked when the pleasantries were over.

"We think someone took some of my memories," Annie said.

"And we need to be sure," Adam said.

"You want me to do my party trick?"

"Yeah, if you can."

"What will it cost?" Bobby asked.

Adam was glad that his brother knew to ask.

"It's on the house," Isaac said.

"How does it work?" Annie asked.

"Remember how you were wondering about vampires?" Adam prodded. "Isaac's the closest thing we've got."

"I just need a drop of blood." Isaac drew one of his knives. "Maybe two."

Bobby straightened.

"Is that thing clean?"

Isaac shrugged.

"Sure, but if you have a needle or something . . ."

"It's okay." Annie squeezed Bobby's leg before offering her hand.

Faster than Adam could track, Isaac pricked her fingertip and licked the bead of blood from the point.

For a long moment, he did nothing, just moving his tongue and looking like a wine snob at a tasting.

"Yeah, there's magic there," he announced after a while.

"There was healing," Adam said. "A lot of it."

Isaac's face twisted when he met something bitter.

"I see that. But, also, there are holes. They're like cuts, a bunch of little slices."

"They'd be recent," Adam said.

Isaac shook his head and opened his eyes.

"No. These go back a while. All the way." He looked at

Annie. "Whatever they did to you, they did it a lot. They've been doing it your whole life."

"What? Why?"

"I don't know, but it's too weird to be a hobby, right, so, uh, *reasons*?"

"We need to fix it," Bobby said. He looked up at Adam. "*Can* we fix it?"

"Maybe," Isaac said. "Magic can . . . well, not fix everything, but a memory broker might have some ideas."

"Then let's go find one," Annie said.

Isaac grimaced.

"There's one west of the city. I can take you there, but it's not a place for tourists."

"They're my memories," Annie said, straightening in her seat. "I'm coming."

"I go where she goes," Bobby said.

"I don't even know what you'd see over there," Adam said. "It takes Sight to navigate the spirit realm, even if you go in body. Bobby has some, but you don't."

"I have an idea." Bobby left the table and came back with a pair of sunglasses.

Adam knew the flavor of the enchantment. Clean and swift, like a mountain river on the edge of freezing.

"That's Argent's magic."

"Yeah," Vic said. "She made those when we rebuilt the eastern tower."

"Will they help Annie see?" Bobby asked.

"They should."

He thought he'd come to terms with his family and friends rebuilding the tower and using it to save him from the last time he'd sacrificed himself.

"We'll need to drive," Isaac said. "Anybody got a car?"

"Yeah, if you can get us across."

"I think the school can manage it," Isaac said confidently.

"Should we bring backup?" Vic asked. "Dautre, maybe?"

"If we're doing this, then less magic is better," Adam said. "We don't want to draw unwanted attention, especially in the west."

"Why not?" Annie asked.

"I'm on someone's shit list," Adam said.

"No," Isaac corrected. "You're on his *hit* list."

He said it like Adam should be proud.

Adam knew that he'd eventually have to settle things with Seamus, the King of Coins and ruler of the western watchtower. He just didn't know how he'd manage it.

They piled into Annie's car, which Bobby had kept driving after her now-alleged death. It was a mom mobile, but Adam couldn't complain, not with five of them. Isaac spoke to the garage door for a moment. Adam did his best to not overhear.

Vic returned from his car carrying his gun case.

"You don't have to come," Adam said.

"Like hell I don't." Vic leaned in for a kiss before pocketing the pistol. "You want one?"

"I've got the sword."

Still, he considered it. The knight had proven that Adam wasn't exactly great with the blade, and drawing it meant invoking the power of the court in hostile territory.

Annie had her glasses on. Vic donned his own pair, likely out of solidarity. That or he knew he looked good in them.

"I'll drive," Adam said.

Isaac and Vic both headed for the front passenger door.

Vic shook his head.

"I know where we're going," Isaac said.

"I'm his boyfriend and I've got a gun."

Isaac jerked a thumb at himself. "Trained assassin."

Vic grinned.

"Grim Reaper."

Isaac lifted his hands in surrender and took a spot in the backseat.

24

The garage door opened when Adam hit the button, but instead of the street they backed into the spirit realm.

"Wow," Annie said, taking in the emerald sky and antique photo style of Denver on the Other Side. "Is it always like this?"

"Yeah," Adam said.

"Sometimes there are dinosaurs," Isaac added wistfully as they drove west.

Adam hoped to avoid any T. rexes—or worse—this time.

He wrapped his senses tight about himself. It blinded him a bit. He wouldn't see something coming, but it also meant he was less likely to get the attention of the western watchtower.

He forewent his usual "we come in peace" announcement.

The roads were simpler here, with fewer traffic lights or buildings crowding them in. The mountains and foothills stood clear of the urban sprawl that the native residents loved to complain about.

The dwellings they passed as they left downtown were pastel-colored blobs dotting a brown landscape like little marshmallows drifting in cocoa. He saw no sign of whatever lived there as they sped past.

Tumbleweeds with a thousand eyes, bigger than elephants,

rolled past. Adam swerved to dodge one and it opened a dozen mouths to flick its forked tongues at them before it went back to pulling itself along with the little hands protruding from its branches.

In the distance a thunderstorm roared. It flashed with neon purple lightning. A strike sent fonts of sparks miles into the air.

"It's getting weirder," Vic said.

Adam nodded. Even with his Sight closed he could feel it. A change was coming.

Isaac called out directions from the back.

Bobby was smiling, caught up in Annie's wonder, which meant Adam and the others needed to focus on keeping them safe. The spirit realm could go from bemusing to dangerous in the blink of an eye.

Once upon a time, he'd have done more to prepare Annie, to let her know what she'd be in for and warn her about the Other Side.

He had to wonder if he was getting too used to it, if he was forgetting its dangers.

Adam had tried to map the city in the time since he'd moved there. It had been a little harder without a car, but drives with Vic had been one way to amuse themselves during lockdown, when traffic had been almost nonexistent.

Things had felt almost post-apocalyptic, with not enough people around.

This stretch felt a bit like that. There were wagons mired in the bone-littered grass. Torn to tatters, their covers flickered and rippling, signaling their surrender.

Then they were heading south, away from Seamus's tower and the dragon lurking atop Lookout Mountain.

The road morphed to something rougher than asphalt, smoothed stone.

"Are we going to Red Rocks?" Vic asked.

"I don't know what that is," Isaac said.

"It's a music venue." Vic squeezed Adam's leg. "Someday we'll see a concert there."

"I'd like that."

They'd avoided seeing a show so far, even when Crown the Empire had come through town. Just because he had way better control of his Sight than he did when he was a teenager didn't mean that crowds were easy.

"It's a big, outdoor space," Vic explained, telling Adam he understood the crinkled look on his face. "But we could leave anytime it got to be too much for you."

"Over there," Isaac said, pointing to a small parking lot and a hiking trail marked by two stacks of ruddy stone.

Adam parked.

"Something is watching us," Isaac said when they'd climbed out.

"Yeah," Adam agreed.

He could feel the eyes on them, but couldn't find the source.

He wished Annie's white box of a car wasn't so obvious, not that there were any other automobiles around. The little parking lot was barren, the asphalt old and cracked. The air smelled of ozone, but the storm hadn't moved closer.

Adam exchanged a glance with Vic and knew he'd help keep an eye on Bobby and Annie.

"In and out," Adam said, leading them to the hiking trail. "We're not safe here."

Vic brought up the rear, and Adam regretted not accepting his offer of a gun.

Back straight, he walked tall. It would do him no good to show weakness. Projecting strength was always the best policy when dealing with the things that went bump in the spirit realm's emerald twilight.

There weren't many trees, just the ruddy-colored stone that gave the amphitheater its name, but the shadows were thick, and the gloom hard to pierce, especially with his Sight on mute.

They reached the peak. The amphitheater stretched out beneath them.

The wide curve of benched seats wasn't empty. At first he thought them art, some sort of wiry sculpture, before he realized his mistake.

The corpses stared ahead, their gazes fixed forever on the stage.

"Isaac . . ."

"This is where you wanted to go," he said with a shrug before leading them forward.

The stage was full of stuff, piles of junk.

The mess held no rhyme or reason. Plates, magazines, newspapers, and stuffed animals were all jumbled together. It was a sort of a hoard, a collection, but one without any kind of order.

"Have you come to buy or sell?" the voice echoed over the space.

"We're here for my memories," Annie called. She pushed her way forward, making her way through the junk and refuse. Her voice only shook a little when she asked, "Can you help me?"

"That depends." The creature that shuffled into view was hulking and hunched, folded into a misshapen robe. "Do you want to remember or do you want to forget?"

Multiple arms sprouted from slits in the cloak, and dozens of eyes gleamed in the darkness inside its hood. What flesh lay visible was coated in a fine layer of purple fur.

"Is that what they wanted?" Vic nodded to the dead observers. "To forget?"

"*Yes.* It's what most of my customers want, most of my trade. They didn't want to remember anything." It sounded sad. It picked a gravy boat out of one of the piles and held it to its ear before setting it aside gently, almost reverently. "It's a thing to be pitied, to wish for oblivion, to be erased."

Isaac shuddered, just a little, before the tough guy persona fell back into place.

"I want the opposite," Annie said. "I need to remember everything."

"Everything?" The thing shook and Adam decided it might be laughing. Its hands shuffled through the piles, sorting maybe, but Adam still saw no pattern to the way it organized its hoard. "That's a lot."

"I mean, everything that's happened to me."

It considered her, then three of its arms extended long, spiny fingers in a *come here* gesture.

Bobby stiffened, but Annie climbed the steps to reach the stage.

The creature set aside the things it had picked up. It put two hands on her shoulders, as if to calm her. Two others wove around her skull, long fingers clasping and unclasping, but never quite touching her.

"Human magics . . . So clumsy. So inelegant. Yes, I can do this for you." Its arms settled inside its cloak. "How will you pay?"

Adam held up a hand, gesturing for everyone to keep quiet.

"What do you want?"

"Memories, of course." Two hands swept across the theater. "Something precious, something rare. Happy or sad, I don't care."

It shook again, amused with its rhyme. Adam had the feeling it used this bit on all of its customers.

"It doesn't have to be yours," the thing told Annie.

Adam riffled through his mind, trying to sort through his recollections, looking for something he could part with.

The day he met Vic? Never.

The trip below, into the Underworld? It had been horrible, but it had changed him. He did not want to let that go. He wanted to remain himself, who he'd become, even if so much of it had hurt.

He sorted and selected. As hard as it was, he'd give up his first kiss with Silver, or—

"I have something," Bobby said, stepping forward and cutting off the train of Adam's thoughts.

"Bobby . . ."

"That day." He shook his head. "You know the one. I don't want to carry it anymore."

"Are you sure? It's a part of you."

"I think about it all the time. I dream about it, and I hate it."

Adam could feel the old hurt and ache leaking out of his brother like blood from a half-picked scab.

"It won't heal it," Isaac said. "Even if you don't remember, the wound will be there."

"I can live with that."

The creature gestured for Bobby to step forward.

"Do what you have to. Just help her."

The creature ran its hands around his forehead. It grinned, its many teeth showing inside its hood.

"Oh yes," it purred. "A murder will do nicely."

Annie blinked back tears as the broker pressed a hand to Bobby's head. It sank its fingers into his skull. Adam braced for blood or for Bobby to scream, but he only blinked and grimaced, not enjoying the sensation but not looking like it hurt as the thing wiggled its fingers, rooting around for something.

The broker pulled something free, a hammer. Blood coated

the head. The broker turned it over in two of its hands. Its eyes shining, it deposited it atop one of the piles with care.

Annie gaped at Bobby.

"It's okay," he told her. "I'm okay."

She hugged him.

The broker politely cleared its throat.

"Will it hurt?" Annie asked.

"The past often does." The thing gestured to the silent corpses. "Why else would they come to me and sell so much that they can never leave?"

Annie stepped toward the broker.

It opened all eight of its arms and wrapped her in an embrace.

25

Annie gasped and fell away from the broker. Bobby caught her as she stumbled.

She took several heaving breaths and shook free of his arms.

"Annie?" Adam asked.

She held up a hand.

"I'm okay," she said. "I promise. I'm okay."

"Do you remember?" Bobby asked.

She fixed him with a wide-eyed expression.

"Everything. I remember *everything.*"

"Thank you for your business," the broker said. It clapped its hands together in pairs of two. "I'll treasure the memory of your visit."

Adam resisted the urge to flip it off as they climbed the steps out of the theater. A glance at Isaac told him the assassin was having a similar reaction.

They went slowly. Neither Annie nor Bobby seemed quite themselves as they made the long, downward climb toward the parking lot.

They hadn't quite reached the car when a crowd emerged from the gloom.

"What's with the masks?" Isaac asked.

Adam spun back and forth, taking in the plastic wolf masks. None of the figures wore a tuxedo, but all were human. They filled the parking lot, a ring of figures in clothing ranging from every era he could think of and a few he didn't recognize.

"What are they?" Annie asked.

"Lost Ones." Isaac sounded sad, but he put his hands to his knives.

Vic drew his gun but didn't raise it.

The crowd kept its distance, but if they charged, there would be trouble. They didn't look armed or even particularly dangerous, but there were a lot of them.

"What are you doing here?" Adam demanded. "What do you want?"

None of them spoke. They just stared back, their faces hidden by the masks.

"Okay then. Good talk. We're going to leave now."

They didn't move nearer as Adam and the others piled back into the car.

The circle parted to let them drive away.

They hadn't dispersed when Adam checked the rearview mirror, but they'd turned, their eyes fixed on the taillights of the boxy SUV.

Annie and Bobby sat close together, their arms wrapped tight around each other.

"How are you doing?" Vic asked them.

"It's like my deck was missing all these cards," Annie said. "Now they're all here and I need to shuffle them and put them in order. It's not just my family. It's being born. It's going to school. It's what I ate for breakfast on the eighth day of my eighth year. I could tell you everything I ever read or saw. *Everything.* It's all here now."

She shook in Bobby's embrace.

"You need to defrag your hard drive," Isaac said.

Adam met his eyes in the mirror.

"I spend a lot of time with Jack."

The drive back was uneventful, and Adam hoped their incursion into the western territory wouldn't come back to bite him. They reached the eastern watchtower, which had no garage door.

"Over there," Isaac said as a warehouse door rolled up, letting in a gleam of mortal light.

It always surprised Adam how he could sink into the perpetual twilight of the spirit realm and return to sunshine in a blink. The sharp shift disoriented him every time.

They were through and back in the garage at the house.

It took everyone a moment to adjust to the shift.

Vic escorted Annie and Bobby inside.

Adam walked Isaac to the coat closet.

"I . . ." Adam stumbled. "Thank you."

Isaac chewed his lip.

"I get it, you know. It's not easy seeing you either. You remind me of him and, well, all of it."

The first time they'd met, Adam had held Isaac while he'd cried over losing Vran. Adam had done his best to hold back his own grief until he'd gotten home. Then he'd found he couldn't weep, and he'd just stared at the ceiling, swept along in the tide of losing someone who should never have been lost.

"Yeah," he said. "I'm sorry. I try not to take it out on you. I know it's not your fault, and I really appreciate your help today."

"You too. I'll always come if you need me," Isaac said. "You know, for his sake."

"I know. Same."

Isaac lingered a moment.

"Do we shake? Hug?"

"Don't make it weird, Binder."

Isaac turned to the closet door and whispered something to it. Opening it, he stepped through to the school.

Adam joined the others in the kitchen.

Vic was already making tea.

"That thing . . ." Annie was saying. "At the hospital. It was so hungry. So much—so vast, and I was connected to it."

"We called it Mercy," Adam said. "After the hospital. We didn't know what other name to give it."

Annie nodded.

She took a moment to collect herself.

"It hated you—us. It couldn't understand us, like we were gnats constantly buzzing around it, annoying it. It just wanted us gone."

"You remember it possessing you?" Adam asked.

"It just slid in, like a door had been left open in my mind. I couldn't stop it. Couldn't fight it." She squeezed the mug Vic passed her in a two-handed grip. "After everything with the babies, I'm not sure I even wanted to. There were times I didn't even fight it. I knew I needed to, but I just . . ."

She teared up as she drifted off.

Bobby lifted a hand like he wanted to lay it on her shoulder, to comfort her, but paused. She reached out and took it.

"I remember what happened on Lookout Mountain. I remember coming to see you, Bobby, to give you a chance. I had to. It *hurt* you."

"What about after?" Vic asked gently. "Do you remember the church in Chicago?"

Annie chewed her lip.

"Yes. They prayed, at least I thought it was praying. Every night, sometimes all day. It hurt. It hurt so much. They wheeled me into that room, inside the circle." She looked around the table. "I remember them dying, burning up from the inside. And . . . it's gone on my whole life. There were parties at the house. I remember my nanny falling asleep. I snuck to the upstairs railing. They were wearing those masks, those red-wolf masks, and black robes. It was like Halloween. They saw me, and my dad . . . he took me into his office and erased it."

So that was the magic Wilcox had been using. He'd been stealing Annie's memories.

"I still don't know why they want me back so badly," she said.

"I don't either, but they're not done. They can't be or they wouldn't have tried to make you go home with them."

"Find out what they want, Adam. Find out why they did this to me. Please."

"I will."

Vic headed for his car. He locked his gun in the safe in the trunk and closed it with a little too much force. He glared at it.

"It's going to be okay," Adam said.

"I should be the one comforting you."

"Not always." Adam moved closer. "We're partners, right?"

"Are we? Because sometimes it doesn't feel like it."

"What do you mean?"

"I saw you. You were ready to give something up for her, a memory. What was it?"

"Nothing about you, nothing about us."

"But a piece of you, a memory. Annie is his wife. If anyone should have paid the toll, it's Bobby. You don't always have to take everything onto yourself."

"I know."

"I'm not sure you do. You're not alone anymore, Adam. Every time I think you've got that, you jump into the fire without backup."

"Are you mad?"

"No. I'm . . . frustrated. It's been a lot. I love you. I'm going to go get some sleep."

"I love you too."

Adam kissed him quickly. He didn't need to hug Vic to feel the tension in him. He stood on the porch for a bit, then went to check on Bobby.

His brother stood in the backyard, having some kind of reverie as he stared at the privacy fence, at some knot or spot Adam couldn't pinpoint.

"How are *you* feeling?"

"It's weird," Bobby said. "I know it happened. I remember telling you about it. I remember thinking about it, but I don't remember doing it."

"I get it," Adam said. "Sort of. Most of my memories of dad are like that. I can see them, but they're fuzzy, like places I can't go."

White hot, they burned to his mental touch. Adam couldn't pick them up for very long without them feeling sick or having all the associations he had around their dad, rage and hate, sticking to him for hours, sometimes days. It would take a lot more therapy and time before he'd moved past it.

Bobby nodded.

"Maybe it was time to stop carrying it, but what I did . . . I don't think you should ever let that go, not completely. It's not like some of the other stuff."

"Like what?"

"Like the kid I made fun of in third grade, that kind of thing. Those I think I can forgive myself for, or should. But some of them, like what I did to you." Bobby hung his head.

"I've forgiven you." Adam had to admit it hadn't been easy and the old resentment still popped up from time to time. "I think it's time you forgave yourself too."

"Thank you, but the other thing—Dad—I took a life, Adam. I can't just dismiss that."

"What you did today, you did for Annie. I'm proud of you."

"I thought she was gone forever. There were times I would have done anything to have her back. Anything. This is the least I can do to help make it right."

Adam didn't know what to say, so he kept silent. He understood. He'd literally gone to hell for Vic, and he'd do it all again.

They stood there for another moment, taking in the square of sleeping autumn yard.

"We should go check on her," Bobby said.

They found her in the den, at her old desk. She'd pulled a stack of blank paper from the printer tray and was writing furiously. She'd already filled a few pages with neat, simple handwriting.

"Whatcha doing?" Adam asked.

"I have to get it down in case it fades again."

"Get what down?"

"Everything I can remember about my parents, about their business, their deals, everything they've built. Can you make me some coffee?"

"Always." Adam moved toward the kitchen. "But why? What are you going to do with it?"

Annie gave him a smile that he could only describe as wicked.

"I'm going to burn it down."

26

Adam pushed himself into Dr. Cahill's couch. He never knew what to do with his hands when he was here. He didn't feel like lying down, so he picked up one of the throw pillows and hugged it to his chest before catching her up on what had happened since their last session. He stuck to the highlights. They only had an hour and a lot had happened.

As he talked, he stared at the painting of the ocean she'd hung on the wall. He'd made a habit of it when he'd started seeing her. Focusing on it, it had felt like he could let the jagged, broken glass feelings that came with the memories float away.

It was a bit of an anachronism. His therapist's style leaned toward a sort of *I do yoga everyday* vibe. There was a wooden mandala triptych on one wall and enough silk tapestries to border on cultural appropriation. It was all very teahouse, which clashed with Cahill's no bullshit attitude.

He finished his story. She pushed her glasses up and said, "Well, that's a lot to take in."

"I never know if you believe me."

It had been one of the things he'd worried about when he'd

agreed with Vic's request that he start therapy. He didn't want someone trying to lock him up—again—because of his Sight.

Nadine Cahill wasn't a witch, but she was sensitive. She knew the Other Side existed, and while he was honest with her, he didn't tell her *everything* he saw.

She seemed to accept whatever Adam told her. She didn't leap to recommending medication and knew he was wary of it. She also hadn't tried to institutionalize him, at least so far, for which he was extra grateful.

"Does it matter?" She wore her long hair loose. It framed her round face in waves of brown.

"Kind of."

"Why?"

"I guess I need to know you're in my corner."

"You're used to not having anyone on your side, Adam—at least you see it that way, but that's changing, I hope. You have Vic. You have your family."

"They still suck."

"Yes, but they're trying, and here's a secret—all families suck, at least a little."

Adam couldn't argue. He'd idolized the Martinez family at first, but the more he learned, especially about how Maria had steered Vic away from his dream of being a chef, the more he realized that no one's relatives were perfect.

He could try to shock her, regale her with the story of his ancestor who'd pruned subsequent generations to prolong his own life, but Adam decided to stick to current events for now.

"You said you feel like you need to move," Dr. Cahill prompted. "And that Vic wants an apartment."

"Yeah, and he's right. It's time, especially with Annie back. It probably has been for a while."

"So why haven't you?"

He knew he had to answer. He paid money to come here, to face the things he didn't want to. This was one of them. The feeling was a vice, a general squeeze around him. He knew it too well.

"I'm afraid."

"Of?"

"The future. What it means for us, living together, all of that."

"Have you talked to him about it?"

"I need to."

It was the number one thing he had to work on. He and Vic couldn't read each other, not anymore, and that meant they had to talk about everything. Sometimes Adam felt like all they did was talk. He wished, only every once in a while, that he could just connect them again, if just long enough to exchange the things they, and he especially, had a hard time saying.

"If it helps, write it down. Living together is a big step, and you want to set some boundaries and understand each other's dealbreakers before you take it."

Just living with Bobby had taught him that it wasn't the big things that got you, it was the little ones—who did the dishes and where you put the laundry, that sort of thing. It was too easy for resentment to build up if you let it.

With Bobby it had been a struggle to get his brother to understand that just because Bobby was a doctor didn't mean that Adam's job wasn't also important, and Adam had to learn to concede that fixing cars wasn't on the same level as saving lives when they were both running late and didn't have time to let the hot water tank recharge.

He thought back to Lauren's apartment and how small it was. In a space like that they'd be on top of each other. Hell, just having to deal with Vic's habit of getting up three to five mornings a week to go for a run was likely to grate when Adam wanted to sleep in.

"Have you two talked any more about marriage?"

"He's still figuring all that out, how heteronormative he wants to be. What if he decides he wants a wife and not a husband? What if he decides that he wants kids?"

"And you don't?"

"No. Never." Before she could ask why not, he added, "I don't want to turn out like my dad, or my mom."

He'd made his peace with Tilla Mae, but she'd never qualify for mother of the year. Uncle, he could do, if that was still in the cards for Bobby and Annie, if they adopted, but he just didn't see himself as a father, even if he and Vic could ever afford it.

"And have you told Vicente that?"

"Not exactly," he hedged. "Um, I kind of hinted at it in Chicago."

"You've been together a while. I think you two have some conversations ahead of you, a couple before you sign a lease, and a couple after. You're only twenty-five, Adam, you don't have to have all of the answers right now, but you owe Vic your honesty, especially since he's given you his. If kids are a deal-breaker, then he has a right to know."

She was right, of course, at least about that.

It had taken him a while to realize that a therapist didn't have the solutions, and he wouldn't have liked it if she'd pretended to. Instead, she made suggestions. Sometimes they landed, sometimes not.

It was like digging for treasure in a big field.

There were insights and truths to discover, but Adam had a lot of ground, a lot of ruddy clay, to excavate.

He knew he hadn't told Vic everything he needed to about what he wanted for their future. He needed to share his worries and his doubts, but he didn't want to rock the boat, to upset the balance of them when things were going so well. Except, now that maybe things weren't going so well.

"I guess I just didn't know I was ever going to be here."

"Because you could die saving the world?"

"Well . . . yeah. Or something like that."

"Adam, do you know what a self-sacrificing narcissist is?"

"I'm guessing me? Is that my diagnosis?"

"No. Though you're a level five smart ass, but sadly that's not in the manual and there's no known cure. In short, it's someone who puts the needs of others ahead of theirs to avoid dealing with their own issues."

"You think that's me?"

"I think you might have that tendency, not because you're self-obsessed, but because you don't value yourself."

Adam thought back to the broker, to how he'd been ready to sacrifice a memory before Bobby had stepped up. He sank back into the couch and squeezed the pillow. Vic was right.

"Don't give away so many bricks that you can't build your house," Dr. Cahill said. "You've been doing that for too long. You're so worried about the future, but if you keep doing it, where will you end up?"

"I think I get it."

"Do you? You're not the king. You're not responsible, not all the time. You can make the world better, but you can't save it, or everyone."

He knew that. He'd failed Vran.

"Maybe I do leap too quickly sometimes, but when I don't someone else has to."

"You're feeling survivor's guilt."

"Maybe."

He didn't say the other thing, the real fear that was bubbling to the surface of his thoughts. It was the thing he didn't think about, that maybe he hadn't married Vic or even moved in with him yet because he didn't want to make a widower out of the love of his life.

27

It always took Adam a while to calm down after therapy. In a lot of ways it felt like coming back from spirit walking—his body didn't quite work right. He had to focus to get home. The bus helped. It gave him time to listen to music and relax his nerves. Vic reached the house about the same time he did, and Adam greeted him with a long hug as soon as he was out of the car.

"Not that I'm complaining, but what was that for?"

"You. Us. I'm sorry. You were right. I've had a bad case of main character syndrome. I promise that I'm working on it."

"Thank you for working on it." Vic kissed the top of his head. "What are you thinking for dinner?"

Adam's phone buzzed in his pocket with a call.

"It's Jodi." He slid the button to answer.

She spoke before he'd even said hello.

"Adam. Where are you?"

"At Bobby's. What's wrong?"

"It's Nicole," she said. "She didn't come home. Something's wrong. I can *feel* it."

Adam didn't question Jodi's Sight. It was stronger, and often more accurate, than his.

"Did she say anything, do anything?"

Adam thought of the Hotel Erythraean, of the doormen that matched a little too well.

"No, at least I don't think so."

"Did anyone come to move her things?"

"She didn't join them. She wouldn't. She just didn't come home. I can't track her. We're too close. Adam, I'm not getting anything, not even with the cards."

"I'll be right there." Adam hung up and looked to Vic. "You heard that?"

"Hard not to. She's pretty upset. Let's go."

"I could take a ride share or—"

Vic silenced him with a quick kiss.

"Let's go," he repeated.

Adam gave directions while Vic drove.

Jodi opened the front door before they'd reached it.

"Nothing?" Adam asked as he and Vic walked in.

"Nobody's heard from her."

"We can file a missing persons report," Vic said.

"Don't you have to wait like a day or something?" Jodi asked.

"That's a myth."

She chewed her lip.

"What if it's too late?"

"I can try to track her," Adam offered.

Jodi gestured toward the coffee table, where she'd already lit a tealight candle in a little iron cauldron. A hairbrush waited beside it, along with a saucer filled with dirt and a cardboard tube of sea salt.

"Thanks."

Jodi gave a worried little nod.

Vic hugged her and they stepped back while Adam mixed the dirt, salt, and a bit of Nicole's hair into a ball.

He tried to focus on her, to reach for what she'd felt like at the park or the last time they'd met.

She'd come across as fiery orange, almost angry—but no, not angry, *determined*. Nicole was driven, hot, like a good black tea, and probably better for you than you realized. When he thought he had a grip on her essence, he dropped the ball into the flame and reached for her.

The spell bobbed in the ether for a long moment until it caught.

"I've got her."

"What do we do?" Vic asked.

"We go get her," Jodi said.

"She could be held somewhere, but it's not the hotel. It doesn't feel north."

"She's my friend. We. Go. Get. Her."

"All right," Vic said.

"I'll drive, but we need to hurry. The connection isn't strong. I don't know how long I can hold onto it."

Vic opened the trunk as he handed Adam the keys.

Adam didn't have to ask. Vic climbed into the passenger seat, gun in hand. He checked the safety as Adam started the car.

His hold on the spell was precarious. It sat like an ember, the last glint of a fire, at the center of his mind. If he squeezed too tight he'd snuff it out. If he held it too loosely it would fly away.

They headed west, stopped at a light. The spell's light, its pulse, began to fade.

The light turned and his foot reached for the gas. A cyclist cut across the front of the car, inches from the bumper, as Adam accelerated.

He let out a long breath and tried not to let it break his concentration.

They zigged and zagged until they came to one of the many

construction sites that had cropped up like weeds in the last few years. It seemed like everywhere you went apartment complexes and condominiums were being built in that quick, four- or five-story style that looked like steel blocks stacked atop each other.

The trail ended and Adam stopped the car.

"This is it," he said.

"Here?" Jodi peered into the gloom of urban dusk.

He understood the question as they climbed out into the night.

There wasn't a building, just the start of one. A tall chain link fence walled away the site. Some dumpsters sat at the side with a pile of trash that likely had been someone's bedding.

"I don't see anything." Jodi said.

"I do."

Vic walked them to the dumpsters. Time slowed. The sound of traffic quieted, and Vic changed.

Black threads, like creeping smoke, crawled across him. His scythe, once bound to a police baton, formed from nothing in his open hand.

Adam and Jodi trailed him. Hand covered by bones that looked like body paint, Vic knelt to pull back the cover of the weather-stained sleeping bag.

Nicole lay pale beneath it.

"No," Jodi said.

"I'm sorry." Adam hugged her.

Vic touched the body, softly laying a hand to her forehead. Something gray and faint, a moth, flitted into the air. He gently wrapped a hand around it and held it to his ear.

"Can you tell me what happened?" It was Vic's voice, but the tones were deeper.

He was the Reaper and the Reaper was also him. It was different than the others Adam had met.

Vic paused to listen to something Adam couldn't hear.

"I'm sorry."

He tucked the moth into his robe and stood.

The Reaper was gone and time started again.

"She didn't see them," he said. "They grabbed her from behind when she got to work."

Adam looked to Jodi.

"She works downtown." She paused to choke down a sob. "One of those charities that gives clothes to women going back to work after prison or welfare."

"We need to get out of here," Vic said.

"Can't we just tell them we found her?" Adam asked, immediately knowing it was a stupid question.

"They won't believe us, or worse, they'll think we had something to do with it."

Vic didn't talk much about his time on the force. When it did come up he'd remind people that he wasn't a cop for very long, but he knew how cops thought.

"We can't just leave her here," Jodi said.

"I'll leave an anonymous tip," Vic said.

Adam looked around for a payphone, but they were rarer than a chicken's tooth now.

Vic began walking the length of the alley.

"What are you doing?" Jodi asked.

"Looking for cameras."

"I can't believe . . ." Jodi trailed off.

Adam moved between her and the dumpster to block her view until Vic finished.

"We're good," he announced. "We need to go."

Jodi clenched her fists. She looked like she was going to scream.

"She won't be here long, Jodi," Vic said gently. "But we need to get you home. They'll come knocking soon."

Vic locked up his gun. Adam let him drive.

"Jodi, if there's anything at the house that shouldn't be there, you need to get rid of it, right now, understand?"

"You mean like drugs?" Adam asked.

"Exactly like drugs."

"You think they're going to search the house?" Adam asked.

"Yes. It's a suspicious death. If there's any evidence of a murder, they'll get a warrant and be very thorough."

"There isn't anything," Jodi said. She sounded numb.

"Okay," Vic said.

"I just . . . I can't believe she's dead."

They didn't speak again until they were back at Jodi's place.

"It might not be a bad idea to put the cauldron and all that away," Vic said, nodding at the altar and the moon tapestry.

"You think they'll have a problem with it?" Jodi asked, a little of her old defiance rising, and Adam knew she'd be okay in time.

"I think anything suspicious could be a factor."

"What if nobody finds her? What if somebody—"

Vic took her by the arms and hugged her.

"You should report her missing," he said.

"Okay." Jodi sat, perching on the couch like she could flee at any moment. "I just don't understand."

Adam took the chair beside the couch.

"Did she know something? Something you didn't tell me?"

"Maybe." Jodi nibbled her lip.

"Jodi, I know she didn't trust the Guardians, but you know me. You know I'm trying to help."

Vic sat next to her.

Jodi looked to him and back to Adam.

"She wanted to know what happened to them. I know you told her not to . . ."

"She went looking for them, at the hotel?"

"Yeah. She said they didn't tell her anything. The front desk said nobody with any of those names was staying there." Jodi looked like she might break down. "What am I supposed to do?"

"The cops will come," Vic said. "They'll ask questions. Be honest, except for, you know, about tonight."

"Okay."

Adam hoped Jodi's past skirting the law would come in handy.

They sat with her a bit longer.

Vic drove them back to Bobby's.

"Are you all right?" Adam asked.

"What do you mean? I've seen bodies before."

"No, I mean about keeping stuff from the police."

Vic let out a breath.

"I don't like it, but what are we supposed to do, tell them you found a body using magic?"

This was one of those moments when Adam didn't know whether to pry more into what Vic was feeling or to let it lie.

"I could call Dale," Vic mused. "We have a suspect, or suspects, but how do we explain any of this?"

He fell silent.

Adam noticed he was taking the long way home, avoiding the highway and letting the city carry them along. Adam kept quiet for a while, then asked, "Do you wish you'd stayed on the force?"

"No—I mean, not usually, but this is one of those times it would be useful to be on the inside. I want to help people."

Adam didn't know what to say to that.

Vic had given up being a cop to live his dream, and he'd said many times that it was likely the right thing, that he wasn't sure he could make a difference. At the same time, he felt selfish for doing what he wanted to instead of thinking about the greater good.

Adam got that. He wanted to help people. He was trying to, but if it came to choosing between playing the hero and a life with Vic, he knew which way he was leaning.

But that could change the next time he drew his sword.

Nothing hurt more than staying on the fence, but for now he had to wait and see.

It was some hours later when Adam felt the scratching at his wards again.

"What is it?" Vic asked sleepily when he stirred.

"I've got a visitor. I'll be right back."

Vic started to sit up, but Adam pressed him back toward the mattress by laying a hand to his chest.

"It's okay. He won't hurt me."

At least Adam didn't think so.

He remembered his coat this time

The figure stood much as before, at the edge of the wards, like a spirit, not quite solid, not all the way in the mortal world.

It was the young one, at least Adam thought he was younger. The mask wasn't as worn. The tuxedo was crisper.

"Why?" Adam demanded. "Why is she dead?"

He reached for the sword to draw it, but the Wolf held up his hands.

"Don't!" the Wolf said.

"So you *can* talk." Adam left his hand on the hilt, the blade an inch or two free of its scabbard. The sword hummed. It wanted to be drawn.

"I didn't kill her."

"Who did?"

The young Wolf hung his head.

"White." He sounded genuinely sad.

Adam had suspected the answer, and he suspected the Wolf was telling the truth. He let the sword go.

"Who are you?"

"Ian."

"Who is *he*, the other Wolf? He said you didn't have the same purpose, didn't want the same thing."

Ian shook his head.

"He's me, another me."

He spoke like it strained him, or like he'd forgotten how to use his voice.

"How is that possible?"

"The Between. I'm there. Him too, but at different points. He's years away from me."

Adam blinked.

He looked again. The Wolf, Ian, was a spirit. He'd been right to call him a projection. He wasn't here, not in the flesh.

"You're spirit walking through *time*?"

"We both are. I can't do it for very long. I just needed you to know it wasn't me."

"Why do you care?" Adam asked.

"Because, it—it just matters, okay?"

Ian pulled at his hair, and Adam wished it made the mask slip. He couldn't get a read on the guy's exact age, but he was young, maybe a teenager. Maybe a bit older.

"I believe you." Adam held up a hand. "What does Wilcox want with Annie?"

Ian shook his head.

"I can't tell you that."

"Why? Because you don't know or you don't want to?"

"I just can't. At least not yet."

"They killed a woman," Adam argued. But Ian was gone, vanished like a moonbeam when a cloud passed over.

Adam sighed and turned back toward the house.

He wasn't surprised to find Vic watching from the living room window.

"Did you get anything out of him?" Vic asked when Adam crept inside.

"A little. I need to look into the Between."

"The place beyond the cracks?"

"Yeah. I don't know how, but it's important to all of this."

Jodi called the next morning.

"They called to say they found her," she said as Adam picked up. "That she overdosed, that there was all this stuff in her system, but she didn't use, Adam. She just smoked a little pot."

He didn't know how to respond. On one hand Jodi wouldn't come under suspicion, but on the other he had no evidence that Nicole had been murdered.

"Her parents won't even call me back."

"What? Why?"

"They hated that she was pagan. They probably think she deserved it."

"I'm so sorry."

"You have to get them for this, Adam. I don't care if the Guardians help you or whoever, but you have to."

"I will." He didn't know how, but he would.

She hung up.

He threw himself back onto the bed and stared up at the darkened light fixture.

He sent an email to Jack about the Between and got back a reply moments later:

There's nothing, not even in the stuff I have from the Elven Academy. I'll send a request to the Archive Infinite, but it could take a while. They're pretty analog.

The puzzle pieces were mostly there, but they would not come together. Adam couldn't see how the cult and the wolves fit with Nicole's death. What were they trying to hide?

What did the Lost Ones have to do with it?

Dressed in loose-fitting clothes, he went to the backyard and drew the sword. He moved through the stances and forms the knight had shown him, hoping the exercise would focus his mind.

The questions remained as he held each pose, probably because he had to concentrate on not cutting himself.

Hopefully anyone watching over the privacy fence would think he'd taken up a weird form of tai chi. He tried to feel the sword, to hear its voice, but he felt pretty sure that any tingle was only his imagination.

Breathing hard, he put the blade away.

This wasn't working.

He needed another perspective.

Adam sighed and called the number for the elven answering service.

He changed and put himself together.

The knock at the back door was expected, but he still tensed. Adam opened it to find Dautre in his pork pie hat and suit.

"I have not heard from you in some time." The elf sounded peeved when Adam waved him into the house.

"Yeah, I've been a little busy, with the murder and all."

"Murder?" Dautre cocked a perfectly formed eyebrow.

Adam caught him up on everything he'd done and found out.

Dautre took the news in.

"You should be careful crossing into the west. Tensions remain high between the towers."

"That's what you're worried about?" Adam asked, trying to keep his voice even. "A woman is dead, Dautre."

"I am aware, now that you've bothered to tell me."

Adam almost shot back that he'd only found out the night before, but he didn't feel like sparring so he took a long breath instead.

"Did you sense any magic about her corpse?" Dautre asked.

"No."

The elf shook his head.

"If the death is strictly mundane then it is outside our jurisdiction. It must be left to the mortal authorities."

"I know that."

"Then why did you ask me to come?"

"I've hit a wall with the rest of the investigation," Adam said. "I thought you could offer a fresh perspective."

"A wall?"

"I mean I'm stumped."

"Another idiom?"

"Yeah. I mean to say that I could use your help."

Dautre's expression said *obviously.*

"We are supposed to work together, right?"

"We are. Where are you *stumped*?" The elf said the word like he'd tasted something bitter.

"Some of the pieces don't—I mean, there are parts of what's happened that aren't like the others."

"How so?"

"Like why are they summoning the boggins?"

"They may not be doing it intentionally. You indicated that the creature you saw outside Emily's abode did not directly attack you, nor did the creatures in Chicago converge on you. If they'd been a trap set to ensnare you or anyone else, their numbers would easily have overwhelmed the three of you."

"I can't argue with that, but it's not like we can go ask them if they were summoned or if they simply wandered out through a crack."

"Agreed."

"What if we had a look at where they crossed over from?"

"Tracking the crossing at Emily's would be a challenge. It was a while ago."

"It's the best lead we've got. Unless you want to go back to Chicago with me."

"We will start at Emily's. I do not wish to be surrounded."

"Can you take us there?"

"What are our other choices?"

"The bus."

Adam tried not to smile at the picture of Dautre on public transportation.

"The queen is fond of your automobiles."

"Well, I don't have one and y'all don't pay me, so it's the bus or—"

He never finished the thought.

They vanished and appeared beside a tall oak on Emily's street. For a moment, Adam could hear the gentle words in the whisper of its leaves. They went out of focus as the world solidified.

It took Adam a moment to find his balance, but all his parts seemed to be where he expected them to be. He was glad he'd worn his jacket, though a bit of a heavier coat wouldn't have been a bad idea. Autumn was already cooling to winter.

He wanted to complain about the abrupt departure, but after his adventure in the Alps he'd prepared for Dautre's sudden teleports. Plus, it was free and speedy, so it would be rude to whine.

"You're very good at crossings."

Dautre nodded.

"Human transportation is inefficient. We may already be too late to track the creature's origin point."

"It came from this way." Adam gestured in that direction. "But I can't find any trace of it now."

"You cannot see it?"

"See what?"

"There is a tear. It is faint on this side, but stronger in the spirit realm."

Dautre lifted a hand to gesture at the empty space in front of him.

"You can See both sides at once?"

Dautre snorted.

"I forget that mortals only have one aspect. Your Sight is admirable for one of your kind, but you cannot double it and be in two planes at once."

"No, no, I can't."

Just the idea of it gave him a headache.

"Here." Dautre took Adam's hand and pulled him forward.

They stepped through the planes again.

The second transition, so quickly on the heels of the first, left him spinning inside himself. He hunched over and put his hands on his legs. He would not puke. Dautre already thought he was an idiot.

Blinking away the dizzy spell, he straightened and took in the place Dautre had brought him to.

"I know this graveyard."

"As you should. It is where we met your cousin and her coven."

The area around the Botanic Gardens was very different in the spirit realm. Adam called it the Bone Garden.

Pale and stripped of bark, the trees grew tall but twisted, their white branches dipping back toward the earth as though they'd given up. They shook and dropped yellow autumn leaves despite the lack of wind. Bats swooped everywhere, snatching insects from the air.

On the mortal side the Botanic Gardens were fenced off from Cheesman Park. A pair of streets similarly divided Congress Park, but once, it had all been one, a massive graveyard, before a fire had pressed the city into moving the dead out of the city center.

The spirit realm remembered the rows of pale granite tombstones, obelisks, and crypts, many of which served as tiny houses for occupants both living and dead. One notable figure walked with a cane, dressed in a top hat and a monocle. Adam didn't know if he'd been someone important, and since the man had no face, he probably never would. He ignored the dead man and the other skeletons to focus on the living.

Lost Ones abounded. They sat or sprawled everywhere, gathered around little cookfires or in clusters to watch the sky. All had the vacant expression of mortals who'd peered too deep into the infinite.

"It's worse than I expected."

Dautre grunted in agreement.

"Their numbers are increasing. They've been coming from all over the realms to congregate here, to colonize this space."

"Why?"

"The court does not know, and they are not forthcoming."

"They're here for the Wolf," Adam said, noting the crude head painted on some of the crypts.

Dautre cocked his head so Adam explained his latest encounters with the figures.

"He said he was in the Between?"

"Yes, but I can't find out anything about it. Does that mean anything to you?"

"You cannot find it because it isn't real. What do you call them . . . fairy tales, I think?"

"You're saying it's an elven myth?"

"Yes," Dautre said as they continued to stroll among the graves. "Used to discipline children. My mother would tell me to behave or she'd send me to the Between."

"The Wolf, Ian, said there were two of him, that he was spirit walking from there at two different points in life, that he was spirit walking through time."

"That is beyond strange. Even if fairy tales were real, what does it have to do with the Lost Ones?"

"I don't know, but he's their patron saint or something. He's one of them, but a spirit. I think he was telling the truth about where his body is."

Dautre sniffed. "I don't see how that's possible."

Adam bit down a retort and changed the subject. "The boggin came from here?"

"No, but it passed through. As far as I can tell, none of these unfortunates has the power to send it to your world."

"At the church, in Chicago, there were a lot of them, but the cult had been active there. Only Amber had been casting spells at Emily's."

"It would seem they are opening these cracks, these tears, on purpose, but why, and where is the plane of origin?"

"The Between?" Adam asked, unable to hold it in.

Dautre shuddered. "Let us hope not. From my mother's stories, it's nowhere you would wish to see, and anything from there would be a terror."

They hadn't seemed so bad, so far, but he did not like the idea of a planar invasion by elven demons.

"I wish we had a piece of the creature to give the king's hound," Dautre said. "Then he could track it."

"Next time I'll prep a monster doggie bag, though I'm not sure how thrilled Silver will be if I call Isaac every time I have a problem."

"That is a wise consideration. Frost has his own duties."

"By the way, what are those?"

"I believe only the queen is privy to that information. You would have to ask her."

Adam filed that away for later as they walked, measuring the size of the encampment.

Most of the Lost Ones kept their distance, sometimes eyeing them with a bit of hostility that said they were not welcome.

Their numbers spilled beyond the borders of the park.

"What does Silver think of all this?" Adam asked.

Dautre sniffed.

"You are more in his council than I, but he has spoken little on the matter. Their presence breaks no law or stricture, so the Guardians have not involved themselves."

Something poked above the trees and crypts, drawing Adam's attention.

"What's that?"

He led Dautre further into the part of the graveyard that would be the gardens on the mortal side.

They'd gone as a group for Maria's birthday, so Adam knew the space fairly well.

Some features from the mortal side remained: the koi pond with its little bridge to nowhere and the twisting trails sloped into the western half.

The square pit where they held summer concerts sported a towering shape. It looked like driftwood or a junk sculpture. Red paint was splashed across the misshapen statue, unevenly coloring the upright Wolf.

Lost Ones gathered in its shadow. Most of them sat or

sprawled on the grass, staring into space. Some looked deep in meditation or prayer.

At least the elements weren't harsh. He'd never known the spirit realm to be anything but mild. It rarely even rained, and when it did, it tended to be warm.

There were other places, other worlds, freezing or molten hells where even immortals wouldn't survive. If the Between was a hell, then no wonder the older Wolf looked so ragged.

Was that why the Lost Ones were here, because they could survive in the spirit realm?

Was that why they'd left Earth?

"Why do the elves come here?"

Dautre faced him. "What do you mean?"

"Your native plane is Alfheimr. The previous king kept his throne, the seat of his power, there, but Silver prefers it here, in the spirit realm."

"The watchtowers are here," Dautre nodded to the white glow on the horizon. "To some degree this realm is neutral ground. No one is from here, as you would put it. The towers change hands depending on the whims of the council of races, or they used to."

"It's kind of locked in now, isn't it?" Adam asked. He hoped so. He did not know what it would mean for Jack and the others if the council suddenly decided the eastern watchtower was no longer going to be a school.

"Few things are forever, Page."

Adam knew that. Death herself had a beginning. That also meant she'd have an end. Still, he hoped Silver and Argent persisted. There was a comfort in that, and a cold blue pang in his chest when he thought of those who should have, but had not lived, as long as they should.

"In many ways the spirit realm is a playground," Dautre continued. "The immortals come here to escape."

"But they fight here."

"Sometimes they play at war."

Adam looked over the graveyard and those camped among the crypts.

"And what happens to them if the immortals fight again?"

"The same thing that happens to anyone caught between conflicting powers. It is one reason I wonder why they gather here."

Adam started walking toward the statue and the Lost Ones crowded around it.

"What are you going to do?"

Adam shrugged. "They're here, let's ask them."

"What do you want?" The question came from a girl dressed like a flower child from the sixties, though her time in the spirit realm had given her a wan complexion and her clothing a ragged edge.

"That's what I came to ask you."

She didn't look inviting, but didn't tell him to go away, so he pointed his chin at the statue. "We wanted to know about the Wolf."

"What about him?" The guy who asked sounded more defensive than hostile.

Dirty, with crazed hair, Adam guessed he'd been a coal miner back on Earth at least a century ago.

"I've seen him. I wanted to know who he is."

"Bullshit," the guy barked, but the girl's eyes went wide with a dreamy hope.

"Really?"

"Really. Wears a tuxedo and white gloves. Oh, and the mask of course."

"He's a prophet. He's supposed to come for us, to lead us to paradise."

"He's spoken to you? He told you that?"

"His acolytes," the man said. "The ones in the masks."

"I've met them." Adam thought of the figures in the discount wolf masks who'd surrounded them at Red Rocks. "But they didn't have much to say. Do you know when he's supposed to take you home?"

"Soon," the girl said. "It's supposed to be soon. He'll return and lead us to heaven."

Adam remembered hearing much the same at some of the churches his mom had taken them to. There'd been a lot of talk about the Rapture and torture and seven bad years for anyone who didn't get taken in the first round.

"There have been signs." The miner sounded almost as wistful as the girl.

"What kind of signs?"

"Angels," the girl said, her eyes wide. "We saw one. Right here."

"Did it kind of look like an octopus, only swimming through the air instead of water?"

They nodded. Several of the others had tuned in. They murmured their agreement.

They thought the boggin was an angel, and he'd killed it.

Adam tried not to grimace.

"Thanks." He gave them a little wave before leading Dautre to a safe distance.

The elf shook his head.

"It's sad, the delusion."

"It does sound well, culty, but the Wolf is real."

"And you believe he's spirit walking to the mortal plane from somewhere he thinks is the Between?"

"Yes, but I don't understand why or what he wants with Wilcox and his family."

"I understand now," Dautre said.

"What?"

"Your expression about hitting a wall. Or stumped. It means a tree cut off in its growth, such as our progress?"

"Yes. I think so."

"Then we need more information. You have exhausted the library at the king's school?"

"Jack is looking into the Between but it's going to be a while."

"There is no more I can tell you that I think would be helpful."

"What does that leave?"

"There are other immortals, other resources."

Dautre's nose wrinkled but he shot Adam a pointed look.

Adam grimaced.

"You're not actually suggesting what I think you are, are you?"

"I am once again uncertain of your meaning."

"All right." Adam almost smiled. Dautre was too much of a rule follower to say it. "How do you feel about biker bars?"

29

Vic grimaced when Adam told him where they were going.

"You sure this is a good idea?"

"Nope, but I can't go to Sara, and it's time to put this to bed, if I can."

"I could come with you," Vic suggested.

Adam took a breath. He had to tread carefully here.

"I want you to, but I can't risk drawing Sara into the conflict if this blows up in my face."

"How do you know Seamus will even talk to you?"

"He's an immortal. They like to play games, and I'm their favorite toy."

Adam had wavered on whether or not to tell Vic where he was going, but keeping news like that a secret wasn't an option. Part of it grated, and he knew that was his old independence, his sense of being alone against the world. It was one more thing to unpack, to heal. Vic wasn't trying to tie him down or trap him. He was trying to be a partner, and for that to work, Adam needed to give up some of his old instincts, his old defense mechanisms. That didn't make it easy, but he knew they wouldn't make it if Adam didn't choose honesty.

"I promise, I'm not having an attack of main character syndrome."

"That's the second time you've said that."

"It sounds better than self-sacrificing narcissist, which is what Cahill called it."

"Okay," Vic said. "Just promise me you'll be careful and that you'll pull the plug at the first sign of trouble."

"I will. I promise."

Adam took off the sword.

Its constant weight had become something of a comfort. Its song dropped into a deeper tone as he set it down.

Not tonight, he told it silently. *I can't say I come in peace and walk in carrying an elven weapon.*

Laying it beside him, he stretched out and rested his hands on his belly, his fingers steepled as if in prayer.

Adam's last impression of the basement was of Vic watching over him.

Dautre met him on the Other Side. They stood on the border of the northern territory, right on the line before the western claims began.

The elf eyed the ground as though the invisible boundary might burn him if he crossed it. He hesitated, his feet firm on the ground.

"You don't have to come," Adam said. "Seamus's issue is with me, not you."

"The issue is with the king, and his intervention in your debt. You are the page of my court. I should not let you go alone."

But Dautre still didn't move. He was worse than Spider when faced with an open door.

Adam held in a sigh and took a few steps forward.

"In or out?"

"We are already outside."

"Are you coming or not?"

Dautre straightened and followed Adam across the line.

They walked. It wasn't far, just a few blocks. Adam had left the sword behind, but he kept his defenses pulled tight around himself.

This part of the city felt rougher, even in the spirit realm, and it was, for all intents and purposes, unfriendly territory.

The houses blended into one another, becoming almost indiscriminate with their single stories and dull bricks. Their yards were full of spikey, whispering weeds and crimson flowers that opened and closed like hungry mouths.

The businesses were lifeless, blocky warehouses. It reminded Adam of the neighborhood around the church in Chicago, and he kept his senses extended.

He didn't bother to try and hide this time. Seamus likely already knew they were here.

The bar lay close to the border, which made it something like neutral ground, but there wasn't any, not when it came to how the immortals drew their borders.

"What sort of patrons frequent this place?" Dautre asked.

"Goblins, or so I hear."

"That seems appropriate."

"Hey, this was your idea."

"I don't remember it that way."

Adam managed to keep from smiling.

The goblins might be useful. They tended to act as go-betweens, performing a lot of petty tasks for various creatures. One of them might have heard or seen something if the King of Coins did not grace them with his presence.

The purple neon sign looped through the lines and letters of the old pen and paper game, spelling out *The Hangman* and the sketch of the noosed figure. Several of the pieces no longer worked, but Adam got the idea.

The row of motorcycles outside were familiar. There had been plenty of choppers and Harley riders around the trailer park. These were in polished, well-loved condition, with pedals and handlebars modified for stouter legs and arms.

"Dwarves . . ." Dautre said.

"Is that bad?"

"In my experience they can be—combative."

"Then let's try not to piss them off."

The interior was a mix of brick and not unpleasant gloom. Old-style yellow bulbs hung over pool tables, all of which had a crank and gears to raise or lower them. A lot of the dwarves congregated there, playing loudly enough that Adam almost couldn't hear the classic rock blasting from the dusty speakers that had been blown out long ago. A few of them smoked cigars and the not completely bitter taste stained the air.

The Steve Miller Band sang about time slipping into the future as Adam and Dautre waded in.

He hadn't spent much time around dwarves. They held the southern watchtower, which was anchored to a brewery in Denver.

The goblins were even less familiar. They crowded the corners of the room, sipping from tankards whose contents smelled like hot pickle juice. Almost as one, they looked toward the interlopers, their yellow eyes large with curiosity.

Adam angled toward the bar.

"We should order something."

"Why? You cannot drink it."

"It would be polite, wouldn't it?"

Dautre considered this.

"Likely."

"Would you mind paying?"

The elf raised an eyebrow.

"It's not like I have beer money in my world. I'm sure Silver will reimburse you."

"If he forgives us for coming here. That is, when he finds out."

"You didn't tell him?"

"One human expression I do understand is 'it's better to ask forgiveness rather than permission.' Since that one makes sense, you might have gotten it from us."

"Dautre. Squire to the Knight of Swords. Eldest of his generation in his mother's noble line of something else I can't remember."

"The snow court of the Selenite Wastes," Dautre said solemnly.

"The snow court of the Selenite Wastes."

"Yes?"

"Did you just make a joke?"

The elf cocked his head in his usual tone of *obviously*.

He left Adam alone to buy two mugs of the steaming juice. Adam tried to notice who was tracking their movements and did his best to appear nonthreatening while also not looking like an easy mark. He had no idea how it was going.

"It is fermented as well," Dautre announced as he returned.

"Yum," Adam drawled. "Are you going to try it?"

"Now you are the one making jests."

They watched their mugs go cold.

"I can't believe you didn't tell Silver what we were doing."

Dautre let out a long breath.

"It seemed the correct decision. He has many challenges at the moment, and he may have forbidden it."

"Do you think this was the right move, coming here?"

"I do." Dautre took an experimental sip of his mug. He didn't gag as he swirled the contents around his mouth before swallowing with a curl of his lip. "Why are you smiling?"

"Because you've got a little rebel in you after all."

Adam decided he might be able to like the elf, given the chance. After all, he'd eventually learned to get along with Bobby.

"I'll give you this, Binder," a voice with an Irish accent cut into Adam's thoughts. "You got a pair on you."

The bar became noticeably quieter.

Adam held up his hands to show they were empty.

"I didn't come to fight."

Seamus scoffed.

The leprechaun wore a burgundy velvet suit that had seen better decades and a hard expression that lent extra crinkles to his already wizened features. He wore gold rings on every finger and another in each ear.

He appeared to have come alone, not that he'd need backup.

You didn't rule a watchtower without a considerable amount of power and guile. Seamus had proved he had both in their previous interactions.

"Why did you come then?" Seamus looked around the bar. "Needing answers for your latest mysteries?"

"Yeah, but I also wanted to talk to you, to clear the air, if I can."

"And yet you bring one of them with you." Seamus nodded to Dautre.

The elf didn't cower, but his usual arrogance dimmed.

"I left the sword."

"Like I said, you've got gonads, that or you're just stupid."

"Maybe it's both," Adam admitted. After all, he'd stood up to a Grim Reaper once, which wasn't a check in the smart column. "But you got what you wanted, the death you wanted. There's no reason for us to be enemies."

Seamus laughed.

"I don't think your king sees it that way. The death of

someone in his care, even a prisoner, showed that he's not as untouchable as his father."

Adam could feel Dautre's anger simmering inside his glamour.

"Was it worth it?" Adam asked calmly.

"What?"

"Your revenge. Is this new Cold War among the immortals worth it?"

"I'm not saying I was responsible for what went down, but if I was, then yes, it was worth it. I'd burn a realm for her."

Seamus's grief and rage pressed against Adam's wards, trying to make its way and become a part of him. He was tempted. Seamus had sent an assassin to RCC to kill a prisoner locked in the basement. The killer had a second job and that task had led to Vran's sacrifice. It would be misplaced to blame Seamus. The assassin would have been there anyway.

Still, it took a considerable force of will to push the leprechaun's anger away.

It felt like a toxic cloud leaking poison into the air where it mixed with Dautre's. If one of them snapped and their glamour dropped, well, Adam wouldn't be there to see the fireworks.

The bar's patrons had come to the same conclusion. A cautious exodus began. Most of them were mortal. Even the dwarves, who were normally up for a scrap, didn't want to be in the blast radius.

"What about you, Binder? What would you do in my place?"

Adam took a breath and let it out slowly.

"Probably the same thing. I'm not saying I don't understand, but there are bigger problems. There are Lost Ones everywhere, for example."

"If you're so worried about them, then why don't you swallow that bilge and join them?" Seamus nodded at Adam's cooling mug. "This isn't your home. You don't belong here."

"It's not yours either, and if you bring war to it, what happens to the ones caught in the middle? I know you care about them. We all do."

It was a risk, playing on Seamus's sympathies. He might act cold and calculating, but the King of Coins had a heart. He'd moved his tower to a mausoleum, a monument to grief, his grief. Adam had to be right. He was betting the farm on Seamus having enough sympathy for the people in his care to not escalate the conflict.

"You're a damn fool." Seamus's rancor wilted and the pressure in the air withdrew.

Beside Adam, Dautre settled into his glamour.

"I know."

"And not just for coming here. You might have bitten off too much this time."

"The Wolf?"

Seamus's grin was enough to make Adam cringe.

"He's a ghost. No one even knows who he is, but he's causing quite a stir among your precious Lost Ones."

"They think he's coming to save them, to take them somewhere else."

"Yeah, they're gathering, like an army of angry peasants. That always ends well."

"You think they could turn violent?"

Seamus played with one of his rings.

"If they do, I'm not sure it's a fight we should win. They've got cause to resent the towers. Things could be changing."

"There are whispers," Adam said. "I've heard the music."

"Then you have a good ear, but I don't think your wolf is what's coming. I think he's just the harbinger."

"Silver said something is rising." It was a trade, information for information, which was a fairer bargain than Seamus usually struck. Adam would take what he could at this price. "It has something to do with the Between, doesn't it?"

Dautre scoffed, but Seamus looked uncomfortable. He cast his eyes side to side, scanning the room to see who or what might be listening.

He gave the slightest nod.

"Whatever it is, it's old. It's patient, and anyone who tries to find out about it disappears. You might want to sit this next one out, Binder."

"Thank you." Adam meant it.

Seamus had given him more than he'd taken, and anything given freely from an immortal, especially information, was truly a gift.

"You should go now," Seamus said, cocking his ear toward the door. "I think your king wants a word."

30

Silver's guards waited on the other side of the boundary line. Adam paused at the sight of the tommy guns and swords.

Beside him, Dautre froze, just shy of the boundary.

It was almost comical. They wouldn't cross to take him but he couldn't just stay here. He was a member of the Court, but at the moment he felt like he had when his mom had caught him drinking beer at sixteen.

Adam had to admit that he was tempted to simply end his spirit walk. Vic had said to flee at the first sign of trouble, but that would mean leaving Dautre, and it wasn't like the elves didn't know where he lived.

"I guess it's time to face the music."

The expression didn't earn him a confused glance or comment from Dautre. The elf looked lost in thought.

"Are you all right?"

"Yes. I am simply considering some of the things the leprechaun said."

The Knight of Swords stepped to the edge of the line as they approached. She did not look happy.

"Come with us," she said. "We will take you to the king."

"Why didn't he come himself?"

"He is preoccupied with the chaos your actions have unleashed." The half circle of elves tensed.

"Thanks, but we can get ourselves there."

"No, Page, we are to escort you."

She stood straight, her armor gleaming. He didn't need his Sight to know that she was not happy.

Adam and Dautre exchanged a glance and stepped over the line.

The knight was not gentle. She pulled them through the ether in a swirl of cold that left Adam shivering.

Adam fell to the ground as the gates of the park swung open.

Dautre wavered between helping him and staying where he stood.

Adam held up a hand and found his feet.

"Come," the knight said, leading their entourage toward the ballroom.

Silver waited alone upon his throne. The courtiers and visiting dignitaries had been cleared from the space.

"Where is your sword?" the knight demanded when the guards had left.

"I didn't wear it."

Her look made him understand the expression *cut her eyes at him*.

Adam let out a breath. He wished Argent were there.

"I wanted to go in peace."

"That was a rash decision," Silver said.

"No. It was considered," Dautre argued. "And the page was right. We needed to speak with the King of Coins."

"What could be so important that you'd risk escalation?" the knight demanded.

"A number of things pertaining to our investigation," Dautre said. "The Red Wolves, the Lost Ones, and the cult responsible for the missing witches."

"You cannot trust anything the leprechaun told you," the knight said.

"I think we can. Seamus talked to me. He gave me intel."

"*Gave?*" She blanched.

"Yes, and even if he lied, talking is better than silence, isn't it?" Adam looked from the knight to Silver and back.

The king's expression was blank, inscrutable, but Adam thought he read a little conflict, or maybe a little hope, around the edges of his pale eyes.

"These are not things for the two of you to decide," the knight said.

"Maybe not, but from the beginning I've been told that mortal matters are my responsibility, mine alone, and this pertained to my case, to the missing mortal witches, which you claim to care about. So which is it?"

"Your impertinence will do you no favors," she huffed.

"Am I or am I not the Page of Swords?" Adam did not look at Silver. "Am I or am I not meant to be a bridge between our people and our worlds?"

"You are," Silver said quietly.

"Then let me act like one."

The knight opened her mouth to say something, but Silver lifted a hand.

"You are right, Adam, though I think you would have shown greater wisdom to tell us of your plans."

"Would you have let me go?" He didn't say "us," wanting to shield Dautre from whatever fallout he could.

"Perhaps," Silver said. "Perhaps not, but in the future, I want you to request permission first."

"I can do that."

"Then you may go."

"My lord—" the knight began.

"All of you." There was real steel in his voice.

"Next time, keep your weapon on you," the knight said before she vanished in a puff of cold that smelled of freshly fallen snow.

Yeah, she was pissed. He'd definitely pay for this later.

Adam walked out of the ballroom and took in the park for a long moment.

Dautre did not look as upset as he expected.

"What?" Adam asked.

"You did well."

"I don't get it—I mean I don't understand."

"Adam, I think you just became the Page of Swords, not merely in title, but in spirit."

"Why, because I stood up to her?"

"Yes. You have always deferred to the other members of the court, which is wise. They outrank you, but there are times when your voice must be heard."

"Thank you. I notice you didn't mention the you-know-where." Dautre cocked his head in confusion.

"The fairy tale?" Adam said.

"I believed it would undercut your case to mention it, but I will make inquiries where I can."

Dautre vanished.

Adam sighed and released his hold on the spirit walk. He slid back into the basement.

Vic was awake and dressed, ready to race into action if Adam needed him. The feeling put a glow in Adam's chest, a lamplight that chased away the last of the elves' cold magic.

"How did it go?" Vic asked.

"Weirdly, I mean, really well. I think."

Vic left in the morning for an early shift. Adam had barely registered the kiss on his forehead and the loss of warmth in the bed.

Spider happily filled the gap, settling atop Adam's legs to pin him in place.

Adam curled and stretched to stroke the coarse fur. The cat felt thin, but he always had. Adam had no idea how long psychopomps lived, but he hoped it was forever. Spider was a piece of Sue. He was a bit of home, as much as Vic was.

Bobby's place never really had been, and he knew with a twist in his gut that was as much instinct as Sight that it was time to move on. He'd put his fear aside. He was ready for the next step.

The house was quiet when he finally showered and emerged from the basement to make his coffee.

He found Annie on the front porch, staring into the distance and the bit of the mountains that peeked above the rooftops. It wasn't exactly warm, but she'd put on a chunky, comfortable-looking sweater, and Adam was suddenly grateful that Bobby had never been able to bring himself to get rid of her clothes.

"Oh. Hi, Adam."

She looked like she'd been crying.

"Is everything all right?"

"Yeah."

She nodded to the second chair.

He took it.

"I was just thinking about my grandmother's hands."

"What about them?"

"They were so pale and papery, almost translucent. You could see all the veins. Side effect of remembering everything. I keep getting flashes of stuff like that."

"I never knew my grandparents. Bobby did, but they were gone by the time I was around."

"I'm sorry." Annie shook her head. "I guess it's not really about her hands. I never got to say goodbye to her. My parents told me, but never took me to the funeral. I used to beg them to go see her, to spend Christmas with her. I wanted to live with her. She loved me, and I think they kept me away, that she might have protected me from them. I can never forgive them for that."

"I'm so sorry."

"It's not your fault, and it's nice, a gift really. I can remember her so perfectly now."

"Have your parents come by again?"

"No, but it's only a matter of time. My dad is used to getting what he wants." Annie looked angry. "But I'm not going anywhere."

Adam liked her a little bit more in that moment. He hated bullies, and the Wilcoxes were the worst kind, the sort who thought their privilege and money made them untouchable. Maybe they were. Maybe they couldn't be stopped, not completely, but at least she could spoil whatever they'd planned for her.

He tilted his head toward her chair and caught the faintest whiff of a cigarette.

"You know, that's my mom's smoking spot too."

"Is it?" Annie smiled. "Robert said she's coming for Christmas."

"Yeah. She has the last few years. Bobby flies her in."

Adam wondered if the PIs had missed that detail or if Annie was just being nice. He picked the latter. He was doing that more and more. It was too exhausting to look for trouble in every conversation or to jump at every shadow.

The drive from Guthrie to the Will Rogers airport in Oklahoma City and then the drive from the Denver airport to Bobby's was so long that they often joked about just road-tripping back home, but then there was Vic's family. Adam was expected at their house at some point, and though there was a bit of an awkward energy depending on which aunts, uncles, or cousins came, he went because it made Vic happy.

It didn't hurt that Guthrie was behind him. It wasn't like he'd never go back, but it wasn't anywhere on his list of priorities.

"I wonder what she'll think." Annie's eyes fell to where her own hands rested in her lap. "You know, about me being here."

"I think she'll be happy for Bobby. She likes you. She took care of you, when you, uh, checked out."

"I remember. She's a firecracker. My mom isn't anything like that. Even when I woke up in the hosp—in the church—she was so cold, so clinical about it all. All I wanted was for her to hold my hand but she wouldn't touch me."

"If we'd known . . ." Adam stared into his coffee. "I'm so sorry. Bobby would never have left you in that place. He'd have come for you. We'd have come for you."

"I think that's the worst part of it all. They wouldn't let me near a phone or a computer. I didn't even think it was strange. They did that to me. I thought Bobby knew. I thought he wanted nothing to do with me, that he hated me for leaving."

"He's not like that," Adam said. "I used to think he was, but he's not. He's a good man."

"I know."

She stared at the mountains for a while. "At least you two are in a better place."

"We are. I'm going to get another cup of coffee. Want anything?"

"No thanks," she said.

Inside, the kitchen felt colder. He needed to turn up the heat.

He reached for the fridge when a gloved hand wrapped around his throat. He opened his mouth to scream when something jabbed his neck.

"You should have taken the deal," White whispered as Adam's world went dark.

31

Adam fought his way back to consciousness and found he couldn't move. He was tied to a gurney, and the ropes holding him burned when he pressed his magic against them.

"You are bound in my place of power," Wilcox stepped into view. He sounded pleased with himself. "You won't be calling on your allies for help."

It came back to Adam. The kitchen, White whispering in his ear.

"Where's Annie?"

"She's fine," Wilcox said. "She'll get her treatment. Then all will be better."

"Treatment? Is that what you're calling it, what you're doing to her?"

"I'm giving her what she wants, or what she *thinks* she wants, not that she'll remember or appreciate it." Wilcox stared Adam down with a look of cold hatred. "She always was too willful. We won't have that problem anymore. When I'm done she won't even remember her name. You're both fools. You could have walked away with what to you is a fortune. You could have been useful, a resource, like the others. Instead, you're going to die here."

White stepped into the room.

"You know what I need?" Wilcox asked. He turned to leave.

"Yes." White pulled on a pair of black surgical gloves.

Patrick closed the door behind him.

White wheeled a metal cart over to the gurney.

He chose a gleaming hobby knife from atop the cart and smiled.

Adam tensed, doing his best to push himself down, away, to get even an inch of distance, but he couldn't move. All he could feel was the cold metal of the gurney beneath him.

"You killed Nicole," Adam said.

"Yes. She came looking for the others." White shook his head, as though it was sad. "I thought it would be you. That surprised me, that I had to come for you instead. Now don't squirm."

White grinned as he pulled the neck of Adam's shirt forward and sliced the fabric with the knife.

Cold air licked at Adam's chest.

Ian appeared in the corner. Translucent, he stood over White's shoulder.

"This is a nice scar." White ran a fingertip across Adam's chest before laying his hand flat, fingers splayed, over Adam's heart. The latex felt dry and powdery. "Should we start there?"

Adam tried again to twist away or call his magic, but the spell worked into the ropes left him trapped. He could not even spirit walk.

White whisked the hobby knife over the line on Adam's chest. There was a second, maybe less, between the motion and the pain. Then the cut opened and blood flowed.

Adam swallowed a scream.

White bent to blow on the cut.

"You work with your hands," he said. He pulled the cart

closer and considered the hammer lying among the other blades and tools. "Shall I crush one. Maybe both? I could remove it completely. No, that would be too much for round one."

"You have to get out of here," Ian said. "You have to."

"How?" Adam asked.

"A saw, of course," White said.

"You have to find a way." Ian stepped closer. His blue eyes shone with panic inside the mask. He sounded even younger than he had during their last conversation.

"Did you know that I wanted to be a surgeon?" White sounded distant, absent, like this was all just theoretical. "All the bloodlust, but none of the brains, I'm afraid."

White moved quickly, slicing back and forth, cutting into Adam's arms and belly.

Adam wasn't able to hold the scream in this time.

"Now, now," White said soothingly. "We're just getting started. We'll have so much time together. I'll gag you for round two. Then maybe, we'll see about that saw."

Adam took gulping breaths. He could smell his own terror mixing with the coppery sweet scent of the blood pooling beneath him. Ian had vanished, and Adam did not know why, but he was relieved that the Wolf wasn't there to see.

"Are you done yet?" Wilcox asked from the doorway. "We're ready for him."

"It looks like we'll have to play later." White set the knife aside. "Oh, wait, just one more thing . . ."

In a fluid, quick motion, he lifted the hammer and brought it down, hard, on Adam's shoulder.

The crunch and snap of something inside was instant. It rang through him. Adam screamed, louder than he ever had. White pressed a gag into his mouth and tied the strap behind his head.

"Yes, that should do," Patrick said with satisfaction. We

need to ensure we have the right resources this time. Another replacement would cost us too much time."

They wheeled him out of the room. Each bump of the bed sent a wave of agony through him and brought another sob. White had left his hand but Adam's right side was fire and agony. He couldn't move his arm, couldn't feel his fingers.

He could barely take in the space. Familiar, but different. These walls weren't draped in black but lined in some sort of generic wallpaper. The circle painted on the floor remained the same.

They wheeled him into the center and the torturous motion finally stopped. He took heaving breaths as robed figures wearing wolf masks stepped forward to ring the room. One of them stepped to Adam, her long hair streaming to her shoulders.

"He'll kill you." Adam tried to speak through the gag. "The rituals—"

She reached to grip his shoulder. Driving her thumb into the break, she twisted. Adam screamed again and saw only red for a long moment.

His vision cleared in time to see the mask descending toward his face.

A different witch lifted his head, gently, to tie the ribbons behind his ears.

In his chest the warlock wound snarled and snapped, straining against the binding. He'd free it if he could. He'd unleash it and let it do whatever it wanted to anyone in the room.

His consciousness began to slip, suddenly, like a glass you thought you had a grip on. It would fall soon. It would break.

How much blood could he lose and remain awake?

He did not want to be here. Everything inside him swirled with white fire, and he could not flee.

The witches began to chant. He felt the circle close. Like a dam, it rose, sealing in the magic.

Light rushed through his body, cold and soothing. In it were thirteen colors, the magic of the witches. This spell held none of Patrick's magic. Of course it didn't. He would not risk himself.

Adam tried to shout for them to stop. He did not want to be the reason they burned away. He did not want for them to die. He reached for the warlock wound but knew it was pointless. He was too tightly bound.

The mask limited his vision. He couldn't see if the witches were all right. He felt pain to the point of nothing, like all of his nerves had burned away.

Then he went with it, carried off in the tide.

32

The smell of fresh-cut grass and burning leaves met Adam's nose. Cautiously, Adam felt his body. His shoulder did not shift when he tested it. The pain had faded to an ache he could live with. He was still shirtless, barefoot, and blood-covered, but his cuts had sealed.

A shallow creek split the land. The grass on this side stood high, at least where the scrub oak trees did not shade the ground. He could smell the sunbaked dirt. The air held the right amount of humidity, like it could rain, like it could thunder. The other side was hard to see, but he knew it. Gray. Dusty. That was west, the way toward the sea.

The banks were ruddy clay that oozed between his toes. Then he recognized this side of the creek. Guthrie. He'd come home.

"Well, this is surely awkward," a familiar voice said.

Sara, Death herself, sat at the water's edge, her bare, Black feet sunk into the mud. A cane with a carved crow's head rested beside her. She wore a loose dress printed with sunflowers and a well-worn jean jacket. She was a large woman, and until he'd learned what she really was, he'd thought her sort of grandmotherly.

"Is this it, then? Am I dead?"

"No." She gestured at the creek and the shadowy forest on the other side. "But you're at the edge, Adam Lee."

"I've never been here before." Crickets chirped in the hollows. In the light, grasshoppers took flight. "Is this the Between?"

"No." She snorted.

"Can you tell me about it?"

Sara shook her head. "Did you forget the rules? You know I don't give anything away for free."

Adam shrugged.

"I had to try."

She smiled.

"You're looking better," he said.

There were lines around her eyes, and plenty more gray in the thick twists of her hair, but the frailty she'd worn like an old coat during their last meeting had receded.

"You, on the other hand, are a sight. You should wash yourself."

Keeping to his side, Adam knelt to dip his hands, intending only to clean them, but the water was warm, just above cold, and he found himself scrubbing his face and body. Its touch did not sting.

"You haven't been to see me," she said, sweetly, like they were old friends, which they were, in a way.

"I didn't want to talk to you. Not after what you did."

"That's more than fair, and it isn't like I won't see you again." She sounded fond. He knew better.

Straightening, Adam took in the sky on his side. It was a brilliant sunset, with clouds of purple and gold, the colors that had mesmerized him when he'd gone camping with Vic. That part did not feel quite like Oklahoma, but more like Colorado.

He could ask her about the wolves, about everything he didn't know but needed to. He could make a final deal with her, but wouldn't.

Adam let the bird calls and cricket song wash over him. They grew large near the lake. Some nights, the crickets covered the shed, turning the white corrugated sheet to a glossy, endlessly shifting black.

He could stay here forever, or maybe just a long while. The pain in his body had receded to something distant, but he chased it, held it tight, lest he slip away.

"Someone's been playing a long game," he said.

"I know."

"Do you know who?"

"No, but I suspect. All I can promise is that it's not me, not this time."

It was another gift, like what Seamus had told him. Still, it would not buy his forgiveness. Nothing she might do would ever be enough.

Maybe he could understand Seamus better than he thought.

"Can I go back?"

"If you must," she said in the tone of a distant relative who never got enough time with you.

There would be pain there, maybe more than he could endure, but there was Annie, in her father's hands.

"Yeah, I have to."

"Then go."

There was no push, no burn.

Adam gently woke and found himself still tied to the gurney. The mask obscured his eyesight, but he could see Ian leaning over him.

"You could have helped." Adam twisted, trying to loosen his bonds or at least the mask. He wanted it off.

"No, I couldn't."

Ian leaned forward and pressed a hand to the ropes around Adam's wrist. He felt nothing at the touch as Ian's hand passed through him.

"I'm sorry."

He sounded so small.

"It's all right. They fixed it." Adam nodded to the sealed cuts. "The Lost Ones worship you. Why?"

"Because a long time ago my older self convinced them I was a mortal who became immortal." He scoffed. "They think I'm a god. They think I can give them the same thing."

"Tell me about the Between."

"Why?"

"Because no one else will."

"There's nothing but boggins here. It's just them and me. It's like limbo."

"What are they doing to Annie? Why are they doing this?"

"Because they have to."

"And you're helping them."

Ian hung his head.

"Not me. *Him.*"

"Why?"

"Because he needs all of this to happen. You have to get out of here. If you can escape, you can stop it. You can change everything. He thinks it's inevitable. I think you're gear or a cog, a pivot point."

Adam strained again. His magic was still locked inside him. He could not loosen the ropes with it. Even if his power wasn't bound, the most he could do in the physical world was slow a feather's fall or toss a handful of dust into the air and have it land in a circle.

"You have to hurry," Ian said. "He'll come back soon."

Adam shifted, twisted. They'd healed his body, testing the ritual on him. He'd worry about why later.

Maybe if his blood hadn't dried, he could have used it to lubricate the binding. He squeezed his hand into a fist, then remembered one of those endless sermons his mother had dragged him to and the preacher going on about how to trap a monkey.

You hollowed out a gourd, put something sweet like candy in it, and make the hole just big enough for the monkey's hand. When it closed its fist, it couldn't pull free and it wouldn't let go of its prize so it remained stuck.

Adam opened his hand, stretched and strained. They'd mended his shoulder, but it wasn't the same, never would be again. Hand open, he pulled his right hand free of the ropes.

Adam ripped off the restraint on his left hand, then freed his legs. The binding spell broke when he loosened the bounds. The mask clattered on the floor when he dropped it.

"He's coming," Ian said.

Adam struggled free. His legs were stiff, asleep. He crashed to the floor.

Twisting, he looked for White's tools and cart, but it wasn't there. He didn't see anything he could use as a weapon.

There wasn't anywhere to hide, nowhere to run to. There was only one door.

White came through it. His eyes lit with happy surprise.

Adam moved behind the gurney, putting the only distance he could between them.

"Remarkable. Not even a hint of harm," White purred. "The fun we could have, over and over. I'd love to see what they could do about an eye or an ear, but I'm afraid Mr. Wilcox is worried you'd be too much trouble."

White patted his suit pocket, almost absently, and drew out a scalpel.

It wasn't that long. Adam might be able to grab White's wrist and kick him—something.

White lunged, faster than Adam could have predicted and certainly more effortlessly than Adam could have moved in a suit.

Adam shoved the gurney with all of his strength, buying a breath as it connected with the killer's waist. White grinned, like they were playing a game.

He was toying with Adam, the way Spider did with the miller moths he caught in the spring before he eventually chewed them up and puked them out.

Help, Adam called into the ether.

He didn't scream aloud. He had no idea who else waited in the wings.

Please, he called again, and felt it deafen against the hotel's wards.

White pushed the gurney aside. It clattered against the wall.

Adam balled his fists, hoping he could get a hit in, and found his hand wasn't empty.

He almost dropped the sudden weight.

White lunged at him as the sword became solid.

There was an instant, a half second or less, when Adam could have dropped the blade. He thrust it forward instead.

White impaled himself. There was no freezing magic, no arcane effect, just the crunch of metal on bone. White straightened, dropped the scalpel, and lurched back, ripping the sword from Adam's hands.

He stood for a moment, staggered, eyes wide with something like surprise and maybe relief. He lunged again, murder on his face, hands reaching for Adam's throat. Adam backed away, scrambling as far as the small space would let him.

White grunted. He swiped in Adam's direction once, twice,

then collapsed. The sword still driven through him, he fell to the ground and rolled to his side.

It took time for Adam to get his breathing under control.

When he had, he kicked White over with his foot and reached for the blade. It dissolved, and Adam felt it settle in its place on his back.

"How did you get through the wards?"

It did not answer, but it thrummed, as if to ask if it had done well.

"Yeah," Adam told it, breath heaving. "Good boy."

Red soaked White's shirt and suit.

Adam wanted to retch, to empty whatever little was in his stomach, but he had to find Annie. He had to get them out of here.

He needed a shirt, shoes. He needed a phone. He could call for help, the cops maybe . . . someone.

Setting aside the tide of revulsion, he reached for White. He had nothing in his pockets. With a grimace, He tugged off the man's shoes. They were a little large, but at least he wasn't barefoot anymore.

He looked at the scalpel, considered it, and decided the sword would be more than enough.

White's blood had soaked his clothes and pooled around him. He lay still, eyes open, his expression soft, fixed and distant. A new tide of sick and yellow-green rose in Adam's guts, reaching his heart, but he pushed it away. He had to.

Later, he thought.

He turned to Ian, who stood staring at the scene.

"Where's Annie?"

"On the third floor."

"Then I need to get up there."

Adam found the hallway outside the room empty. This was

one of those backspaces, the places behind the facade, with naked cinderblock walls and exposed electrical piping.

"We're in the basement?"

Ian nodded.

Ahead were a pair of steel doors, much like the ones in Chicago.

"Wait here a second."

Ian stepped through the doors like a ghost, passing unimpeded through the metal, and emerged again a moment later.

"Not that way. There are guards. They've got guns."

"Okay." Adam took a long breath and carefully backed away.

"Why are you trusting me?" Ian asked.

"I don't have a choice, do I? Which way?"

Ian pointed to the end of the hall. "There's a freight elevator. And a laundry room with a janitor's closet."

"Let me see the laundry room first. Is it unlocked?"

"I don't know."

They passed the room with the gurney and he didn't, couldn't, look.

Ian stood outside the laundry room.

Adam exhaled when the handle turned and the door opened.

Inside were massive washing machines and a giant roller for pressing sheets. There was a bin on rollers full of dirty towels.

He almost cried to see some coveralls hanging in the janitor's closet. The name on the patch said *Kurt.* Adam shrugged into them and let go of his disappointment that there weren't work boots, but there was a toolbox.

Adam eyed the dryers.

"How many people are up there?" he asked, nodding to the ceiling.

"A few dozen."

Resources, Wilcox had called them. Human resources.

He didn't think of them as people, but still, he'd paid for them. He wouldn't want to lose them. There couldn't be much time. Someone would find White. The guards with guns would come for him.

Adam walked toward the dryers. He winced at the scrape and clatter as he pulled one away from the wall.

"What are you doing?" Ian asked.

"Being a mechanic."

"You're going to fix it? Is this the best time?"

"I'm not fixing it." Adam knew his smile had to be grim. "I'm going to break them."

He didn't know how long it would take, but they were industrial strength.

Jammed up with the towels and with their ventilation blocked, it went quicker than he expected.

"Go see if they take the bait," he told Ian.

The young Wolf ran through the wall.

Adam got the rest of his breath back. He was gambling Annie's life, his own, and anyone else's who might be staying at the hotel.

The smoke reached his nose an instant before the alarm started.

Ian popped through the wall a moment later.

"They're running."

"Then it's time to go."

Adam headed for the freight elevator.

33

He knew you weren't supposed to take an elevator in a fire. Hopefully, everyone else knew it too. Another gamble then, that he could outrace the flames.

The alarm, a piercing buzz, chimed in tune with white and red flashing lights when the doors opened on the third floor.

Ian waited on the other side.

"Have they moved her?" Adam asked.

"No."

"Any sign of Wilcox?"

"Not yet."

"Thank you," Adam said. "For helping me."

Ian nodded.

"She's in room 315. This way."

"What are you doing?" a voice demanded.

The older Wolf waited ahead.

"I'm helping him," Ian said.

"You're going to ruin it."

He leaped, tackling Ian. They fell through a wall.

Adam hurried on. He found 315 and tried the door.

It didn't open.

He kicked, planting his foot in the center, but it held.

The two wolves rolled back into the hall, kicking and punching in a blur of black tuxes and growls.

A woman rounded the corner, pushing a maid's cart. She passed through the wolves without noticing them.

"Can you open this?" Adam asked her.

She took a white earbud out of her ear and seemed to notice the alarm for the first time.

"There's a woman in there." Adam gestured to the strobe lights.

"It's only a drill," she said with a full body shrug. "And the do not disturb sign is up."

Adam ripped it off the door handle.

"It's not a drill. There's a fire in the basement. We need to get her out of there."

"All right." The maid reached for her card key.

She knocked and called, "Housekeeping!"

"Really?" Adam asked.

"Habit." She swiped to open the door.

The bolt slid back with a grinding sound.

Annie sat slumped in a chair, her eyes closed. Adam hurried to her.

"Annie. Annie." He didn't want to slap her. "We have to go."

She didn't stir. Adam reached for her with his Sight. A spell was wrapped around her mind like a heavy spider web.

"No!" a voice shouted from the doorway.

The older Ian rushed into the room. Adam turned, drew the sword, pointed it at him, and opened the warlock wound.

"You might be in the Between, but if you're spirit walking then I can still do some damage. Now back off."

The Wolf stopped.

With a whirl, Adam turned and sliced the enchantment holding Annie asleep.

The maid was already dialing 911.

"I'm calling the police!"

"Thank you. Make sure the fire department's coming too."

Annie stirred, but remained groggy as Adam helped her to her feet.

"What—where? What did they do to me?"

"We're at the hotel," Adam said. "We have to go. I started a fire."

"Huh?"

"Burn it all down, remember?"

"Oh. Good." She smiled.

They were in the hallway when the sprinklers came on. Water sprayed from the ceiling, soaking everything. Adam's sockless feet slid in the oversized shoes, but it roused Annie.

"Do you know this man?" the maid asked her.

"He's my brother. He's here to help."

They took the stairs to the first floor.

A fire door lay ahead.

Adam reached for it, but the maid shouted, "Stop!"

She held a hand to the metal and shook her head.

"It's hot."

"Is there another stairwell?"

The maid nodded. "If we cut across the ballroom on the mezzanine."

They went up another floor.

The maid breathed a sigh of relief and pushed the bar to open the door.

They were in a little hall, with restrooms. The sprinklers weren't on here.

Annie had her feet beneath her now.

The lights were out. Adam paused.

"Wait here," he told them. "Let me make sure it's safe."

He stepped inside and the door closed behind him.

"Hey!"

"Adam!" Annie called. She pounded on the door behind him. "Get away from me!"

"Run, Annie! Run!"

The lights came on above him.

Patrick Wilcox stood at the other end.

"I must admit, you surprised me. I didn't think you'd manage to kill White."

Adam took in the room. He'd assumed the ritual space had also been in the basement, but this was it. Pillars held up the vaulted ceiling.

Figures were tied to three of them.

"Jodi?"

She did not look conscious. Emily and Cole were in a similar state. Adam could see the same spell that had entranced Annie wound around them. Jodi's was a little off, and he suspected his cousin was fighting it. He only hoped she had time to win.

"They were kind enough to come to us," Patrick said. "They're like beetles. Crush one and the others run to you." The maid stepped into the room, her face worried as she pulled off her apron.

"She got away, Magus."

"No matter, so long as she is safe. We do not need her for this part."

The rest of the coven, Lauren and the others, moved into the room. They began to chant, casting. The spell was strange, glassy.

Adam drew the sword. He reached to open the warlock wound but the trap sprang closed first.

The spell erupted in threads of power that writhed like tentacles. He dropped the sword and it protested, a long whine in his mind. The cords of magic wrapped him tight and pulled him down, away.

He tumbled, head over feet, his perspective going blurry as his body fell. He saw the ground coming a blink before he crashed against it.

Groaning, his shoulder still aching, he sat up.

Instead of the spirit realm, a twisted, funhouse version of his reality appeared; this place was almost sterile. The mountains on the horizon, when they didn't drift through the sky, were jagged, claws of curving rock. The ground, a sea of dust, lay pale and lifeless.

The spirit realm was life. Adam had seen Death from the inside. This wasn't either.

Boggins drifted through the colorless sky. Some were like the one he'd seen at Emily's. Some were like the one who'd come through at the church in Chicago. Others were even larger, dwarfing their kin.

One of them, with dozens of wings, squared off against something like a giant squid lined in barbed spines. Adam did not know if they were mating or fighting as they crashed against the horizon and shook the ground.

"Welcome to the Between." The Wolf stepped out of the mist.

He looked almost as rough as Adam felt. His tuxedo was torn. He was missing a sleeve, and the exposed skin was heavily scarred, like something had bit into him, over and over. His mask was cracked. Half its mouth had broken off, revealing a scraggly, unkempt beard of dark blond hair.

"Where's Ian?" Adam said.

"Oh yeah. I forgot about that." The Wolf chuckled. "The hotel—that fight—He's long gone, Adam. It's just you and me now."

"What do you want? Why did you bring me here?"

"You still haven't figured it out? You were supposed to be

smart, at least smarter than this." The Wolf pointed his chin at the bleak mountains and soulless sky. "I want my freedom, and you're the only one who can give it to me."

"Why me?" Adam looked to the sky. "I can't cross planes. I can't open a way out of here."

"No, but you carry the key. You can take us home."

"And how am I supposed to do that?"

"Your sword. It's an anchor, much like what you had with Vic. It can find you anywhere. It can point you in the right direction. Call it, and the way will open."

"And you'll be free."

"We both will."

"Then what?"

"I'll take my rightful place. I'll lead the Lost Ones to their promised land, to paradise, a world of beauty and plenty, where they will never starve, never want, where their lives are too respected for them to be killed."

"Alfheimr? You want to take them to Alfheimr?"

"Yes. We'll colonize it, do to them what they've done to the spirit realm. We'll let them see what it's like for a change."

"What happened to you?" Blue filled Adam's chest. "How did you become this?"

The Wolf lifted his hands and mimed playing a violin.

"I was a musician. She liked that. She brought me to Alfheimr to play for her. I'd never seen anything so beautiful, not even her. She fed me fruit like I had never tasted, glass apples, so sweet. She gave me wine. I was just a boy, a toy for her. She *broke* me, and when she was done she tossed me away, into the Between, the basement where the immortals throw their garbage. I *fell*, and none of you ever came for me."

"I am so sorry, Ian. I am. I know you're angry."

"Oh, I am decades past angry and years past rage. I will

be *free*. I will bring them down to our level. I will show them death and mortality on a scale their heaven has never seen, and you'll help me."

"I can't do that." Adam shook his head. "The elves won't stand for it. Even Silver couldn't stop them if you invaded their plane. Everyone following you will die. You must know that."

"I'm not leaving you a choice." The Wolf's grin was cruel. "Time moves strangely here. You may already have lost your place, lost Vic. Even if you won't budge, you'll eventually have to eat, and the food here will make you a Lost One. Even if you escape someday, find another way, you'll never go home again."

"How long did it take you to make this happen? To set me up?"

"A lifetime. It started with Silas Wilcox. All he cared for, all his children and their children care for, is money, but I guess that equals power in your world, our world—and I'll have that too. I have bent their will for four generations."

Adam shook, but he could feel that the Wolf was right. He could call the sword the same way he had when he'd killed White. It would come. It would obey him and point the way home.

"I can see you're hesitating. Let me give you an incentive. Your friends are still at the hotel. They're innocent. They need you and I know you won't let them die."

"Did you even know their names?" Adam asked.

"Who?"

"The witches in Chicago—Nicole. All the people the Wilcoxes have stepped on or White murdered so you could bring your grand plan together."

"They don't matter. Only right now matters. All of it, everything I did, was to get us here, to this point. Come on, hero. Don't let them down. Do what you have to do."

Adam squeezed his eyes shut.

The Wolf was right. He knew Adam, knew he wouldn't let Jodi and the others die. He had to make certain Annie was safe. It was what Argent said about him, that he'd do the right thing, every single time.

Then again, maybe they didn't know him as well as they thought.

Adam opened his hand and called the sword. It slid into his palm, slicing through time and space, opening a jagged way.

Adam closed his fist around its hilt.

"I'm sorry," he said. "But you're right. You're not leaving me a choice."

He opened the warlock wound.

34

Patrick was still there, standing outside the circle, when Adam reappeared in the ballroom. The witches either lay sprawled on the ground or staggered, exhausted or dead from the ritual they'd used to cast him into the Between.

"We await your—"

Patrick sputtered to a stop when Adam dropped the broken mask to the floor.

"He's not coming." Adam brought his foot, still wearing the dead man's shoes, down and crushed the mask.

He slashed at the circle with the sword, breaking it. The lingering magic snapped like a broken power line. It whipped through the air, shedding sparks of power.

Wilcox turned to run but Adam was ready this time. Freshly fed, the wound snapped out, ripping through Wilcox's defenses and knocking him to the ground.

Jodi growled when Adam cut the binding on her mind.

"Damn it," she said, her drawl thick. "I almost had it."

"Yeah, you did. Get Emily and Cole free."

She didn't ask what he was going to do as he stalked toward Wilcox.

Patrick had rolled onto his back. He tried to scramble away even as he raised his hand in a warding gesture.

Adam cut the spell from the air. Wilcox threw a curse and the warlock wound swallowed it whole.

"What are you going to do to me?"

"Far better than what you tried to." Adam brought the blade down in a slash.

It wasn't proper form. It wasn't anything the Knight of Swords had taught him, and it took everything he had to do it right, to mix the wound with the blade and not let the sword stay fully solid, to end Wilcox forever.

The metal passed through him and vanished. Adam felt it settle onto his back with a satisfied hum.

Wilcox gripped his heart.

"You . . . you . . ."

"Stopped you." Adam leaned over him. "Be glad I left you alive."

He could see the cut with his Sight. Wilcox's magic was broken. It might heal in time, but for now it sputtered inside him, the threads of life and power neatly severed. He might as well be mundane, only he'd always feel it. He'd always know what he'd lost, his impotence, and in the moment, Adam could not bring himself to feel even a little bit bad about it.

Jodi, Emily, and Cole came toward him but kept their distance.

"I didn't know you could do that." Jodi stared at Patrick, Seeing what Adam had done.

"Neither did I." He surveyed the fallen cultists. "Let's go call Argent."

A crack split the air.

"What the—" Jodi started.

"Oh my gods," Cole said.

The boggin that squeezed through was one of the giants. The ballroom shattered as it sucked up the floor and ceiling.

"Run!" Adam screamed.

"We can't just leave them," Emily protested, nodding to the downed witches.

Adam eyed them. They'd nearly killed him. They'd let White do what he'd done. He could just go. He should just . . . go.

"Adam . . ." Jodi said, reading his expression. "Coz?"

"Damn it," he said. "Emily, do you have your thread?"

"No, but this will do." She pulled at the corner of her crocheted coat.

The boggin ripped plaster from the ceiling and padded chairs from the banquet tables.

Some of the witches had found enough strength to flee. Some were trying to help their fellows.

"Help them," Adam said. "But get out as soon as you can. It's too much for us. We need backup."

He didn't even try to track Wilcox as he rushed forward, lifting the sword. He couldn't cut through the debris, but he used his will to push the blade halfway solid. A tentacle made of ugly fabric and plywood table parts swept toward the witches and Adam sliced, cutting into the spirit but not the matter. The sword sang, happy to be of use. The junk fell to the floor.

The thing made no sound as he severed its appendage. It spun, faster than he had expected, and knocked him back with another arm. He hit a support pillar, hard, and sank to the floor.

The thing's twisting mass of pseudopods and debris all pointed toward him, ready to drive through him, when Emily and Cole got her yarn around it.

"We bind you. We bind you . . ." they chanted with Jodi.

So did Adam, pouring his will into the spell.

"We bind you."

The spell began to take form, but it would never hold. The thing was too massive, too much.

Then other voices joined in. From the edge of the room, the cult witches added their casting to the binding.

It sealed, pinning the boggin in place. It crashed to the ruined floor.

"What are you waiting for?" Jodi asked. "Kill it."

She was right, of course.

The thing flexed. The strands of power holding it in place began to snap.

"I'm sorry," Adam said.

He opened the warlock wound and let it free.

It took him a moment to realize that the fire alarm had stopped ringing.

Jodi stared down the witches who'd joined the cult and Adam was relieved that she was not the one with the sword.

"Let's go call the Guardians," he said.

She nodded.

They were nearly to the front door when a rush of cold magic filled the air. It was like a blast of snow on a July day. The hotel's wards collapsed, shattered by the gentlest blow of a power that no mortal could match.

"What is that?" Emily asked.

Adam let out a long breath.

"The cavalry."

The front doors shattered, their glass atomized.

Argent, Dautre, and Vic stepped into the lobby.

The Queen of Swords took in the water-logged space as several elves filed in behind them.

"Great timing, y'all."

It took everything he had not to drop into Vic's arms.

Argent surveyed the group.

"It would seem that you have the situation well in hand."

"Don't be so certain. We've got a ballroom full of cultists, and at least one body in the basement."

"Y'all took your time," Jodi said angrily.

Argent narrowed her eyes.

"We have been preoccupied by the *boggins*."

"There was more than one?" Adam asked.

"The cult's ritual unleashed at least a dozen across the city," Dautre explained.

"We've got to find Annie," Adam said.

"She's safe." Vic stepped to Adam. "She's at the hospital with Bobby."

"Why hasn't the fire department come?" Emily asked.

Adam took another long breath. "Wilcox probably disconnected the alarms. He wouldn't want any authorities poking around."

"You mentioned something about a fire?" Argent asked.

"I started it as a diversion."

Argent lifted an eyebrow. "You have been busy. What was that about a body in the basement?"

Adam tried to look her in the eye when he told her, but he couldn't. His limbs felt heavy, like the floor pulled him toward it.

"I killed a man, a mundane. I used the sword."

She froze, still as stone. Her expression remained glacial when she nodded.

"Then I must take you to the king."

"Why?" Jodi demanded.

"I killed someone, Jodi. It's what has to happen."

Adam stared at his stolen shoes.

"Yes," the queen said, but not ungently. "There must be a review, and a judgment."

"Judgment?" Vic asked.

"It is called the king's *court* for a reason, Vicente."

"So it's like an Internal Affairs thing?"

"Yes."

"I'm coming with you," Vic said.

"That would not be wise." Argent spoke firmly. More gently, she added, "I think you should sit this one out, Baby Reaper."

Adam cocked his head at her, but her expression gave nothing away. He'd probably never know if she'd meant to echo Seamus's words to him or not.

"What about the witches?" Adam asked. "Some of them are hurt, but they're responsible for the boggins."

Argent turned to one of the other elves.

"Tell the king we are coming and that he must convene the court."

"Yes, Lady."

"The rest of you, finish what needs doing here and take the cultists into custody."

Several elves entered the lobby.

From the charge in the air, Adam guessed they'd been casting glamours to contain the situation.

"What about Wilcox?" Adam asked. "Did you see him?"

"He gave us the slip," Vic said.

"You have to get to the hospital. You have to make sure he doesn't get to Annie and Bobby."

"Baby . . ."

"Promise me, Vic." Adam turned to Argent. "Give them protection and I'll go anywhere you want."

She cocked her head at him. He felt the power in her, the magic that had made him shake and cower at their first meeting. Now he shook for other reasons.

"Please," he said gently. "You don't know what he's capable of."

Argent turned to Dautre.

"Take the Reaper to them," she said. "No one else, mortal or other, comes and goes from the hospital."

"That will be hard to—"

"Fake a gas leak, or a plague. I don't care which or what. My command is given."

"Yes, my queen."

"Thank you." Adam bowed.

Vic stepped to him and hugged him hard. Adam winced and Vic pulled back.

"Are you all right?" He ran his hands over Adam, gently searching for the hurt.

"I'll . . . I'll tell you later."

Vic moved to arm's distance. He looked like he wanted to hug Adam again but did not want to hurt him. Adam watched the conflict play out across Vic's face.

"Just tell them the truth. I know you did what you had to."

Adam nodded.

It was the most he could do without breaking down. He hadn't realized until that moment how much he'd feared that Vic wouldn't understand. He'd been a cop, and for a long time he'd seen things in black and white.

Adam tried to conjure a smile, to say it would all be okay, but he couldn't.

Dautre laid a hand to Vic's shoulder and they were gone in a flash.

35

The full court was present when Argent marched Adam into the ballroom.

Silver sat on his throne of ice, his sheathed sword resting with its point against the floor. His suit of perfect gray was much the same but the jacket was long and flared like a cape. The knight stood to his left. Argent left Adam and took her place to her brother's right. The crowded room fell silent. They weren't alone this time. The dignitaries and courtiers had gathered to watch. Adam forced himself to stand straight until he came within the appropriate distance of his king, just outside of striking range. He bowed, and for once gave it the extra few inches as a way of saying he was sorry.

This could not be easy. He was the Page, and his actions reflected upon the court. All the realms were watching, and he knew Silver could not afford to be seen as weak.

"You have called us to court, sister. Explain."

"Adam Lee Binder, Page of Swords, has confessed to the killing of a mundane with his weapon of office."

Adam had expected a murmur or a few gasps would pass over the crowd, but the silence was heavy, and somehow so much worse.

"Adam?" Silver asked, and despite everything he'd thought walking in here, he wasn't prepared for the note of concern in his old love's voice. "Is this true?"

"It is." Adam fixed his eyes on the floor, where the point of Silver's scabbard touched the wood. "The man, White, killed innocents, I don't know how many, but that was not why I took his life."

"Then why did you kill him?" it was the knight's question, asked with icy curiosity.

"It was him or me. My life or his, and in that moment, I chose mine."

"Give me your blade," the knight said.

Adam drew it and knelt, offering it toward her with both hands.

She brandished it, swirling it through the air experimentally. "You have been practicing."

"Yes."

"It came to you across the wards where you were held."

"Yes."

The knight turned to Silver. "He speaks true. The one he killed was mundane and he intended the page's death."

"There is more to it," Argent said.

Adam lifted his eyes to meet hers, silently asking her not to make him say it, not to make him show them.

"Isn't there?" she pressed.

"Yes."

"It matters not," the knight said. "It is not the role of the page to pass judgment, to decide who lives and dies."

"It is in battle," Argent said. "Adam, remove your shirt."

"Lady . . ."

"Do as I say."

She glared at him with the full force of her snowy eyes.

Adam unbuttoned his stolen coveralls and peeled them to his waist.

The court did gasp then. The slashes were already sealing to scars, but the lines were red and angry. The blood caked, dry and itchy, across his skin. The bruise of the healed hammer blow made a galaxy of purple and yellow across his right shoulder and arm.

Silver's eyes traced the worst of them, the line of the wound he'd once healed, and fumed.

Adam could smell himself, the pain he'd experienced, the sweat of the battle since, and the faint odor of whatever soap had been used to wash the coveralls. Something with lavender. Maybe Kurt had a wife. Maybe he just liked frilly soaps.

He knew he was distracting himself, trying to put some distance between the feeling of exposure that threatened to have him drop to the ballroom floor. He might as well be naked, putting his hurts on display like this. He pictured the painting in Dr. Cahill's office, the one of the ocean, and imagined himself drifting away in that blue water.

"The man you killed did this to you?" Argent asked.

"Yes."

"Cover yourself," Silver said gently, bringing Adam back to the now.

Adam shrugged back into the garment.

"There is no argument that the page was attacked and harmed," the knight said. "He is not before us for that, but for the use of his blade to kill a mundane."

"A mundane who knew of magic," Dautre said, stepping into the ballroom. "Whose master used magic to harm others."

"And this master?" Silver asked Adam. "What of them?"

Adam swallowed.

"I severed his craft," he said. "As Dautre said, he harmed

others. He intended to do so again, so I bound him in a way that would stop him from doing it again."

Silver turned to Argent.

"Sister?"

"Without magic he is no longer in our jurisdiction," she said. "We must leave him to the mortal authorities unless he is foolish enough to try such spells and rituals again."

Silver did not react. He might as well have been part of his throne.

"This is no simple matter," he announced after a long pause. "While the death of a mundane at our hands is a serious concern, so is a mundane who knew of magic and visited cruelty upon his own kind."

"Yet the law is the law," Argent said. "There must be consequences for Adam's actions."

She'd always been on his side. The turn now, away from him, stung.

"I am the law." Silver stood and swept his gaze across the court. Adam could feel the force behind his words. The cold light of the tower whitened, almost blinding even with Adam's wards and Silver's glamour. His fury landed on the knight. "That is what you and the traditionalists believe, is it not? If the king is all, then your council is meaningless and any arguments as to the fate of my page carry no merit. That is how my father would have responded."

Silver surveyed the court. The knight did not look cowed, but she had the brains to stay quiet as Silver continued, "We named Adam to the role of page to bring our worlds together. Perhaps that was a mistake. Perhaps not. I will take this case under consideration and pass my judgment in time. For now, Adam, you will leave your weapon with us and return to your plane. Consider yourself on probation."

"Yes, my lord."

"Dautre, take him home."

"I will do it," the knight said. "His training fell to me, so part of his failing is mine."

"As you wish."

Dazed, Adam followed her out of the ballroom. They were outside the gates when she laid a hand to his shoulder, more gently than he expected.

The world shifted to white then blue. They were in Bobby's backyard, beside the patch of iris bulbs.

"Why?" Adam asked.

"I disdain the human habit of single sentence questions. Speak clearly."

She met his eyes and despite the danger of it, he didn't turn away from her.

It was just the two of them, but still he checked over his shoulder.

"Why did you do it?" he asked. "Why did you help the cult and the Wolf?"

She did not deny it, but she cocked her head to the side, telling him to continue.

"Those rituals—the healing and plane crossing, they're ancient. They're not even in the library at RCC, but they're in the elven archives, aren't they? You gave them what they needed to heal Annie and to open the Between."

"Yes and yes," she said flatly.

"And you told the Wolf about the sword. That's why you pushed me to train with it, to bond with it. And Annie. You saved her. You took her out of the spirit realm and to Chicago."

"Yes and yes again."

He blinked, surprised she'd admit to both things.

"People were hurt. People *died*. So why did you do it?"

"For North, because he cannot live in the world as it is. He cannot simply be among humans or elves. In so many ways, he too, is a Lost One. The Wolf promised change, to make somewhere my son could thrive."

"He was going to colonize Alfheimr. He wanted a war with your people."

"And it was one he never could have hoped to win."

"Then why help him?"

"Our king is progressive, but our people are not. Almost none of them leave their palaces, their green fields or crystal beaches. They live untainted by mortality, by death, or struggle. I knew, the moment I held North in my arms, that he would require a different world, a new one, even if I had to break the old one to make it."

Adam closed his eyes.

He did not know what to say. She'd done a terrible thing, more than one. So had he. The worst thing was, like with Seamus's thirst for vengeance, Adam could understand. He really wished he couldn't. Maybe he was just getting older, or maybe he'd seen too much shit, but he understood.

She was a lot of things, but she loved her child, so much so that she'd almost started a war for him.

"I killed the Wolf," he said. "I'm sure the sword told you. You lost."

"You killed *a* Wolf. There are two, and even if the other never rises, the Lost Ones have gathered. They are massed in the spirit realm, where all the towers and Guardians cannot help but see them. Victory can come in many forms. In the end, I may have the outcome I desired without further loss of life. If so, I will owe you a debt of gratitude."

"And the boggins? The Between? They'll keep coming through. The mortal world is going to notice them eventually."

She shook her head.

"There are doors that are never meant to be opened," she said distantly. "That is one consequence I hope we can prevent."

"I don't know what you mean."

"I know, and I suspect that is why the Queen of Swords wanted you here, safe, and away from the court."

Adam blinked.

"Argent was trying to protect me?"

"Why else would she argue for your removal as page or the king be so passionate in his fury? They wanted you safe, and so you are. No elf will touch you while his judgment remains unspoken. More than ever, it marks you as his." She turned to go. "I will leave you to your consequences."

"Wait . . ."

She looked back at him.

"Who is North's father?"

She surprised him with a bitter laugh. "Did you think it was the Wolf?"

"Kind of, yeah."

"He was a soldier," she said sadly. "A warrior after my own heart. He died in one of your wars."

"Which one?"

"It does not matter. It was pointless, all of it, as most wars are."

"Even though you're a soldier?"

"Especially so. My son is gentle. I don't know where he gets it."

"You could send him to school, you know. He'd fit right in at RCC."

"He's not like anyone else there."

"No one is like anyone else there. That's sort of the point. Let me talk to Silver for you . . . you know, when he's speaking to me again."

"Why would you do that? I used you, Page. You were hurt because of my actions."

"But North wasn't involved, and I know better than anyone that we're not our parents. I think it would be good for him to have friends."

"I will consider it. You are kind, Adam Binder. Some might see that as a weakness to use against you."

"Somebody already tried. It didn't work out so well for him." He said it with a bravado he didn't quite feel.

"Then I might make a warrior of you yet."

She vanished.

36

Adam showered. There wasn't as much pink in the runoff as he'd expected. He found that strange.

He kept staring at the clothes he'd left piled on the other side of the glass door, the coveralls, the jeans, the shoes.

He did not know what he would do with them. Throwing them away seemed like it wouldn't be enough. Burning them seemed too dramatic.

Adam started when the door to the bathroom opened, his heart racing like he'd heard a gunshot.

"It's okay," Vic said. "It's just me."

Adam tried to pull his heart rate back from the stratosphere.

Vic reached in and turned off the water. It had gone cold, and Adam realized he was shivering.

"You've been in here a long time."

Vic wrapped him in a towel and gently started to dry him.

"Why don't you come out now?"

Adam gave a little nod. Vic took another towel and ran it over his head, drying it carefully, not using any force or strength.

He led Adam back to the bedroom, past the pile of clothes, past the shoes.

Trying not to cry at the cuts on Adam's body, Vic scowled and helped him into a pair of running shorts and a black tank top. They were Vic's clothes, a little too large, but perfect in the moment.

Adam went through the motions like a doll, letting himself be guided, steered. Foot up, foot down, arms over his head, then lowered.

Vic sat him on the edge of the bed and sat beside him, not quite at arm's length, just near enough to put a hand to the small of Adam's back, but he didn't touch him. Adam hated that he felt relieved by that.

"You have to talk to me," Vic said. "Or if you want, I can call Dr. Cahill and see if she's got an opening."

Adam shook his head.

"I know I have to tell you about it . . . I just . . ."

He trailed off, unable to continue.

"Breathe, baby. Just breathe."

Adam did, and after a while, he let the story pour out of him, everything he'd learned, but especially what he'd done.

"You did what you had to," Vic said. "You know that, right?"

"I do, but it doesn't feel right."

"It shouldn't, but this job you're doing—it's going to come with stuff like this."

"I'd do it again, Vic. I'd make the same choice again. Does that make me a bad person?"

"No. It was him or you and I can't say I'm not glad you were the one to walk out of that room."

"I don't mean White. I mean the Wolf, in the Between. I couldn't let him out. I couldn't be responsible for that, for all the people who'd die in his name, so I killed him."

"You said he was the older one, right?"

"Yeah."

"Then he doesn't exist yet. You may have stopped him from becoming that. It can all go another way."

"That doesn't mean it doesn't count. It doesn't mean it won't still happen or that I didn't do what I did."

Vic tried to pull him close, but Adam couldn't take it then. He stood, paced a little, and balled his fists. He needed to go, to drive, but couldn't. He had no car. He couldn't breathe.

Vic watched him from the bed.

"What do you need?" Vic asked.

"Time."

Vic nodded, then stood.

"Okay. I don't like it, but I get it. I'll . . ."

"You don't understand." Adam stepped into his space. "I need time with you."

It was the gentlest it had ever been between them.

Vic lay kisses on each of Adam's new scars.

When he stretched across him, Adam squirmed, and Vic sensed that now wasn't the time for any kind of pressure or wrestling.

Something sank inside Adam. He liked the weight of Vic atop him. He'd always liked the playful rocking back and forth, the push and pull of it, but now his skin itched. He wanted to run away. He shoved the feeling aside. He had to be here, now. That was the only safe space, to not think, to just be.

Maybe they weren't linked anymore, but Vic seemed to know what he needed, even though Adam couldn't ask for it. Vic kissed him for a long moment, and when Adam was about to break it off to catch his breath, Vic did.

Adam could have cried, but he let the moment carry him forward.

Afterward, lying together but not entwined, Adam pulled free of the bed long enough to find his phone.

"Whatcha doing?" Vic asked sleepily when the light woke him.

"What about this one?" Adam turned the phone to show Vic the screen.

Vic grinned when he saw the apartment listing.

"Yeah. I like it."

"Let's go look at it tomorrow."

37

"Is it weird, coming back here?" Vic asked.

"A little."

They were out of the car, staring up at the house.

Adam would have taken Vic's hand, but each of them had a pan in his arms, and the last thing Adam wanted to do was slip on the sidewalk and spoil Vic's hard work.

"Are you sorry you left?"

Adam laughed.

"Never."

They were still figuring out how their stuff fit together. Vic had too many pots and pans. Adam had none. Still, they were settling in.

Thankfully Vic had always expected his time at his mom's to be temporary so he'd brought out the stuff he'd been storing. They had towels, a shower curtain, and most of what they needed for basic furniture.

So far Adam had contributed a stack of used paperbacks and a shiny new coffee pot that Bobby had called a housewarming gift, while he had joked that it was actually an "I love you now get out" present.

The apartment wasn't home yet, but it had bright white walls, and it was theirs.

It was only one bedroom, but the living room was long enough for Adam's desk, and there was enough cabinet and counter space in the kitchen for all of Vic's cooking gadgets.

Most of all, it had Vic and Spider. They were what mattered most.

"You think Jesse's bringing his new girlfriend?" Adam asked as they reached the door.

Vic shook his head. "He still hasn't said anything about her. Mom's dropped a lot of hints and gotten nothing."

The door opened before Adam could ring the bell.

"Adam Lee!" his mother said excitedly. "Get in here. Both of you."

"Ma'am," Vic said as she held the storm door for them.

They were quick to put down their burdens and embrace Tilla Mae. Adam's mother had softened, just a bit. She'd never be a ray of sunshine, but she looked good, and happier than he'd ever seen her. Adam nodded to Early, who took up a good amount of the kitchen's corner while he sipped a beer.

Bobby had called Tilla to talk to her about Annie's return. He'd been worried about Early, who even in jeans and a polo still looked like a sheriff, but she'd assured him that he had nothing to be concerned about. Their mother was good at keeping secrets. The darker they were, the deeper she buried them.

"You know the tree's history, right?" Jodi was asking Bobby as they emerged from the den. "It's a pagan tradition."

"Yeah, yeah," Bobby said playfully.

"Hey, coz," Adam said, opening his arms for her.

He could feel the bit of sadness, the grief for Nicole, but it had receded, becoming a lower strata in his cousin's complex layers of self.

The doorbell rang and Adam jumped a little.

Vic gave him a look and Adam forced a smile.

He knew it would be this way for a while. It might be forever. It came on at the oddest moments. He'd be at the garage and someone would drop a tool, or one of the neighbors could slam their door too loudly, then it would all rush back: White, the room, the blood, and the dead man's shoes. They sat in a cardboard box at the bottom of the bedroom closet. Someday he'd know what to do with them. Someday, but not yet.

No one had come around to ask about White. He figured the Guardians had swept his death under the rug. It wasn't like anyone would ever find the weapon that had killed him. Adam could still feel the sword, but it was a quiet, distant link. He let it be.

Silver had not pronounced judgment, and Adam wondered if he ever would. Maybe he'd forgotten how brief the lives of humans were. Maybe he was sparing Adam some punishment, or perhaps the knight had been right and this was Silver's way of keeping Adam safe.

The Hotel Erythraean was closed for remodeling when Adam had worked up the courage to drive by it. Its wards were gone, as were its doormen. If the boggins were causing havoc, well, being on probation meant he wasn't told anything.

Maria and Jesse entered, her with a bottle of wine in a colorful bag and him with a wrapped package that he furtively went to tuck beneath the tree in the den.

"We said no presents," Vic called after him.

"It's not for Christmas," Jesse said. "It's a housewarming gift."

"The wrapping says Happy Holidays."

Jesse shrugged as he came back into the kitchen. "It was the only paper we had."

It was odd to see them without Chaos, but the house was

full and Adam was at the edge of what his senses could bear without the drama the dog would bring.

His sensitivity was worse than it had been in years. He knew why. He kept trying to unpack it in therapy, but so far he'd edged around the issue, unable to face it directly. He had to, he knew that. It would be there, and he'd jump at shadows until he did.

"What did you make, Vicente?" Maria asked.

"Tamales, arroz con leche for dessert, and something special that Adam can eat."

"He doesn't know?"

"He wouldn't let me in the kitchen to peek," Adam complained. "He wouldn't even let me in the apartment. He made me go to work."

Vic shrugged.

Adam had a guess. They'd driven over, and the smell, like cornbread and honey, had given something away, but he'd pretended not to notice and tried to let himself enjoy the surprise.

"I still don't know how you don't eat meat," Early said, though without rancor.

"Hey, just means more bacon for y'all, right?"

Adam had promised himself he would not be *that* vegetarian. What he hadn't expected was how concerned the carnivores would be about him not getting enough protein or something.

"I heard about someone who tried to feed their cat a vegetarian diet," Early said. "Poor thing died."

Adam tried not to bristle at the remark and told himself that Early was just making conversation. He knew he was being touchy. He took a breath.

"Spider eats what he eats, and I eat what I eat."

"Speaking of eating," Bobby said. "Places everybody."

They'd added the extra leaves to the dining room table, the one they never used, but the house had never been this full.

Annie had woven Christmas lights into fake green garland and hung it around the doorways.

She'd put electric candles on the table, adding a warm glow. The music was a playlist of Christmas carols sung in a New Age style, Jodi's proud contribution to the party. It soothed Adam's frayed senses.

"I like this, Jodi."

"It was this or Hillbilly Ogre Orgy," she said with a smirk.

Adam did not ask about Annie's parents and hoped everyone else in the room knew not to either.

The case was still ongoing. The visit from the FBI had been a surprise, but not to Annie. She'd taken everything she'd remembered, everything she'd written down, and sent it to them.

Her parents were in the wind, probably off in the Caymans, where Adam hoped they stayed.

He took his seat and dishes were passed or served.

He smiled to see Early take a scoop of what Vic had made for Adam. The big man shrugged when he caught Adam looking.

"Is it okay?" Vic asked after Adam had tried a bite.

"It's perfect," he said, trying not to tear up.

Vic had taken something Sue used to make, what she called Mexican cornbread, made with cheap salsa and plastic cheese, and elevated it to art. This was more like a deep dish or Detroit-style pizza, with a thick layer of honey-sweetened, golden bread, a sauce of homemade salsa with cheese and roasted onions and bell peppers.

"You should serve this at the restaurant, baby bro," Jesse said.

"Someday," Vic agreed.

"Someday," Adam promised. He had what he wanted. He had his dream. He'd do everything he could to make sure Vic got his.

Vic squeezed his leg under the table while Maria poured the wine.

Annie shyly put a hand over her glass. Bobby did the same, and Adam *knew.*

He knew it like he did when his Sight told him something with perfect clarity, illuminating a truth he never should have seen.

Tilla was not so subtle. Her excitement thickened her accent when she drawled, "Wait. Why aren't you two drinking?"

"Ma," Bobby protested, but Annie put her hand atop his.

"It's still really early. We weren't going to tell anyone for a few more months, you know, especially after last time."

"We wanted to be sure," Bobby groused in his mother's direction, but Adam could feel his excitement, the bubbly, golden hope he was trying to contain.

"Do you know what you're having?" Jesse asked.

"Jesse," Maria chided.

"It's too soon, but we want to know," Annie said. "We'll find out as soon as we can."

"No burning down the neighborhood with a gender reveal party?" Jodi teased. Everyone looked at her, but Bobby laughed.

"No," he said. "Not for us."

"You really want to know?" Adam asked.

His Sight was usually silent when it came to people close to him, but maybe it was because the baby wasn't born yet, or maybe because it had all finally clicked into place.

Everyone looked at him.

"Yes, please," Annie said.

"Tell us!" Bobby barked, bringing a round of laughter.

"It's a boy."

A collective murmur of happiness spread across the table as they took in the news.

"Have you thought about names?" Tilla asked.

"She wants to name him Vail," Bobby said, teasing though he was beaming.

"Because that's where you proposed to me." Annie gave his hand a gentle slap.

"I'm open to suggestions," Bobby said.

"His name is Ian," Adam said.

And he would play the violin. He would have his uncle's eyes and his Sight. He would, if they were not very careful, fall somewhere that would break him. Then after a lifetime there, somewhere he should never have gone, he would die by his uncle's hand.

Under the table, Vic squeezed his hand. Adam understood the silent promise.

They would love this impossible boy, born because he had to be, because his bastard grandfather wanted more when he already had so much.

They would love him, protect him, and do everything they could to stop that terrible day from coming.

"Ian Vail Binder," Bobby tested the name aloud.

"I like it," Annie said.

"See?" Bobby asked. "You can have your hippie name so long as it's in the middle."

Annie shook her head, but she splayed her fingers over her belly and grinned.

38

The dishes were cleared, the washer loaded, and the leftovers divided. Jodi had already left with a grocery bag of food. Early had taken to the basement, now a guest room, to catch up on the game between the Baltimore Ravens and the 49ers. He'd invited Vic to watch with him, but Vic had politely declined. Ever the peacemaker, Bobby went with him.

Annie and Tilla were upstairs, talking about paint and nursery colors.

Adam loved to see Annie so excited. He'd been their test case for the second coven. They needed to know they could finish what they'd started, healing her, and ensure the Wolf was born.

"Wonder Bread . . . bro," Jesse said, nodding for them to follow him to the den.

Maria drifted along, her curiosity piqued by her eldest son.

"Sit," Jesse ordered, pointing to the futon Vran used to occupy, now folded into its couch form.

Adam obeyed and sniffed, trying for one last hint of salt and sea, but the elf was gone from here. He'd miss him forever.

Vic sat to his left, Maria to his right.

Jesse looked nervous as he handed Adam the little package

he'd put beneath the tree and sat on the floor across from the coffee table.

"Go on," he said. "You're killing me. I've got a dog to go let out."

Adam unwrapped the little package and blinked. He could feel it already, but he opened the box and let them tumble into his hand.

"Jesse! These are . . . breathtaking."

"Vic said you needed one. Sorry it took so long."

"That's how you've been spending your nights?" Vic asked.

"Yeah. I figured you gave your dream a second chance, why shouldn't I?"

Adam pulled out card after card.

Jesse had drawn them in a style Adam had never seen. They looked like street art, but the themes were there: swords, coins, cups, and wands. He'd woven in swirls and skulls, subtle things that made him think Vic's brother might have a little Sight of his own. There were, of course, a lot of cars and black cats.

The Chariot was a Cutlass Supreme.

The Empress bore more than a passing resemblance to Maria.

Adam paused at the Lovers.

He'd captured them, Adam and Vic, clothed thankfully, but perfectly, standing face-to-face, heart to heart.

Adam stood and rushed to hug Jesse.

Vic joined in before Jesse shook them off with a muttered, "Get off me."

"Thank you," Adam said, because he didn't know what else to say.

It was one of the kindest gifts he'd ever received and his magic hummed at just the brush of his hands.

"So . . . no girlfriend?" Maria asked, sounding disappointed.

"No girlfriend," Jesse said. "If you want grandkids you'll have to settle for Chaos, at least for now."

Maria smiled. "I guess she'll do."

Adam and Vic walked Jesse and Maria to their car.

"Ready to go home?" Vic asked as his brother and mother drove away.

"Almost," Adam said. "I'm gonna just take a minute, if that's okay."

Elves were stationed on the neighbor's roofs. He did not know if they were there for his protection or to keep him under watch, but he raised his coffee mug toward them when Vic slipped outside long enough to press it into his hands.

Adam's phone buzzed with a call.

The screen read *Unknown Number.*

"Binder," Wilcox said when Adam pressed the phone to his ear. "I hear congratulations are in order."

"And here I thought your Sight was gone."

"Money has a longer reach than magic. He taught my father that, and then he taught me."

"Did you want something?"

He had no way of telling the FBI who was on the line. They'd probably have no luck if they tried to trace the call.

"I merely wanted to gloat," Wilcox said. "You think you won, but you didn't."

Victory can take many forms, the Knight of Swords had said. Adam's stomach sank a bit, not because Wilcox was right, but because he might be. It was all still ahead of them, still yet to come.

"So you got what you wanted, a grandson. Good for you."

"Yes. He will be my heir, and he will be powerful."

"One question—if that was your goal, then why did you try to take Annie back to Chicago?"

Wilcox laughed.

"Because I know my daughter. Mr. Binder."

Adam wondered if the title was a sign of respect for a man like Patrick Wilcox. Maybe Adam had earned that when he'd made an enemy of him.

"All I had to do to make certain that she stayed with your brother was tell her not to."

"They're going to name him Ian," Adam said. "In case you care."

"He will have all of my strength," Wilcox continued. "And I will guide him."

"*If* Annie lets you near him." It was Adam's turn to laugh. "And even if she does, you're forgetting something else, a variable you can't control, no matter how much money you throw at it."

"And what is that?"

"Wolf or not, your grandson or not, that boy will be a Binder. He's my family too, and I'll do everything I can to make sure he doesn't turn out like you."

"You—"

Adam hung up.

The coffee hadn't gone cold when he sipped it.

He should have worn his coat outside, but he wanted to feel the wind, the winter. He never wanted to stop feeling anything.

Up the street, two figures emerged, rounding the corner. One walked, the other rode a mobility scooter.

Adam didn't know where the second sister had been, but he smiled to see her. He waved to them. The sisters waved back and walked on.

The storm door slid shut behind him.

Vic put his arms around Adam. He didn't grip too tightly. Adam put his hands over Vic's, pressed them to his chest to say he was okay, to give a little consent.

They were working through it, talking through it, and Adam knew that even if he never stopped feeling the way he did, they would be okay.

"You're gonna freeze out here."

"Probably," Adam agreed. "But I think I'm ready. Want to go home with me, Vicente Martinez?"

"Always."

EPILOGUE

When Adam dreamed, he dreamed of the Between. It wasn't quite a spirit walk, wasn't quite a memory. Maybe he'd gotten it from the Wolf. Maybe it was just his imagination, but Adam knew that was a lie he wanted to tell himself. He'd left a piece of his heart there, a bit of innocence he couldn't get back.

In the dream he walked alone beneath that washed-out sky. He had no moon, no sun or stars, no way to mark the miles or the direction. The watchtowers did not light the horizon, but he followed the music, the wordless tune he'd first heard in the spirit realm.

He'd thought it was the Wolf's song, Ian's, but knew now it was something far older.

When he came at last to the mountains, they were nothing like the foothills in Colorado, which started gradually, sloping upward, giving you time to adjust to their height. These were like a wall, sheer and tall, curved and jagged, like the claws of some titanic, petrified thing.

A door was carved into the rock. Taller than most houses, it was made of pale stone and ice. Adam moved no closer. He knew, without knowing, that there were places he was never meant to go, that this was a door never meant to be opened, and yet it was.

It was just a little, just a crack, but he knew it was enough to let whatever had been locked within escape. That was the song he heard. Whatever was now free, was singing, and its tune reached across the realms.

"You can't have him," Adam called to the sky, to the dusty ground and jagged mountains. "I don't know who or what you are, but you can't have him."

Because he understood Seamus now. He understood the Knight of Swords and why she'd done what she'd done for North.

He'd break as many worlds as he had to, as many rules as he had to, if it kept his nephew safe.

ACKNOWLEDGMENTS

To everyone at the Educe Group. I loved working with you all.

To the entire Blackstone team, who always make my books shine and make me feel welcome.

To Rohnn Holder, for being the first person to set me on a path to therapy, and to Cathy Cahill for being my first therapist.

To Marilyn Kretzer, Sarah Bonamino, The Brothers Green, Isabella Bedoya, Lesley Sabga, Charlie Kauffunger, Brenda Johnson, Phyllis Dores, Phillip Fitzsimmons, Bryan Haworth, Bronwyn Kelly-Seigh, Chris Cooper Ceary, José Orlando, Cody Church, Jessica Posey, Jeff Dahlem, Christopher Freeman, the ever-delightful Madame Askew, Ashley and Kat at the Pueblo Library, everyone at Coastal Magic, Phillips Fitzsimmons, all the incredible booksellers and librarians who tell people about my work, and Valerie Eddy, for all you do for authors.

THE ADAM BINDER NOVELS, BOOK 4